A Step into the Dark

Ollie Wit Book One

DONNA AUGUSTINE

ISBN-13: 978-1945946011
ISBN-10: 1945946016

1

Knuckles hit the wood of my front door.

Over, and over, and over again.

That was the sound that woke me from where I'd been asleep on the couch. Not an alarm for work. I'd stopped showing up there weeks ago. Not family. I didn't have one of those anymore. And not friends. I'd never had many of those, and this past month had taken care of the few I'd had left.

As always, consciousness hit like a hammer striking a stubborn nail that didn't want to sink in. The knuckles continued their uneven cadence as I lay there and gritted my teeth through the pain of being awake. Awake meant I was still alive. Alive meant I had to live another day, even though the chore of getting off the couch seemed akin to climbing Mount Everest.

But climb I must. There was no out. This was it. I'd have to keep going, waking up day after day, whether I wanted to or not, because of a promise I made fifteen years ago before I'd had the maturity of knowing how bad this life could get. But it was a promise I'd keep to a man no longer among the living.

"Ollie?" Dr. Martin called from the other side of the door.

If I'd wanted to talk to someone, I wouldn't have thrown my phone off the bridge weeks ago.

I reached out a blind hand to feel for a water bottle that wasn't empty. After tipping over a couple of empties, my hand landed on a winner.

If I'd been a normal person, I would've glanced over and located one easily. But I wasn't ready to open my eyes and deal with *them* yet. And they'd be there. They always were. They'd been my constant companions, the only ones I couldn't seem to lose.

Swallowing a swig of warm water, I realized the knocking had stopped as the silence spread out like a lifetime of doom before me. Maybe if I fell back asleep now, I wouldn't wake up again? If the mind didn't want to continue, it seemed logical that the body would eventually agree to go along with the plan.

My dream of an eternal peace was disrupted by the jingle of keys and at least two sets of feet walking down the apartment building's hallway.

The knocking started back up but stopped after a couple raps. Dr. Martin was speaking again, but not to me this time. Then there was the voice of my super, saying something or other about how he wasn't supposed to let him in. Of course, that didn't stop the jingle of keys and the sound of my deadbolt shifting.

"Olivia? Are you in there?" Dr. Martin's voice echoed through my apartment, bouncing against the bare walls and wood floors, filling the apartment with his voice.

I didn't move or make a sound, but that was pretty easy. Wasn't sure my voice was working anymore, and the permanent indent I'd created in the couch hugged my tired body like a well-worn catcher's mitt ready to be retired.

There were only a couple of steps down my hallway before they'd find me. The bedroom was a few steps away but still too much effort. He'd only search for me there next anyway.

I rolled from my side to my back, a precaution against seeing *them* if I opened my eyes. The one predictable thing about my constant companions was they didn't float.

The steps got closer, and then there was nothing but silence for another moment. I imagined the two middle-aged men taking in the picture I made.

"Is she alive?" Dan whispered, as if his voice would wake the dead.

Dan, my super, the one who'd been hitting on me since the day I moved in, was now afraid to get within a few feet of me. Seemed there *were* a couple of brain cells rattling around in that head after all.

"Her *chest* is moving," Dr. Martin said in a tone that made it clear that, although I might've changed my assessment of my super, he wasn't very impressed. "I can handle it from here."

Dan, or at least I assumed it was Dan, let out a long whistle, before I heard him retreating back down the hallway and shutting my door.

Dr. Martin's steps were coming closer.

The sound of a cardboard pizza box skidding across the wood floor preceded a rustle of papers and a thump as they fell. The sound of the chair creaking under his weight told me his diet wasn't working out too well since the last time he'd mentioned it.

There was another stretch of silence before a drawn-out sigh filled the air, which sounded nearly as tired as I felt. His conscience might've dictated this visit, but his stamina wasn't quite on board with it all.

"How are you doing, Olivia?"

It was such a simple question, one people asked all the time, and yet I'd never really known how to answer it, even before it had gotten this bad. Still, if he was going to put out the effort, I felt compelled to muster up a response.

"I'm fine." Lying there in clothes stained with my dinner from three nights ago and still not opening my eyes, "great" seemed like it might've been a stretch.

Another long slow, exhale. "It's normal to feel like this after what you've been through."

"I know, doc." I didn't need a degree in psychology to know there was nothing normal about this, but it was easier to go along and get along. I didn't have any fight left to spare.

"It's going to take time after… Well, after any tragedy it takes a while."

Accident—that was the word that had been on the tip of his tongue before he swallowed it back. That was what the police, the fire department, and even the arson expert had called the explosion. An *accident*.

Couldn't blame doc for not saying it. I'd be afraid to say that word to me, too. Last time someone had said it, they'd had to shoot me up with enough tranquilizers to take down an elephant as I screamed that there were monsters everywhere coming to kill us.

No one, not even doc, wanted to hear about the monsters anymore, and I knew continuing to talk about them would eventually land me in only one place. A dark padded room might not be too bad, but *they* would follow me in there too. At least free, there was the illusion I might escape them one day.

"Olivia, you haven't opened your eyes since I've gotten here."

He knew the reason for that too. I'd been seeing doc since I was a kid, before I'd begun to edit my life story to fit what people expected. It was easier for all involved if I lied—after all, my recent lapse screaming about the monsters had gotten me nowhere but an overnight in the psych ward. "Sorry about that. Nasty migraine."

Give him an excuse to believe I was okay. That was what he wanted. It was what we both wanted so we could wrap up this little meeting.

"Olivia, please look at me. I'm worried about you."

Damn doc and that stubborn vein of duty running through him. He was going to make me work for my peace.

I forced myself upward, knowing I was going to have to put on a better show than this if I wanted to earn my quiet. Dropping my arm, I saw doc sitting there staring at me, and also what I'd dreaded. One of the monsters had sprung up beside him. They were always varying shades of grey to the inkiest black. This one looked the way I'd imagine a troll would, standing near the doc's shoulder, its eyes a silver-grey—eerily like my own when I thought about it, which I preferred not to. It was still better than the ones that had red eyes.

The monster leaned closer to him, and the doc shivered. He glanced behind him at the old single-pane windows. It wasn't a draft from the windows. I could've told him it was the companion beside him, but he wouldn't have believed me anyway.

When he looked back at me, the sun shining through the window showed off the fresh lines around his eyes and the dark shadows beneath. He looked like he'd been sleeping about as much as I had, and I knew I had to wrap this up for both our sakes.

He leaned forward. "I stopped by your work when you didn't answer the phone. They said you quit." His eyes wandered around the room. "When was the last time you left your apartment?"

"Doc, I'm going to be fine. I'm sorting through this and need a little more time before I'm willing to open up. But I'm not going to snap my cap and do something crazy. I'm not suicidal or homicidal or any other word that revolves around killing."

He squinted, and I saw the pity in his eyes. It was the one emotion I hated most.

I ran both hands through my hair, pushing back the dark curtain it had formed around my face as I stared at my feet, my big toe hanging out of the sock on the right foot. I was going to have to get a little tougher if I wanted to get him out of here. This wasn't something he could fix, so I was doing him a favor driving him out. These creatures were dangerous. I knew that now. Was positive of it.

I only paused a second before I turned back to him. "I know I don't seem okay right now, but to be honest, neither do you."

The doc shifted and the monster laughed. I threw it a dirty look as the doc's eyes shifted downward.

I looked back down at my big toe, wondering if I should've given him a few more minutes to leave on his own before I went there. I still remembered the session when I'd told doc that the monsters had said his wife was cheating on him.

I'd been seeing him for a while, hearing how it was all in my head for longer than I could remember, and the tedious nature of it all made me feel like my brains were turning to mush.

It wasn't like I'd ever wanted therapy. I knew *they* were real. Everyone else needed the therapy. But, to make my parents happy, I'd gone once a week to see the doc, and he'd asked me over and over again what the monsters did, what they looked like, did they speak? Well, ask a question enough times and you better be prepared for when you get the answer.

Doc shifted in his seat and leaned back, farther away from me. I shifted slightly down on the couch, helping him out by widening the gap more. "I'm sorry."

"For what?" he said. "Nothing to apologize for."

I nodded, not arguing the point but sensing my opening. He was ready to leave. I'd sufficiently primed the pump. "I'm okay. I'm just sad. I'm sad to the depths of my bones, and sometimes when I wake up in the morning, I wish I hadn't. But I still get up, I eat, and I get by. I'll be fine."

Fine. Not good. I didn't think I'd ever be good, but I'd live.

I watched his face as he took in my words. I'd thrown in enough hurt for him to realize the rest had been truth as well. I didn't know if I was going to be good anytime in this life, but I'd keep living it, for whatever it was worth.

I knew we were in the home stretch when he rattled off the normal questions—was I sleeping, was I feeling threatened, blah, blah, blah…

It was a test I knew all the answers to. It was amazing how well you could get by with just "sure" and "fine."

After a promise to call the office and set up an appointment, he stood like a vanquished foe accepting his defeat. He could leave me here alone, feeling like he'd done something. I could be left alone. Somehow in this scenario, I was the victor. All I'd won was my solitude, but that was enough.

I saw him out and walked back to the couch, avoiding the dark figures that seemed to be looming in the most unexpected corners, and slumped back into my dent, my eyes downcast. That was when I noticed it, an envelope with "important" handwritten on it.

I hadn't seen the doc leave anything behind, but he must have. I grabbed the envelope, withdrew the sheet of folded paper, and opened it to see a single sentence.

Don't speak to the monsters.

No signature, no name. This wasn't from the doc. I glanced around the room, avoiding looking at an especially large monster near the kitchen.

How long had this been sitting here? Had I grabbed it in my mail? I couldn't remember the last time I'd gotten my mail. How long had this been sitting here?

One month ago, I'd spoken to the monsters for the first time in a decade, and someone out there knew.

2

If I hadn't gotten that note yesterday, then I wouldn't have jumped off the couch the second I heard something slither underneath my door. I dodged left around a little furry monster and grabbed the note lying facedown in my hall.

They were back. Note in hand, I didn't bother reading it as I flung the door open and saw Dan walking down the hall, about to turn the corner.

Wait, Dan saw the monsters?

I looked down at the paper.

You need to get your mail out of the lobby. The mailman can't fit it in your box anymore. It's all over the lobby and I'm getting complaints.

Dan

A month ago, he would've stalked me to deliver this message in person, maybe delivered it himself to show me what an upstanding person he was. Now I got notes under my door so he didn't have to get too close.

I walked back into my apartment, crumpled the piece of paper, and threw it on top of an overflowing pile of trash can. It bounced to the floor, setting off a garbage avalanche as I settled back into the dent in the couch.

It took a solid twenty minutes—or, by my new method of telling time, two-thirds of a *Seinfeld* rerun—of internal debate before I decided that getting my mail might not be the worst idea. When you didn't leave your apartment, having heat and electricity became more important than normal, especially in a Boston February.

My holey socks were sopping wet before I made it down the single flight to the lobby. Didn't anyone know how to wipe the snow from their feet?

I let out a breath strong enough to puff out my cheeks as I eyed the soggy pile of what I presumed to be my mail under the metal boxes in the wall, unless someone else in the building had died and I didn't know.

Wet magazines almost created a Slip 'N Slide as the key to my mailbox gritted in and then resisted turning. Dan had said he was going to fix this two months ago, back when I was still worthy.

After a couple solid tugs, the box vomited up more of my mail in a splatter onto the lobby's puddled floor.

Scooping up my wet mail, I kept my head down as people entered behind me, resisting the urge to check and see if they were wiping their feet.

I was the antisocial freak of the building, and saw no reason to break that impression now. If I spoke in my current mood, it would only serve to diminish my standing. I hated the world and everyone in it, and I didn't have to get to know you first.

A pair of male hands reached down and began helping me gather up my mail. I bit back the groan as the consequences of his kindness hit. Now I was going to have to speak to him, even if it were a single word. I could only hope that wouldn't somehow morph into conversation. The odds were in my favor, considering I hadn't brushed my hair in three days.

He handed me his share of the soggy pile as I turned and rose. My helper stood beside another man who appeared to be with him, partly because I couldn't figure out another reason for them both to be standing there staring at me. They also appeared to have been churned out of the same cookie-cutter machine, with long wool coats over suits and ties, but both had forgotten to groom their hair or five o'clock shadows. Not that I could climb on a soapbox and preach, but at least I was consistent in my appearance.

It might have been their unblinking attention, or the way they stood a little too close, but something about these two tripped my inner alarms. It wasn't a *take off at a run* alarm. It was more like a *milk that was on the brink of turning that you had to smell a couple of times* sort of problem. A monster that had lingered in the corner's shadow crept over and started sniffing one man's shoes, almost like the dog it appeared to be, then sneezed.

Yeah, something wasn't right with these two. That was my cue to get out of there.

"Thanks," I said, taking the long path around them toward the stairs.

"Wait," one of them called, as I climbed the first two steps back to my floor.

I turned, against my better judgment, to see why I was supposed to wait.

"We'd like to speak with you."

I took another step up, the smell of something rotten getting stronger. "Why?"

"Don't run," one of the men said. "We just want to talk to you."

Run? Most sane people with a lick of instinct would've been hightailing it away from them. They were lucky they were talking to me instead. All I had left in me was a leisurely stroll away.

The idea of them possibly being the murdering types ran through my mind, and instead of wanting to flee, I imagined a guilt-free exit. Murder would mean I hadn't given up. My life had ended by no fault of my own, and if everyone I loved were in heaven right now, I'd be with them instead of here, alone. If there were no heaven? It wouldn't matter anyway, because I'd be dead. Except would putting myself in harm's way screw me on a technicality?

I leaned a hip on the stair railing, my hands full of mail, and decided this needed further investigation. "Who are you? I've never seen either of you before." I looked them over closely. Could it be them? They hadn't seen the monster sniffing around them. I would've noticed a sign or a glance. But maybe? "Did either of you write me a note?"

They looked at each other, checking to see if one had done it without the other's knowledge. "No," they finally answered after their silent deliberation finished.

"Then what do you want?"

The two looked at each other as if they needed to clarify their answer—again. I didn't have time for this. Well, technically I had all the time in the world, but I didn't have the patience for anything. "If you've got something to say, I suggest you spit it out. I've a TV show coming on in five minutes."

The slightly taller, and, if possible, scruffier of the pair finally spoke. "We're here to offer you employment."

I coughed to cover a bark of laughter. Prior to my world collapsing, I'd been a cashier at a very reputable convenience store. To my understanding, cashiers weren't hard to come by, even if you did want experience. Maybe they presumed this was a good line because of where I lived, having no idea that I'd inherited the place from my grandmother and could barely pay the taxes on it. "What position are you offering me?"

"It's a communications position," the shorter but broader one said.

I made a short humming sound, as if giving this some thought. That was the beauty of not fearing death. You weren't so terrified in a situation like this that you couldn't have a little bit of fun with your would-be attackers.

"How much does it pay? I've got a high standard of living." I crossed my ankles, putting my holey socks on display.

They both glanced down at my feet. The shorter one pulled it together quicker, while the taller one seemed to get hung up on a stain on my sweatpants.

"A million," the shorter guy said as he tried to nudge his buddy out of his stare.

"A mil? Like, you mean a month, right? You can't mean a year. I could never live on that." I huffed, and added a couple shakes of my head, sending knotted locks swaying.

The taller guy's eyes narrowed as if he were having a hard time playing my game, but the shorter one kept rolling right along with me. "You'd have to negotiate that with our employer, but you'll have to speak to him yourself. You'll need to come with us."

Would going with them qualify as suicide? It was sort of a murky area.

Too murky. Nope, this wasn't going to work out. Couldn't break the promise. "Sorry. I don't have time today. Maybe next week."

I turned and began climbing the stairs.

"You have to come with us," they said before I hit the fifth step.

"No, I don't think I do," I said in a singsong voice as I got to step six. You never knew— maybe if they chased me, I'd fall down the stairs and break my neck. Could a girl get that lucky?

I heard a couple more people entering the lobby, and glanced back out of curiosity when I heard one of them groan. Another two men I'd never seen before walked in.

I would've remembered either of them. They were the antithesis of my current company, with their suits. One of the new guys was at least a half foot over six feet, and had flaming red hair that made me imagine leprechauns. His companion, although tall, was closer to six, and had the craziest blond beard I'd seen since ZZ Top or Gandalf.

Between their worn leather jackets, which couldn't do much for them in the frigid cold, and the hard stare of their eyes, they appeared like they might've just come from beating someone up in the alley. What was going on?

Had the whole building been taken over while I'd slept on the couch?

"What are you doing here?" one of the suits asked the thugs.

"You're early and you know it." Red tapped his watch as he held it up. "Eight hours left, and don't tell me you didn't know." He spoke like a father chastising his son who was late for dinner.

Beard turned to me and said, "What are you listening for? This conversation has nothing to do with you."

I moved back down to the fifth step. "Who are you? Do you even live here? This is my building and I was speaking to them." I would've pointed condemningly if my hands weren't full of soggy mail.

"Not anymore, you aren't," Beard said, waving his hand at me as if to shoo me upstairs.

"I'll hear that from them, thank you." I looked directly at the two I'd been speaking to. "When does this gig start?" I took a step back down the stairs. "Let's go meet your boss."

The suits were rapidly shaking their heads, and the more assertive, shorter guy said, "No. Sorry. Misunderstanding. We'll see you—"

Red cleared his throat. "You know the rules."

It appeared to be a standoff between the suits and goons. Then, as if coming to some sort of silent conclusion, they all walked out of my lobby without so much as a goodbye.

I took my soggy mail and climbed the stairs. If the scary people didn't want to speak to me then that was fine. They could all go find themselves another victim.

3

Top Gun or *The Neverending Story*—those were the best picks the bargain bin at the corner store could offer up. Great movies, except I'd seen each one more times than I could count.

Both went in the basket. I only had the concentration of a fish these days, so it didn't make much difference what was on. Binging on pizza while watching movies on a screen only a foot away might've been a slump for most, but it was a step up for me at the moment.

It was all about baby steps away from the abyss until I no longer wanted to leap into it with abandon. Since death was off the table, I'd have to go about living to some extent. I'd even showered today and put on clean yoga pants and socks without holes. It was enough progress that I felt justified in going back and falling into the permanent dent in my couch for the next twenty-two hours before being compelled to take some other small step but gigantic push forward.

Movies selected, I ignored a monster hiding in the shadows as I headed toward the conveniently placed chips and candy. Stalling a few more minutes so my pizza would be finished by the time I walked to the pizzeria, I threw some salt and vinegar chips in my basket, along with some Reese's Cups and a pack of Twizzlers. I took a step toward the register before I backtracked and threw in some Laffy Taffy too.

Another dodge around a monster trailing in a fellow shopper's shadow and I was in line at the cashier. I stared up at the chipped ceiling paint and pretended to be pondering some great philosophical question, or maybe I appeared to be pining after a boy. Didn't matter. Monsters didn't float.

The smell of mothballs wafted over from the woman checking out in front of me, carried by a draft from the door opening. Even staring up, I caught sight of the top of a red head that was too tall to stay out of my vision.

No way. Don't look. Keep my eyes on the ceiling. Who cared if it was them? It wasn't like they'd wanted to speak to me anyway. Probably just bored or chilly in the alley.

I hummed Canon in D as Mothballs took her sweet old time emptying her basket.

Red and Beard approached until they were so close that, even staring at the ceiling, it was hard to ignore their warm breath, letting me know someone liked to drink coffee at night.

"Our boss needs to speak to you," Red said, his head bouncing around as if he'd had one cup too many.

"I thought no one wanted to speak to me?" I wasn't sure if it was the fact that we were in a public place that gave me the balls, or the little issue of losing the fear of death since my life literally blew up in front of me. Having a death wish was sort of liberating like that.

"That was *yesterday*," Beard said. "We couldn't speak to you then."

"Sorry, but I'm not in the mood for anyone crazier than myself today. I've already got plans for the evening." I held up my basket so they could see the movies before I turned forward again.

That was when I noticed that Mothballs had paused in emptying her cart so she could see what my new company was about. Great, just what I needed today, for her to let off the gas when she'd already been crawling by on fumes.

Red and Beard remained where they were, practically entrancing Mothballs with their presence.

"You don't understand. He *really* wants to speak with you," Red said.

"Well, if he *really* wants to meet me…" I turned. "It's still no." I looked back to Mothballs. "If you could keep it moving, I'll make sure I give you the CliffsNotes after you're done so you don't miss a word."

She huffed but went back to emptying her cart.

Beard cleared his throat. "We'd like to do this the nice way, but there's other options."

Did they not realize we were in the middle of a store? With an audience? Mothballs was all ears, and she looked the type to have nine-one-one stored in her favorites.

I tilted my head to the side, making sure they had a good view of the eye roll. These two had better work on their act. I wasn't looking to school anyone, but somebody had to help these two out. "Look, I don't want to tell you how to run your business, but shouldn't you two be waiting in a dark alley? This isn't the way to go about things if you want to be successful in your current line of work."

Beard looked at Red. "I'm really sick of doing this, and her being a wiseass isn't putting me in the mood."

"You think I'm in the mood?" Red asked him. "It's enough work when they're scared and do what we tell them to."

I'd gone back to ignoring Beard and Red as Mothballs started arguing with the cashier. "That's the wrong price. It's on sale."

A groan worked its way up out of the depth of my annoyance to settle on my lips. Every time I thought maybe there might be a god, something like this would happen and smash it all to pieces. I tried some deep breathing, like

Dr. Martin had always suggested, but it wasn't making the urge to swat her with my Twizzlers any better.

"Look, can you come nicely?" Red asked. He was nearly screaming as Mothballs was insisting the cashier go to the aisle and check the price.

I dug a quarter out of my pocket and placed it on the counter in front of her. "Here. Here's the quarter. Can we move things along?"

"No. It's on sale," Mothballs said, eyeing my quarter as if it were a pile of rat poop and not the very thing she'd argued for.

I moved back into my spot in line at purgatory, and Beard stepped closer. "You need to come with us."

"Not happening. You need to back off." I hooked a thumb toward Mothballs. "This is making my mood worse, and I didn't start off so good to begin with. Now bugger off." Bugger off? Where had that come from? I'd had the BBC playing in the background a lot. It must've been seeping into my subconscious.

I turned, giving Red and Beard my back. These two whack jobs could go find another victim. I wasn't letting any crazy person kill me if they weren't willing to put in some effort. *You need to come with us.* That was it? That was the best I got? How insulting. They could go wait it out in an alleyway like any other self-respecting thug and try to lure me in, not approach me in the middle of a store.

I felt hands grip my upper arms, and then I was losing my movies and goodies to the floor as they lifted me off my feet in between them.

"What are you doing? Let me go," I said, trying to wriggle out of their grasp, but we were on the move already. "Call the police," I screamed toward Mothballs.

Mothballs, who hadn't been able to get her fill of my business before, didn't seem to care at all as I was being manhandled out of the store.

"Hello! What is up with you people?" I screamed at the cashier, Mothballs, and a few other patrons who went about their business.

"They can't hear you anymore."

"What? Why?" I went limp from shock, and they used the opportunity to ease their transition out the door. It didn't last long, as I swung my legs wildly at the two of them now.

"The way it works," Red said as we crossed the parking lot. They didn't put me down until we'd made our way over to an old Caddy. It was midnight black, pristine, and looked like a seventies model. These guys knew how to roll, I'd give them that, but they were a little dense as far as picking targets.

These two needed a wakeup call before they invested too much more time on me. "Just to lay all our cards out on the table, I have no money." The stained sweatpants and holey socks the other day should've tipped them off, but I wasn't taking anything for granted with these two.

Red almost seemed insulted. "We don't want your money."

Actually, they both were acting like they tasted something sour now. "Then what do you want?"

"You need to come with us and meet someone."

"Why do they want to meet me?" I had nothing. I was an utter nobody. No one wanted to meet me.

"Kane will explain," Beard said, tilting his head toward the car.

I was probably counting down the minutes before they manhandled me into it anyway, but I'd never been one not to push a situation as far as I could go. "If he wanted to meet me so much, why couldn't he have come to me?"

"Because that's not how this goes. It's been a month and now you go see the boss," Beard explained, giving me his full attention until he was distracted by Red popping the trunk on the Caddy. "Why did you do that?"

Red turned and pointed toward me. "Because it's my turn to sit in the back, and I like space. Plus, the last one peed her pants."

"You know, every single time you pop the trunk, it freaks them out and it's not funny. We aren't allowed to put them in there since…" He glanced at me. "Since the incident."

"Even if she's not freaking out? Maybe we can give it a try. It's real roomy in there."

"No. No this time and no for the next fifty times. Stop asking."

They continued to bicker over where I'd go, but all I cared about was what he'd said about a month. It was a month today since everything had fallen apart. How did they know that?

"You said a month?" I asked, looking between Beard and Red. "Why a month? What do you mean by a month?"

Red glanced over at Beard. Beard shrugged in a *why not explain*-type gesture.

Red turned back to me. "A month since the explosion."

"That's why you came to find me?"

"Yeah," Read said as Beard nodded.

I grabbed the front of Red's jacket. "Did you write a note?"

He took a step back, the jacket taut between us. "Didn't write it. Only delivered it. Boss wrote it." My hands dropped as he continued, "By the way, you're going to get bugs if you don't do something about all those pizza boxes."

Could it be that after all this time I'd found someone else who saw the monsters? "He knows about the monsters?"

"Of course he does."

Since I'd been a small child, I'd known things weren't as everyone had told me. Now I finally might have someone who had answers.

"Take me to Kane." I walked over to the car and opened the front passenger door.

Red yelled, "I get shotgun!" as I was closing the door.

Beard opened up the driver's side, calling to Red as he did, "Get in the back."

Beard settled behind the wheel. Red got in behind me, huffing the whole time, and then complaining the seat was too far back as he kicked his legs sideways.

An excitement I hadn't felt in years coursed through my system as Beard pulled out of the parking lot. "How far?"

"Fifteen minutes," Beard answered.

Fifteen minutes. That was all. I glanced out the window, amazed that this person had been so close, answers just out of reach.

I'd thought I knew every part of Boston there was. I'd been born and raised here, but after ten minutes, we were turning onto streets I'd never seen before. They were empty except for what I could only assume were gangs.

"Where are we?"

"About a block away," Red said from the back seat.

"But where? I've never seen this area of town." We drove past two men in a fistfight in the middle of the street.

"This is No Man's Land."

Beard pulled the Caddy into an empty alleyway, and I followed them out of the car.

Beard and Red waved me forward to a steel door that sat at the end of the alley. The building it belonged to looked like an old factory. It was hard to tell what was in it from ground level, since there weren't any windows until the second floor.

I stepped forward to where they were waiting in front of the door. "Your boss, this Kane person, he's here?"

"Yes. This is his building," Beard said as Red started banging on the door.

I looked around the place, but there wasn't much to see as Red banged over and over again.

"Damn, Jerry. He always leaves his post." Red was shaking his head as he pulled out his phone. "Hey, fucko, answer the door," he screamed into it after a second. He pocketed his phone and looked at Beard. "He was winded when he answered."

Beard shook his head, sending his beard into a little waggle as he did. "That boy cannot keep it in his pants. He still hooking up with the vamp?"

Vamp? As in vampire? I kept my mouth shut, afraid to stop the flow of conversation.

"Either that or he's running marathons in under five minutes. You know what they're like in..." Red looked over at me. "You know what I'm talking about."

I kept my head turned slightly as if I weren't interested, but the conversation seemed to have halted in spite of my act.

Vamps. It had to mean vampires. If there were monsters, it wasn't a huge leap to think there were other things. Were these two vampires? Nah. Didn't seem so from the way they'd been speaking about the "vamp."

I was ready to start bouncing on my heels if I didn't get in there and to this Kane person soon. I'd been waiting years to get answers, and now I had to wait for this Jerry to have sex? It was near unbearable.

Rubbing my arms to ward off the chill, I asked, "You sure he's coming?"

The door swung open before they could answer.

A strapping kid in his mid-twenties opened the door, all tan and glowing, as if he belonged in the islands and not this frigid winter. He seemed happy enough, with a smile on his face as he apologized with perfect white teeth, to have been doing exactly as they'd assumed.

At least, I thought he was apologizing. It was hard to hear with the heavy bass blasting out of the door.

"You going to leave us out here all damn night?" Red asked. Him I could still hear.

"You know how boring this shit is," Jerry said as he backed up and I followed Red inside the place, Beard following behind me.

The place was not what I'd been expecting from the outside. It was teeming with people and looked more like a club than a factory.

It was a humongous open floor with a two-story ceiling, and steel-topped tables scattered about. Some people were lounging around with drinks in front of them, a few were dancing, and some played cards with stacks of chips in front of them. A bar ran the length of the wall, with no bartender in sight, and there were a few booths hugging the corners.

"Lower this shit!" Red yelled. I hadn't noticed a DJ, but someone was handling the music, because the decibels immediately came down a few notches.

Beard motioned for me to follow him farther into the place. No one gave us more than a passing glance as we walked toward the back of the room, where a set of stairs led to a second-story walkway that ended with a door to a room that was above the main floor.

The people in here might not have been interested in me, but I couldn't help being mesmerized by them. They all seemed a bit...*odd*. Not in a way I could put my finger on...they just were. It was like when you caught sight of a strange person on the street but someone had gone and gathered them all up in the same place. Were some of these people vampires?

"What is this place?" I asked Beard, Red lingering behind and, from the looks of it, trying to unsuccessfully chastise a smiling Jerry.

"*This* is the Underground," Beard said.

"Like, a club for...underground types?"

He smiled. "Exactly."

As if they somehow sensed the need to demonstrate just how different they were, two men in the center of the room stood up, almost upending the table full of cards and chips in front of them.

"You're a fucking cheat," one of the men said, and I was close enough to see his fangs drop down as his lips curled back.

Holy shit, there *were* vampires in this place.

"Prove it!" the other shouted, and then his clothes were tearing off him until he morphed into a huge, snarling wolf. It happened so fast that I almost didn't believe what I'd seen. Except I knew I'd just seen it. A vampire and a werewolf were about to rip into each other before my very eyes.

Beard reached forward, wrapped a hand around my arm, and tugged me back a few feet. "This is why they shouldn't be able to play cards together, but nobody listens to me. Every damn week."

Jerry, the handsome, smiling doorman, quickly made his way over and inserted himself in between the two about to go at each other as Red made his way toward me and Beard.

"Shouldn't one of you two be helping him?"

Beard waved a hand in Jerry's direction. "He's fine. Kane will be out any second anyway. No one's allowed to fight on the floor."

"Pisses him off real bad," Red added. "He's sick of replacing furniture. Rules are, if you want to kill someone, you've got to take it out to the alley, where you can't break anything. Also, it's good to point out that you need to hose down any blood or fleshy bits left over. Those little pieces get stuck in the concrete nooks and crannies, and they'll build up after a while. You get a bad stench then."

Red was looking at me as if I'd understand what he was talking about, and I nodded, having not one idea what a rational answer sounded like in this situation. What the hell had I just walked into?

Beard took one look at me and must have read the shock there, even as I tried to hide it. He turned to Red, speaking over my head to him. "How many times do I have to tell you, too much information? Little bits at a time."

Growling in the center of the room drew my attention back to the pair squaring off. Beard and Red were continuing to argue about how much I needed to know at the moment, when a light from above halted everyone in the room.

A man stepped onto the landing outside of the room above, and all eyes settled on his broad frame. He didn't say anything, but the vampire's fangs snapped back in and the werewolf let out a whimper as it sat back on its haunches.

The man on the top landing glanced around the room. His eyes landed on me briefly before he looked at my companions. He nodded before walking back into the room, this time leaving the door open.

"Who was that?" I asked, already sensing I'd found my destination.

"That would be the boss," Red said as he moved toward the stairs.

Beard's hand at my back suggested I follow. I was sandwiched between the two men as we made our way toward the stairs.

Peace returned, people turned occasionally as we walked past them, and I picked up the words "paper doll" more than once as they looked me over.

Why in the world would they call me a paper doll?

4

The room above the chaos turned out to be an office. A single lamp sat on a desk and shed just enough light to see how well used the space was as I took in the piles of papers and boxes with more papers beside it.

There were lots of papers and boxes, but no monsters? Where were the monsters? I turned, searching for them just as he spoke.

"This her?" The voice was deep, with a slight gravel to it, and although this man had spoken softly, he easily dominated the room.

I turned toward his voice, seeing him walk from one of the darkened corners across the room. He was taller than I'd realized. The smell of sandalwood and cedar, and something indefinably male, drifted toward me in his wake as he moved toward the desk.

He spared me a glance. Deep-set hazel eyes seemed to size me up in that instant and determine my value, before he settled behind the desk and his attention was drawn to one of his many papers. With his dark head turned, only a strong profile was visible.

The brief attention gave me a pretty good idea what he'd deemed my value to be. The last time I'd been dismissed so quickly by a man was before I'd gotten my first training bra.

"Yeah, Kane. This is the new one," Beard said.

Kane's perceived value meant nothing as I stepped forward on my own and took the chair in front of his desk, keeping my chin up and my shoulders square. It didn't matter if he'd dismissed me as if I were a rat scurrying across his floor. That wasn't my purpose here. Hopefully this man had the answer to a question I'd been asking my entire life. "Are you—"

He held up a hand, as if to tell me he needed another minute, except without being polite about it in any way. I held my tongue, but only because I needed him.

He finally laid the paper he was so engrossed by on his desk and gave me his full attention—for another half-second, anyway, before he turned to his man who was busy making himself a Keurig coffee on the side of the room.

"Butch, did you drop off that other thing before you fetched her?" he asked, looking at the man I'd been thinking of as Red.

"Yeah. Had to scare off the others before we got to her." Butch rustled through a small drawer of little cups before he turned to Beard. "Leon, did you take the last French vanilla again?"

Leon walked over and peered over Butch's shoulder. "I might've."

"You might've, or you *know*?" Butch asked.

Kane kicked his feet up on his desk. "Leon, you forget to tell Isabella again?"

"Might've." Leon's cheeks bunched up.

Butch grabbed a little plastic cup out of the drawer, shaking his head the whole time he loaded it into the machine. "This is the third time you've done this in a month. You keep using all the French vanilla and then not telling Isabella."

"You're going to go out and get more before tomorrow morning," Kane said to Leon.

Leon shrugged as he put up his hands. "I know. I'll go. I swear."

Butch took his coffee from the machine. "No, you're really going this time. If I have to drink that other shit tomorrow, you're collecting the next one on your own."

Next one? Did they mean people? This wasn't the first time they'd mentioned having done this before. How many times had this happened? Looking about the room and their attitudes, it certainly didn't seem as if I were a novelty.

Leon moved in front of the machine. "I said I'd go. What else do you want from me?"

Butch didn't' stop shaking his head until he took a sip of his new coffee, which seemed to start him back up again. "I swear, no French vanilla and you are on solo."

Leo wasn't even speaking anymore, but gesturing with his hands, as if to say, *I can't do anything else about it.*

I'd watched a vampire and a werewolf nearly kill each other a minute ago, I'd confirmed that my monsters were real an hour ago, and all these people were worried about was having the waft of French vanilla clinging to their morning coffee? Enough with this. "Excuse me."

When that didn't stop the coffee quibbling, I repeated myself, a hair shy of a scream. "Excuse me."

They all turned toward me as if they had forgotten I was sitting there.

I nailed this Kane with a glare worthy of my cashier days, when a customer didn't help bag. "I'm sure your coffee is very important, but *you* wanted to talk to me. Are we talking or not, because I've got other things I could be doing." I didn't bother mentioning that I'd probably want to talk to him more.

Kane's attention was back on me, and his head tilted slightly to the side. "More backbone than the others. I dare say a little prickly, even? You sure you grabbed the right one?"

His goons had a good chuckle.

Butch sipped his second-choice coffee. "She's a bit feistier than the others, for sure, but she checks all the boxes."

"She does looks like one—black hair and grey eyes." Kane's gaze ran the length of me now that I had his attention. I gripped my hands on my lap, refusing to straighten my hair or look at the hole in my shirt. I shouldn't have worried. The appraisal didn't last long before he turned back to his thugs. "Where did you pick her up?"

"Store near her apartment," Leon added, searching for his own K-cup as he struggled to make a choice.

Kane looked down at his desk again, holding up a sheet of paper. "Your name is Olivia Wit, correct?"

"I'd hope you would know that after your men stalked me for the last two days." "Stalked" might've been a little strong, but I needed to make my point. He was the one that wanted something, as far as he knew.

Kane let out a small laugh before adding, "She is amusing."

For someone who looked to be in his early thirties, he'd really been spending a lot of that time growing a hell of an ego on him. If I hadn't needed answers, I might've told him to go screw and walked out. But I did, so I sat silently and glanced around the room again.

Where were they? They never went away, ever. I leaned back, making it look like I was checking out where Butch and Leon were as I checked out every corner of the room again. They had to be here. Had to.

"Are you looking for something?"

I swung back around to see Kane had gotten out of his seat and perched on the desk right in front of me. It reeked of an intimidation tactic. Wouldn't work. You can't scare someone with a death wish. Only thing it did was confirm that the two of us were about as alike as the North Pole and the equator.

I lounged back in my seat, muscles as languid as ever, and I could see from the way his eyes took in my form that he got the signal. This Kane guy was full of himself, but some of the ego might've been earned. He was not going to be easy to navigate.

Decades worth of questions were rattling around in my mind, but spewing them out rapid fire wasn't a good way to ensure I'd get the answers. He'd been searching for me. He needed me for something. That was the most important question at the moment.

"I'm not looking for anything. Your men said you wanted to speak to me?" I raised my eyebrows, letting him know that I wasn't to be toyed with. Game on.

"If you're honest, this will go much smoother. You don't want to lie to me." He didn't break eye contact, his legs a foot from my own.

I stared back. "And if I don't answer?"

"This chick ain't only crazy, she's got a death wish," Butch whispered to Leon while they drank their coffee. They were watching the standoff between us like we weren't just prime time, but prime time on premium cable.

The thing was, I wasn't crazy. I needed answers, and badly. I couldn't blow it by getting my back up because maybe this guy wasn't so likeable.

We watched each other for another couple of seconds before he made a second attempt.

"You're seeing a psychiatrist because of visions?"

I knew I had to meet him halfway. I couldn't leave without answers… I just couldn't. "If I answer your questions, will you answer mine?"

He nodded. "If I can. Tell me about the visions."

I glanced to the corner behind him, still looking for the monsters that had gone missing, before I looked back at him and said, "I see things in the shadows."

"What types of things?"

I slumped in my chair, pulling away as much as I could, from the questioner and the question, out of reflex. I'd said I wanted answers, and I did, but years of hiding the truth was a hard habit to overcome. I didn't talk about this, not unless I had to, and certainly not to someone I didn't know.

But this was the cost, and I'd never been so close to the truth before. "It varies. They come in all shapes and sizes. The only constant is that they seem to form in the shadows of things. Sometimes a person's shadow and sometimes the shadow of things like a bookcase or a house."

He crossed his arms as he leaned back. "Do they speak to you?"

"Sometimes." I crossed my arms. "My turn. The monsters I see in the shadows, do you know what they are?"

"I know about everything."

That was one of those statements that would've driven me crazy before the explosion, before I'd learned what really mattered. He could keep his arrogance as long as he could manage. He'd learn, just as I had, that nothing and no one in this world was safe. Once you learned that lesson, it was hard to feel like anything grander than an ant moving along and waiting to be stepped on.

Didn't matter what delusions he had. They weren't my problem.

"Then what are these monsters that…" My brain always got stuck on this part, like a mental tic or a skip in a record, as if my mind was trying to delete that verse of the song.

"That caused the explosion?" he added.

He hadn't helped out of consideration, but out of expedience. This man was as cold as a January frost.

"Yes." Every other time I'd broached the subject of the monsters in the shadows, I'd been laughed out of the room. It was hard to believe that after twenty-two years, I might finally get some answers.

"They're called crawlers, and they're real enough to take out an entire building full of people. They're creatures from another dimension that leak out into this world. Most can't see them. That doesn't mean they aren't real.

"That's how I found you. There's certain telltale signs of their presence. Mass casualty events with only one survivor tend to be a flag."

"That thing, the one that I saw right before…" Fuck. I was not going to get choked up now. I needed to pull it together.

So much for game on. If I kept going like this, it was going to be more like cry on. My entire life I'd been told I was crazy. I'd lost everything and people had said I was having a psychotic breakdown. And just like that, in a blink of an eye, all my beliefs were validated, and in the worst possible way.

"Ah, fuck. She's gonna cry now. They always cry," Butch said.

"I hate this part," Leon added.

I turned and nailed the thug brothers with a look that would've fried bacon. "Do I appear to be crying to you?" And I wouldn't, especially not now.

Turning away from them, I tried to concentrate on the information Kane was giving me, but I couldn't stop myself from getting sucked back into the swamp of emotions. They nearly drowned me every time I thought of that day.

I could still see the blast, feel the heat as I stood there and watched, knowing in that moment they were all gone—my father, my mother, and my sister. "I tried to get them out."

My skin warmed as I realized what had slipped out, and I wished I could reel the words back in. I seemed to have a problem with shutting down completely whenever I remembered.

Whenever I had talked about the incident, whoever the unlucky bystander was who might've been nearby, they always tried to make me feel better. I'd watch as they'd searched for words that would fix this. Some things weren't fixable. You merely learned to live with them.

I glanced up and could see this man didn't have that issue. He wasn't searching for words. He took what I'd said in as if it were a statement, and made no effort to fix it. I wasn't sure if it was because he knew he couldn't or if he was so cold he simply didn't care enough to try.

Maybe it should've been hurtful, but it wasn't. It was a relief. I'd spent too many years trying to ward off other people's fixes even before this, and nothing was preferable.

When he finally spoke again, it wasn't to me, but to Butch and Leon.

"Definitely Shadow Walker."

They grunted their agreement.

"A Shadow Walker?" I asked, looking at him, then to Butch and Leon, then back to him. "How did this happen to me?"

He straightened and walked behind his desk, as if he were losing interest again, but he kept talking. "A Shadow Walker is an anomaly of the human race. They pop up randomly from ordinary families all the time for no apparent reason."

"Can you all see them, too?"

"I can." He pointed at his men. "They can't."

"Are you a Shadow Walker?"

"No."

The answer was abrupt enough that I knew there would be no other details forthcoming about how he could see them too. I didn't care. The importance of it was dwarfed by the magnitude of the reality that he was confirming for me.

"So, what do you want from me? I'm sure you didn't bring me here for my own enlightenment." I doubted this man did anything for anyone but himself.

He laid another piece of paper he'd been perusing on the desk and looked back at me. "I need you to talk to these monsters."

"Why don't you talk to them yourself?"

"Because they'll only speak to a Shadow Walker. For this, I'll pay you five million dollars. Enough so that you can go lock yourself into a dark room until you die, if that's what you want. I also know of a way to get rid of the crawlers after you're done, if that's also something you want."

He could get rid of them? Was that really possible? I bit the side of my mouth so as to not spurt out what I was really thinking. If he had any idea how much I wanted them gone, who knew what someone like him would ask?

"Ten million," I said, not caring if he gave a dime. I'd hold a conversation with my shoes for fifty bucks if he wanted. I'd talk up a storm, like a drunken parrot on a pirate ship, if that was what it took to get rid of these crawlers.

"Done," he said, as if it were of no consequence.

If he was lying about the money, he might be lying about getting rid of the monsters too. "I want to see proof of funds."

His eyebrows rose, as if he doubted what he'd heard. "Proof of funds?"

"Yes. I think that's a pretty standard request, considering the transaction you're proposing. Don't you have a bank statement or something?"

"There's other ways to accomplish this."

"I'm sure there are." I knew an implied threat when I heard one, and I thought on it for a moment. Then decided I didn't care. "From what I'm hearing and surmising from you and your men, I'm not the first Shadow Walker you've...*approached*. Maybe not even the twentieth?"

He leaned an elbow on the arm of his chair, not admitting or denying. I peeked over my shoulder, and the thug brothers both shrugged. Good enough.

Turning back around, I leaned forward as if I were about to share a dark secret with Kane, then whispered in a sort of loud way, "Doesn't seem like it's been working out so hot, so I think you should work with me."

His jaw shifted slightly; he clearly wasn't appreciating my humor. "I'm tempted to throw caution to the wind and let you go self-destruct on your own."

It was the first time I'd seen anything other than a frosty exterior, and the heat he threw off nearly singed me across the desk.

He was pissed, but I wasn't playing make-believe that he could do what he said without some sort of proof. "Is that a no?"

"I'd show her proof," Leon said from the back corner of the room. "I think this one might actually last a while."

Kane's eyes flickered over my face, and I knew he was judging me by some measure I couldn't possibly guess at, as this was my first go around, and who knew how long these people had been doing this?

"You're pretty fearless," he said.

My eyes widened a hair at the unexpected compliment. "Thank you."

He wasn't smiling when he added, "Probably to the point of stupidity."

I crossed my legs as I mustered up my best glare. "I've been scared a long time and it's gotten me nowhere. Useless emotion."

"I hope you can hang on to that attitude, but I'm not optimistic. There's a lot to be scared of."

He was speaking to me as if I knew nothing of the world, as if I hadn't lived through my own personal hell. Maybe I was barely hanging on, but that didn't mean I still wasn't holding. "I don't break easy."

"Break?" he scoffed as if I'd made a bad joke. "You think what you've been doing is living? You're already broken."

I looked at the handsome bastard who seemed to think he knew it all, and couldn't stop myself from jabbing back. "Yeah? Well, I'm not so optimistic about you, either."

I wished my insult took root, but it didn't seem to even nick his surface.

He reached down, and I heard the sound of a dial moving then the noise a safe makes as its locks disengage.

"Here," he said, dropping the contents of a velvet bag on the table. "There's proof of funds."

The diamonds sparkled in the light, but that didn't mean they were real.

"How do I know they aren't cubic zirconia?"

He relaxed back on his reclining chair, and I got the sense he wasn't going to argue with me anymore.

"Supposing you do have the cash—"

"Why, thank you for that leap of trust."

I nodded, not really caring about the money so much, but the next thing was a deal breaker. But if he was honest about the cash, he was probably on the up-and-up about being able to get rid of the crawlers. "So, I get the money, you'll get rid of the creatures, and all I need to do in return is speak to them?"

"Yes. They have information I need." He was leaning back in his chair again as he sorted through more papers, as if this negotiation was taking up too much of his time.

"What information?"

He didn't bother looking up at me as he answered. "A spell. I'll let you know more as needed."

"I can get spells? As in magical spells?" Magic. I could do magic? While I was in awe, he seemed uninterested.

"Yes." He reached over and pressed a button on the phone on his desk. "Bella, can you come in here, please?"

A stunning blonde, probably about the same age as Kane, if I had to guess, walked in a moment later. After a quick glance at me, she stepped around the desk to stand so close to Kane that her pencil skirt and blouse brushed his arm.

"What rooms do we have available?" Kane asked, glancing at her.

She opened up the book she had in her hands and blew out a little stream of air as her eyes widened. "We're pretty packed since the fire sisters burned down the building on eighth."

"Is there anything? She's a Shadow Walker, so…" His voice was soft as he spoke to her, and I wasn't sure if it was because of who he was speaking to or the subject matter.

"Oh." She glanced over at me again as if she'd missed something, then went back to her book. "Well, if it's not going to be for long, there's always the suite on sixth if you want to put her there."

"I don't need a room. I haven't agreed yet, and I definitely didn't say I'd stay here even if I did."

Kane and Isabella glanced at me as if they thought they'd heard something, but then went back to speaking to each other.

"Nothing else?" His voice, which had been softer, now held a slight edge.

"I know you like to leave that open, but it's the only thing available."

"Fine. Give her the rooms on sixth." He was addressing her and motioning toward me with his hand.

"I haven't agreed to stay. You can't keep me here. It's against the law."

"Whose law?" He shook his head while Butch and Leon laughed, and even this Isabella woman was smiling.

"You people can laugh all you want. I'm not staying here." I made sure I looked at everyone in the room so they saw this wasn't a joke to me.

I'd just finished glaring at Leon when Kane said, "And I'm not going to force you to. You're going to come back here of your own accord within days. Your kind always do. I'm doing you a favor."

I stood, getting ready to make a run for it if needed, in case he was lying. "You can keep your favors. I don't need them."

I heard the thugs exhaling loudly. The woman rolled her eyes, and Kane didn't seem to care either way.

"I knew she was going to be more difficult than the others," Butch said. "She came too easy. It didn't bode well."

I turned in time to see his friend shake his head in commiseration. As if noticing me watching him, he added, "Cut her some slack. She doesn't know any better."

I was certain that was for my sake alone.

Kane cleared his throat. "I don't have time for this right now. Don't speak to the monsters without me and don't get involved if you see something. The rest we'll work out when you get back. You can go now."

"See something?" I asked.

His attention had already moved on to something Isabella was showing him.

"See what?"

"You'll understand." He pointed to Butch and Leon. "See her home." He went back to his paperwork and waved a hand toward the door, dismissing me.

As I walked from the room, the only thing that kept repeating in my head was, *What a dick.*

Didn't matter. I knew what I was now, and I had a name for the monsters. I might not have to ever come back. If he knew a way to get rid of these crawlers, then I'd be able to find it too.

5

"Come on, let's go bring you home," Leon said as we walked away from Kane's office.

"For now," Butch added.

I nearly tripped over my feet by the sudden reemergence of the crawlers, but caught myself before I fell. "Why weren't there crawlers in the office?"

"Me and Butch don't see them. Couldn't tell you why they're one place and not another," Leon said.

I moved forward, walking down the stairs. Butch and Leon were walking behind me as I heard Butch saying to Leon, "How do we keep pulling this duty for the last goddamn six months?"

"Because you pissed him off and I tried to cover your ass. You did this to us. It's your fault," Leon replied.

"Exactly how many women have you kidnapped?" I asked as Leon moved past me once we hit the main floor.

"Not only women. Men too. We like to consider ourselves equal opportunity abductors," he answered with a chuckle.

"How many people, then?"

"I don't know, a few hundred?" Butch asked Leon.

Leon nodded. "Yeah, about that, give or take fifty. But they weren't all abductions. I mean, you came mostly willingly, if you think about it."

"What happened to the others?" I asked as we made our way through the main room that seemed to be in full swing now. I saw a couple of pairs of fangs hanging down, and the man who had turned into a wolf.

"Shadow Walkers never last long. They seem to be born inherently weak. That's why they're called paper dolls. It's not like humans tend to be strong, but nothing like paper dolls," Butch said.

Leon turned and shot Butch a look.

Butch said, "It's not like she wouldn't have found out."

I didn't bother mentioning that I'd already heard the name on the way in, and it wasn't a huge leap of logic to put that together. That wasn't the thing that caught my attention.

"Why do you say human like I'm the only human here?"

Leon cleared his throat. "That's not what he said." He was staring down Butch something awful.

"Nope. You misunderstood. Me and Leon, a hundred percent human. Kane too." Butch moved in front of me, and then Leon, with a sudden burst of energy toward the door.

The cold, brittle air gusted through the alley as we made our way toward the Caddy, Butch speeding forward and yanking open the front passenger door.

"You're such a child," Leon called. He motioned me toward the back seat.

I couldn't seem to remember how we'd gotten here, or I would've headed off on foot. But I didn't know how to get back, and it was really damn cold, so I climbed in the back seat.

It didn't take long for Butch to start chatting to Leon. "One of these times I say we just keep 'em. I'm tired of escorting them all around when I have plans. We lock 'em up in one of the closets until they are willing to do whatever he says."

Leon waved his right hand all around. "You know how Kane feels about that. Waste of energy when they all come back on their own."

I ignored their chatter. It didn't matter what they said or what they wanted, and they could talk about closets the whole way back if they felt like it. I wasn't going to see either of them again anyway. I was going home with the answers I'd gotten, and it would be enough to find my own way out of this mess.

I settled back and tried to commit the scenery to memory as we rode away from the building to parts of Boston I recognized. By the time we hit the North End, I couldn't remember how we'd gotten there.

They pulled up to the curb right in front of my building.

I got out of the car, never so happy to see my building.

I glanced back at them as they got out of the car. "That's a tow away zone." As far as I was concerned, a ticket was the least these two should get, but maybe that would make them leave.

"Yeah, it's great you have one right in front of your building," Butch said, as they both followed me inside the lobby.

I kept walking forward, still hoping they wouldn't follow.

"No elevator?" Butch asked as I walked past it and to the stairs.

"It's only one flight, and you don't need to see me up." I climbed. They followed.

I managed to open up a gap of space between us as I got to my apartment. I opened the door and the two suits I'd seen, the ones who'd approached me yesterday in the lobby, were sitting on my couch eating my Doritos.

"What are you doing?"

One of them looked up mid-crunch.

"Sorry. You've been gone a while, and we got hungry." His shorter friend put the cookies he was holding down on my table, next to what I knew to be my last bottle of water.

"What I mean is, what are you doing in my apartment?" I walked over and jerked the bag of Doritos away. Between the cookies and the Doritos, they were eating what would probably be my dinner tonight, since the pizzeria had surely tossed my pie hours ago.

One of the suits' mouths dropped open, as they caught sight of Butch and Leon entering behind me.

"You two," he sputtered.

"Time to leave. Already brokered a deal." Leon waved his hands in a grand gesture toward the open door that was partially visible through the hall.

"You brokered a deal with them? But we saw you first," the shorter one whined as they stood.

"Yes," I lied. I thought I lied, anyway. I hadn't signed anything. "Get out and leave my cookies."

"You heard her," Butch said.

I watched as the two men got up and made a path for the door. They were leaving, but it wasn't quietly.

The shorter of the two mumbled, "I told you not to eat those Doritos. Told you she wouldn't like it. Now look."

"I was only going to have one chip when you dug the cookies out."

"You started it."

"Was I supposed to watch you eat?"

I could hear them arguing all the way down the hall.

"You too," I said as I watched Butch and Leon making their way to the couch. "I want to be alone, and I don't need you people here."

"We cleared your apartment and now we have to go?" Butch asked, as if somehow insulted.

I pointed toward the door.

Butch shook his head but turned to leave. "Just once it would be nice if it went down differently," he said to Leon.

"I know," Leon said, following him.

I watched them exit and shut the door behind them, but just as with the first two, I could hear them speaking as they walked away.

"She didn't seem so bad," Leon said.

"She's talking a good game, but she's still a paper doll. She's not going to be around long, anyway."

I locked the deadbolt and opened my laptop. My fingers flew over the keyboard as I typed, *Shadow Walker and Crawlers*.

Unfortunately, this wouldn't be easy, since all three of those words were common enough to draw thousands of hits.

I grabbed my bag of Doritos and a half-full bottle of water I'd left in the kitchen, settled into my dent, and started reading.

I looked at the monster closest to me curled up on my couch like it was a pet cat, and was tempted to ask the little shit how it spelled its name. Even if it did answer, I'd given up on making heads or tails of most of their words years ago. It was an odd day when they spoke anything resembling English. Plus, Kane had warned me not to speak to them. Maybe it was for the best to err on the side of caution.

After I'd spoken to them the last time…

Nope, not going to think of that.

No matter how many articles I pulled up, nothing sounded remotely like what I was dealing with. There was that weird occult shop on the corner. I'd stopped in there a very long time ago, but I hadn't had a name then. Might not hurt to stop in there now. I found their hours online and shut my computer.

Eyes burning from lack of sleep, I checked the time. A couple of hours and they'd be opening for the morning.

I leaned back into my indent, hoping they'd have answers and I wouldn't have to go talk to that nasty man again.

6

Even though I'd tried to catch some sleep in the couple of hours left before dawn, I was as wired as if I'd had jumper cables hooked up to me. Having another person say the monsters were real somehow made them all the worse. By the time the clock hit twenty to nine, I was out the door and heading to the mystical shop on foot, not wanting to get stuck in a cab with a crawler.

I got there ten minutes earlier than their opening time, but the lights were already on and the door was unlocked. There was a lone woman sitting behind the table. Her hair was a mixture of blond and grey, with all sorts of wavy pieces trying to break free from order.

"Can I help you?" She had a manner about her that invited confidence, and there was a price list hanging behind her that offered tarot readings by Susie for thirty dollars.

I glanced at the back wall of the shop, which was lined with books. "Do you have any books on Shadow Walkers?"

Her face scrunched like a paper bag, adding ten years to the already forty-something. "Shadow what?"

I leaned a hand on the glass counter that housed all sorts of stone baubles, fearing I'd already gotten my answer. "Walkers. Shadow Walkers."

"Never heard the term." Her head tilted. "What is that?"

I rested both hands. "What about crawlers? Have you ever heard of them?"

She pursed her lips and shook her head. "Never. Are you sure you have that right? I thought I'd heard of everything."

I dropped my head. "I don't know."

"I've heard of a lot of stuff, but not that," she said.

I nodded. I was going to have to go back. If I couldn't find out any more on my own, I wasn't going to have a choice. I took a couple of steps away and then sat on the wooden bench not far from the register as an especially ugly crawler sidled up beside Susie.

I had the names, and they did nothing for me. Had he made them up? Resting elbows on knees, I dropped my face into my hands. What choice did I have but to go back?

"You know, I've got a friend, a fella that owns a shop on the other side of town. I could give him a call if you want?"

She was probably offering because I presented such a pathetic-looking figure. Maybe she was afraid I wasn't going to leave as I sat there pondering my options on her bench. I didn't particular care why. I popped my head back up. "That would be fantastic."

She nodded, not looking overly happy she'd mentioned it, but digging out her cell phone and calling anyway.

"Hey, Pete, I've got a girl over here that's asking if I've got any information or books on something called a Shadow Walker or crawlers?" She looked at me as she said the words, as if to make sure she had them right.

I nodded.

She let her eyes wander around the shop the way people do when they're only half listening to a conversation. Then something was said that caught her attention, her brow furrowed, and her eyes shifted back to me.

"Yeah, I'm still here," she answered. "Okay."

She hung up the phone but kept it in her hand. She licked her lips and mustered up a fake smile.

"Sorry, he didn't know anything, so you should probably get going." She was going to lose some skin on her hand if she didn't let up on the knuckle rubbing.

I slowly rose to my feet. "You're lying."

"You need to go now." She took a step back, her eyes darting around the shop as if looking for an escape route.

"Not until you tell me what you know," I said, walking over to the counter.

"Will you go then?" Her voice had acquired a whine.

"Yes," I answered, and hoped I wasn't lying.

"All he knows is it's some sort of dark magic and that really bad things happen around you people."

"You people?"

"He said if you were asking, there was a good chance you were either one or connected to one somehow." She pointed toward the door. "That's all he said. I swear. Now please leave or I'm going to call the police."

"Thank you," I said, and turned to leave. She followed me at a distance, and I saw her locking the door through the windows a moment later, and then pulling down her shades.

What kind of monster was I?

I walked a few blocks away, coming to terms with the fact that I might need Kane. I might have to go back there.

No might. I *was* going to have to go back.

I dodged a monster that vaguely reminded me of Snuffleupagus from *Sesame Street* and was walking along in a small girl's shadow, and found myself heading toward the mall. I didn't know why, but the monsters tended to not like the place that much. Maybe if I could get rid of some of them, I could think clearer. There had to be some other way than him.

After dodging another twenty or so monsters, it wasn't long before I was swinging open the door to the mall entrance and getting hit with a blast of warm air, just in time to keep my toes from freezing. I hit the main floor and headed toward the candle shop. Not only did the crawlers not like the mall, they seemed to hate the smell of candles. It wouldn't buy me too much time, because their like for me seemed greater than their aversion to smelly wax.

I turned a corner, five stores away from smelling some pumpkin spice and berry blast, and saw them.

A teenage girl, maybe seventeen or eighteen, was leaning with her back against the wall in between a sporting goods store and Sarah's Secret Undies. A man, about twenty, was facing her, his hand planted on the wall beside her shoulder. I was only ten feet shy of them when I watched as the man curled his lips back, his fangs descended, and he sank them into her throat.

There, in the middle of the mall. During the day? There wasn't a drop of sunlight in this place, though. Could be?

As I fought back a scream, people walked past as if it weren't happening.

His head was positioned in a way that made me think his teeth must've been in her. The girl started pushing on his chest, and then switched to hitting his shoulders and back when that didn't work.

Kane's words came back to me. *Don't get involved.*

"Fuck. That."

I wasn't a total novice. I'd watched Buffy. I knew what I had to do.

I searched the immediate vicinity for a weapon. A stake; I needed some sort of stake. Luckily, I was next to a Tim's Toys. There was a miniature pool table set up outside, with tiny cue sticks. I grabbed one off the table and ran up behind the creature before he killed the girl.

I gripped the cue with both hands over my head. I only had one shot of killing it, and that was while the vampire was transfixed on sucking everything this girl had out of her.

The disgusting results from slamming a makeshift stake into the heart of the creature were immediate. The man was gone, replaced by a pile of goo and clothes in front of me, and I was left holding the miniature cue. I'd just killed my first vampire.

People kept walking past as if nothing were amiss. The girl, who'd been screaming, was now calm and rubbing her neck as if she had a cramp.

Her eyes settled on me as I stared at her, waiting for her to start gushing thanks.

She looked down at the ground between us. "Ew, did you just, like…throw up? Gross." She curled up her lips and walked away, as if I were a drunken bum.

I dropped the stick in the pile, my hands shaking. What the hell was going on here?

It took ten minutes to run back to my apartment, and I almost wiped out as I ran up the stairs because of all the puddles. Someone needed to put up a damn sign. As soon as I reached my apartment, I slammed and locked my door behind me and then sagged against it.

Then I looked down the hallway and saw my living room.

My blinds had been pulled down and the cushions of my couch ripped open. My table was broken, only three legs left, with a stray one across the room.

I half walked, half bounced off the walls, on my way to the bedroom, to find it was no better, my drawers emptied, the mattress off its frame. Not to mention the place was crawling with monsters, and I didn't have time for them.

"Get the hell away," I yelled as a large one stepped in front of me.

I clapped a hand over my mouth, but the words were already out. Great. Now I'd done both of the things that Kane had asked me not to, just as I was coming to terms with him being my only option.

On my way out, I shut and locked the apartment, more out of habit than anything else. I could leave it open at this point. What was the worst that would happen? They'd cut my couch into *four* pieces?

I walked down the stairs and made it across the street before grinding to a halt. I had no idea where Kane was. I couldn't remember the first thing about getting back to his building, and I'd tried to commit it to memory.

My mind was filled with nothing but gaping holes when the explosion happened. Instinct had me crouching and covering my head as debris rained down.

Not again.

I stayed there, huddled on the sidewalk, as I heard people yelling and running past me.

My arms were still wrapped around my head, and I might have stayed like that all night if someone hadn't stopped in front of me.

"You okay, lady? Were you in there?" a boy asked.

I coughed, trying to clear my throat enough to sound confident.

"I'm fine. I was just walking by."

The kid, probably only ten or eleven, nodded and moved closer to the scene that was still at my back.

I stood but didn't look, only moved farther down the block until I would appear to be more of a spectator to the fire than a victim. There was a little unoccupied stoop I crouched into, preparing for what I'd see.

The entire building, from the first floor to the sixth, was blowing flames. Large chunks of the brick wall were missing; the largest section was where my apartment had been.

People were coming out of the nearby building like ants out of a disrupted nest, all swarming to see the tragedy. The crawlers watched beside me as if mesmerized by the flames' dance of destruction, as the last of my life seemed to smolder away.

* * *

The hours churned on as the fire department fought a flame that refused to go out. People came and went, drifting closer until they'd gotten their fill of the disaster and left to go to their own cozy homes. I stopped noticing them as I sat there. I didn't notice much of anything other than the flames, until the monsters started to scatter. Since I'd been old enough to remember, they'd been with me. There had only been one time that they'd been absent.

Down the road, a man, silhouetted by a streetlight behind him, headed my way.

Kane stopped a few feet shy of me. He watched the building burn without saying anything, not a "sorry" or any other condolence. Just like the first time I'd spoken to him, I found his lack of emotion and empathy to be a relief. It was the one quality I did like about him. I didn't have to respond to the normal platitudes. It just was.

When he finally spoke, it wasn't what I'd expected. "I told you not to do two things. You did both."

When he'd first approached, I figured he'd seen this on the news, but they hadn't been there for the vampire killing.

"How'd you know?"

"Leon and Butch have been tailing you."

Should've known that. I leaned back against the door of the empty building.

"Why hadn't I seen a vampire until you got involved in my life?"

Even in the early evening lack of light, I could see the look in his eyes.

"Because you've reached your magical majority. For some it comes in their teens; sometimes, like with you, it's early twenties. Others it isn't until their thirties. You're going to see a lot of things now because the veil has lifted."

He took a couple of steps away from me and then stopped. "You won't be able to get back without me showing you, and I think you know your options have shrunk to one."

He was right. I'd tried to remember where the Underground was before and my mind had drawn a blank, as if I'd never been there. There were some people out there that had a bad sense of direction, but I wasn't one of them. I only need to go somewhere once and it was as if I had a burned path in my brain, but not with that place.

The sound of his feet hitting cement made it clear he wasn't waiting. Unless I wanted to sleep on the street tonight, I needed to get moving. He knew it and I knew it. Wasn't anything left to argue.

I thought bottoms were reserved for drug addicts and gamblers. Apparently not, since I was pretty sure I was wallowing in the muck of the lowest denominator.

I stood up and let out a string of curses, every one I'd ever heard, and loud enough that the people still watching the fire looked over at me.

He stopped and glanced back at me too, before looking at a gold watch on his wrist. Monsters had just blown up my apartment building, I was on the verge of losing whatever sanity I had left, and he was concerned about having a few more minutes of his time wasted. If this wasn't the bottom, I was afraid to see what that underbelly looked like.

I caught up to him, and we walked away from the disaster still roaring behind us. Instead of dodging monsters in my path, I was dodging groups of people showing up to see the fire that just wouldn't quit. No one and nothing stepped in front of Kane.

He had a car waiting a block away, and I climbed into the passenger seat of the black sports car, a type I'd never seen and certainly couldn't name, which had a strange-looking B on the steering wheel.

As we drove into the area that was way too quiet to be a part of Boston, but was somehow, I asked, "Why is it that I don't remember how to get back to the Underground?"

"Because you aren't supposed to."

"How can I stay somewhere I can't get back to once I leave?"

"You'll remember after you sign."

"Sign?"

"Standard nondisclosure form."

I watched as we drove, determined to remember anyway. He parked the car in the alley as I tried to think of the last three or four turns. I couldn't remember anything before parking.

He walked inside the building, and I got the feeling he would've left me in the alley if I hadn't hurried along. People glanced over, but nobody batted an eye as we walked across the main floor and up the stairs into his office, lending credence to the idea that this probably happened over and over again. Now that I was firmly stuck, I wasn't sure I wanted to know how many times.

I took the now-familiar seat in front of his desk. He walked behind it, opened a drawer, and pulled out a sheet of paper.

He laid the paper and a pen in front of me.

You are hereby bound to not disclose anything.

This was the nondisclosure? No threatening of libel or suing in court? Was this some sort of joke?

I held the sheet up. "There's no names on this, not even a date?"

"It's covered." He pushed the pen toward me.

"What about my conditions?"

He rested a hip on the desk as he said, "I'm good for them."

I laid the sheet down again. I had nothing left to argue with, and nothing to lose. I took the pen and signed my name and then slid the paper toward him.

He picked it up, crumpled it into a small ball, and then threw it into the air. It didn't come back down in one piece, but broke apart and disappeared into smoke.

As it did, it felt like a vise was wrapping around my chest. It wasn't quite crushing, but it wasn't easy to draw a breath, either.

"It'll pass in a few seconds."

As he was saying the words, the vise that had wrapped around my chest had already started to diminish. Note to self: it might be pertinent to ask a few more questions before I signed anything else. Seemed there were worse things than fine print when it came to signing contracts with Kane.

He looked down at the watch on his wrist again while I waited for my chest to expand fully.

"You could've warned me."

He shook his head and stood, walking toward the door. "No, I couldn't. Every time I have it's taken an extra five to ten minutes to finish up this business. I'll show you to your rooms."

Wow, five or ten extra minutes. What a bitch that was.

I followed him out of the office as the reason I hated him so much struck home. It wasn't that he was rude. Although he was. It wasn't the coldness about him. I actually found that easier to handle. It was that when he talked to me, it was always like I was a colossal waste of time. That was what bugged the hell out of me, but I kept following him anyway, because I wasn't up for living on the streets.

We made our way through the main floor and a hallway off the back, where two elevators stood side by side.

He pressed a button next to the one on the right. "This is the one you need. It only stops at the sixth floor. The other one doesn't go that far."

The doors slid open as I was about to tell him I didn't take elevators.

He stepped into the elevator, free from crawlers. What was the deal with this guy? He was a walking crawler repellent.

He stood waiting as I eyed up the box. What if they showed up after the doors shut?

"They won't get on."

I stepped into the elevator with him. "It wasn't them I was worried about." It wasn't a complete lie.

I knew this was "Kane's level," as Isabella had suggested as much, but I hadn't thought it was only Kane's level. But for as large as the hallway was, there were only two doors, which pounded home the impression I'd gotten the moment I'd stepped off the elevator. I was in his domain.

He walked to the door on the right and opened it.

It looked like a hotel suite, a very nice hotel suite with generic greys and whites. A sectional dominated the living room area, and a door off the back probably led to an equally generic bedroom and attached bath. Generic or not, it was a lot nicer than where I'd been living and wished I still was.

"Let Isabella know if you need anything."

"Is there a key?" I asked.

"You don't need one up here." He walked toward the other door that I assumed was his place.

"Kane, one last thing."

He stopped and turned.

Did I have the nerve to ask? Did I want an answer to this question? I wanted to know so many things…but this was the one thing that had kept me sitting there and watching the fire for hours on end.

"You told me not to speak to them without you. Why?" When he'd said it in the office, on some level I'd thought it had to do with keeping whatever magic he was searching for all to himself. Then my building had blown up.

He paused before answering. "Because you've hit your magical majority."

It was an evasive answer, and I had a strange feeling he wasn't doing it for his own sake. "But why does that matter?"

He turned fully toward me and paused again before saying, "You sure you want to know?"

"Yes."

"You can see crawlers, but they're still bound to that other plane. Now that you're of age, once you speak to them, they can use that contact to put a toe into our world."

"So when I talked to them…" I swayed on my feet as he watched me, not moving toward me but standing where he was about five feet away. I reached out a hand to the wall.

That night, the evening of my sister's gallery opening, I'd talked to one. I'd known it— even with everyone telling me it wasn't my fault, I'd known it was. They'd said it was a freak accident with the heating system, but I'd never truly believed that. I'd known it was the monsters; I just hadn't realized I'd been the one who gave them the opportunity.

I didn't care what I looked like as I half slid, half fell onto the floor.

He was probably judging me. From the little I knew of Kane, I could already tell he wasn't the type to fall apart over anything. He was probably thinking I was weak.

He could judge all he wanted. I didn't care. I didn't care if he stayed in the hall or left; either way, I was as alone as a person could be— except for the guilt.

I heard his footsteps as he approached. I saw his shoes as he stopped in front of me. I wasn't sure what he was looking for—maybe tears? I didn't have any of those left. I was entering a drought season after a rainy period.

"You'll get over it," he stated as if it were fact. "If you last."

I let out a strange laugh that sounded like it came from a different person, one on the fringe of hysteria. "Must be nice to know everything."

He didn't shoot a comment back the way I thought he would. He just left.

7

My stomach woke me, reminding me that I hadn't eaten since yesterday morning. I kept my eyes closed, trying to ignore it. I wasn't a big fan of waking up these days, and yesterday hadn't improved that at all. My stomach didn't seem to care as it growled louder, an intestinal version of the middle finger.

The next growl didn't come from my stomach. I was pretty sure it was a small one. The larger ones tended to be quieter. The little ones reminded me Chihuahuas with Napoleon complexes. I made sure I was lying on my back as I opened my eyes, increasing the odds of only seeing ceiling.

Eyes opened, there was nothing but ceiling, which meant it couldn't be too bad. I slowly turned my head until it came in to view. As expected, it was small and only a few feet away, sharing the queen bed with me. It was crouched down and let out another low growl, but I didn't care. It was hard to get too rattled by something I could envision wearing a rhinestone collar.

I lifted my head higher so I could see over the little growler and get a look at the supplied clock on the nightstand. Eleven. No wonder my stomach wouldn't stop.

Next came a quick scan of the room, designed to take in the entire space but not absorb too many details. All I wanted was a lay of the land and what spots to avoid without looking at the strokes of the picture. Nothing good came from details. Medium-sized scaly one in the corner, but it was tucked out of the way.

Coast relatively clear, I made my way into the bathroom, where I found an unused toothbrush in the drawer and some other essentials.

Desperation drove me to go through the drawers and closets next, looking for something left behind by a previous inhabitant. It was one thing to be in the same dirty clothes while you lay on your couch alone contemplating all the ways there were to die. It was another to go about in the general population—or among these people—dirty and possibly smelly. It didn't seem like a good way to make friends. Not that I was looking for friends, but alienating myself didn't seem to be such a good idea either.

After searching every drawer and closet in the place, seemed I'd be making my entrance with the clothes on my back. They had the added wear and tear of being slept in, since I'd taken every precaution against unwanted visitors in the night.

The lack of kitchen in the suite meant I'd have to go in search of food.

Outside the apartment and to the right was the elevator and Kane's door. Looking to the left, all the way at the end so it nearly blended, was another door. It wasn't marked, but I'd done this enough to know when I'd found a stairwell.

Even though there would probably be monsters in there too, my sanity had always clung to the illusion of an escape. It was sort of like getting on a cruise ship and not knowing the life rafts all had holes.

I took the stairs all the way to the bottom, where it let me out into the hallway adjoining the Underground main floor. A few steps forward and I stopped. I'd seen this place and its people a couple of times already, but the electric nature of the place still gave me a jolt.

Similar to last time, the majority of the heads in the place swung toward me, and again looked away almost as quickly, as if I were random blue jay at an exotic animal zoo.

That was fine by me. I'd never been a meet-and-greet sort. I was fairly certain even if I hadn't been my own brand of freak, I still would've been a touch reclusive by nature, and the only thing I was interested in right now was food.

Keeping to the perimeter of the room, I noticed a handful of people with plates in front of them. Odds were there was food somewhere in this place.

Instead of finding the source of nourishment, I caught sight of Butch waving his hand toward where he was seated alone at a booth in the corner. I continued my path along the outskirts, and he nodded to the seat across from him as I got close.

"How you settling in?" he asked, and then took a sip of what appeared to be a mug of beer.

"The rooms are really nice." I scanned the place, wondering where the waiters were. "How are people getting food?"

"I can order for you. What do you want?"

I looked about the place again. "Is there a menu to choose from?"

"No. Order whatever you feel like having."

Whatever? That was a wide range. It couldn't be anything. "Can I get scrambled eggs?"

"Sure. I'll order. It's better if I do it, at least the first time until you get used to them." He cleared his throat. "I need a gargoyle," he said, his voice rising to just about the level of the music.

A horrible-looking creature appeared suddenly. I wasn't sure if he were truly cement or just appeared that way, but his features seemed frozen in a scowl. The apron hanging from his bare cement torso didn't do much for him either. "What do you want?"

The voice didn't soften the appearance.

"Scrambled eggs and a coffee." Butch glanced over at me, and I nodded, understanding how it might take a time or two before the startling nature wore off.

The creature disappeared.

"What the hell was that?"

"Gargoyle. They handle the service here. You know, food, laundry, in return for their rent and staying here. Most of the ones here were homeless. As their buildings got renovated or torn down over the years, they ran out of places to go. They struck a deal with Kane in order to move here." He looked about the place before he added, "They're great, but not without drawbacks. Don't ever complain about the food or drinks. Bad things happen when there's a complaint." He checked about again and then leaned in closer and whispered, "And don't ever go in the basement."

The gargoyle popped back up, and Butch jerked back as if he hadn't been whispering to me. The gargoyle placed a plate and mug in front of me. I usually took my coffee with milk and sugar, but the way Butch was making a face, I decided I'd learn to drink it black.

"Thank—"

Butch shook his head, in a clear *don't bother with the niceties* gesture. Didn't matter, as the gargoyle disappeared before I finished speaking.

Drinking my coffee black and convincing myself it was better this way, I kept my eyes on the rest of the place. It was fairly full considering it was a Tuesday afternoon, but these people probably weren't your typical nine-to-fivers.

The crowd served me well, though. I'd noticed over the years that the crawlers didn't appear to like sharing their space, although I knew from the times I'd accidentally walked through a few that they weren't solid.

With Butch on one end of the booth and me on the other, the crawlers would have a hard time getting in between. There was enough traffic past the booth to discourage them from standing nearby. It wasn't as good as it was when Kane was around, repelling them all somehow, but it was enough to allow me to eat my eggs in some measure of peace.

"So, what's the deal with all the people here? Do they work for Kane or something?"

I glanced up to Kane's closed office door, wondering if he were in there and when our "work" would start.

"This is one of the only places they can come hang out and be themselves. Some of them live in the apartments. It's taxing to always have to mainstream. In return, they do him favors from time to time."

Kane sounded like the godfather of the underworld. I ate a bite of my eggs, wishing I hadn't asked. The abstract picture had been bad enough.

Butch lifted his beer and took a sip before using the mug to motion toward a table dead center. "That group over there are your basic shifter types, mostly run-of-the-mill werewolves. Of course, there's always some other breeds thrown in as well, couple cats and a possum, oddballs who don't have anyone else to hang out with."

It was clear when you looked at them which shifters didn't seem quite as cohesive in the clique. I didn't voice an opinion, only nodded as I ate. I needed to avoid any opinions accidentally leaking out. It was like being in a foreign land and not knowing what the locals might find insulting.

He shifted his to look at a group in the corner. "Witches, warlocks, basically anyone that works a spell."

Now I had to stop eating. "If I'm going to be getting spells, does that mean I'm a witch?" Witch, like a real witch. That might actually be pretty interesting.

As I watched Butch's eyebrows rise, I knew it wasn't going to work out that easy.

"It's not exactly clear-cut. It's real weird with the witches. They're a little picky about who they consider a witch and who's not. What magic they deem is appropriate and what might be considered dark. It's sort of complicated." He leaned forward, his eyes intent on me. "There's one thing you need to remember, and this is very important." We were disrupted by Leon joining our booth, and Butch slid farther in to make room.

I gave Leon a smile and then moved my attention fully back to Butch. "What's the important thing?"

"Whatever you do, don't ever ask anyone what they are if you can't tell," Butch said. "That's one of the most important rules you need to follow."

Leon blew air out of pursed lips before adding, "Yeah, never, ever ask. People get real weird about that stuff."

I nodded.

"And no magic in the building. That's another biggie," Butch explained while Leon ordered something from a gargoyle.

I ate a few more bites of eggs as I made a mental note of all the rules, while trying to ignore the table of witches that, reading between the lines, didn't really approve of my magic. Dark magic, Butch had said. What was dark magic? Did he mean evil? I was a good person, relatively speaking.

Butch nudged my arm with his elbow. "That's Flip heading over. Maybe you can be friends with her? Most people don't like her either."

What? My fork clattered onto my plate. "Either? What do you mean, either? Do you mean they already don't like me?"

Butch scratched his red hair. "No, of course they'll like you…some of them, anyway."

"I'm sure a couple here and there," Leon added. "You're new, is all. Takes time to make friends."

As soon I turned to look at Flip, I caught Leon giving Butch the evil eye.

Flip was a tiny thing, with a smile on her face and the biggest pouf of blond hair I'd ever seen. The oddest thing about her, though, was the way she walked as she headed over. It was almost as if her feet barely touched the ground. "Why don't they like her? She looks like a happy sort."

Leon salted the club sandwich the gargoyle had dropped off as he explained. "Because Flip is a mutt. This is the way it is—if you were to find a vamp and a werewolf in a predicament outside of here, they'd help each other out. But that doesn't mean they like each other. There's been bickering and fighting for generations."

Butch took over explaining as Leon starting eating. "Flip is the illegitimate offspring of a drunken night between a fairy and a leprechaun during a party here."

"Best New Year's Eve party *ever*, if you ask me," Leon said, around a large bite.

Butch took another sip of beer as he watched Flip getting closer. "She does nothing to help her cause. Don't let the smile fool you. She's got a dragon's temper."

Flip strolled up to us and smiled wide. "Hey! You're the new girl?"

I smiled and nodded. They had to be putting me on. It was the nicest greeting I'd gotten from anyone I'd met so far.

"You mean the new paper doll," a shifter sitting at a nearby table chimed in.

The smile was wiped from Flip's face, and a completely different person seemed to be standing there. She swung around on the shifter and screamed, "Shut the fuck up and stop listening to my conversation, you shifter trash!"

Flip kicked the air near her chair. The shifter cowered, pulling her chair farther away from where Flip was as the rest of her group told her to let it go.

Flip turned back and motioned for me to scoot in.

I would've scooted in if that hadn't happened. I might've scooted a little quicker because it had. I had too many issues going on already. I didn't need a pissed-off half fae, half leprechaun wigging out on me.

"Some of these people are very rude. Don't mind them." Flip took the empty spot, and I was quickly moving even farther over as she arranged herself cross-legged.

A light from above drew everyone's eyes as Kane's door opened. As if he'd known right where I'd be sitting, his eyes landed on me and then Butch. He held up both of his hands, fingers splayed, before he walked back inside.

"Looks like your number's been called." There was a sad little sigh that followed, the kind you'd expect when someone was doomed to some unfortunate fate.

"It's that bad?" I asked.

"No, of course not!" Butch said, as if catching himself.

"Nice meeting you." Flip stood, even though she'd just sat, and half floated away.

"I've got something I've got to go handle," Leon said with a quick wave as he stumbled out of the booth.

Butch stood too. "Need some help with—"

"Of course, come on," Leon said, waving Butch along.

Butch stopped and turned toward me. "Oh, make sure you're ready at ten tonight." Then he hightailed it after Leon before I could ask what to be ready for.

It wasn't long before a monster scooted in, and, crazy or not, I could've sworn he was smelling my food. I shifted my plate a little closer. My day was looking bad enough. Nobody was stealing my eggs.

8

I heard the door open in the other room and wondered if no one knew about knocking in this place. Good thing I hadn't opted for washing my one set of clothes in the bathroom sink along with my underwear.

"Hello?" I called out. The shadows in the room scattered, telling me who it was without an answer.

Kane walked into the bedroom as I was walking out of the bathroom, dressed but sans underwear.

"What if I were getting dressed?"

He stood there. He made a point of looking at my bare feet and letting his eyes trail all the way up to my face before saying, "I've seen the female body before." He turned and headed back into the living room as I made faces at his back.

"Isabella is having some things brought up. Come down to my office afterward. It's time to get to work."

I followed and stopped him before he could walk out. "Wait. What is work, exactly? What does this entail?" He'd said I'd be talking to the crawlers, but that didn't seem to match up with the mass exodus this afternoon or the "paper doll" comments.

"Sit," he said, pointing at the sofa I'd just been about to sit on.

"I'd prefer to stand."

"Fine. Stand."

I eyed up the sofa and sat.

"I thought you wanted to stand?"

"I'm entitled to change my mind." I curled my legs underneath me and rested my arm on the back of the sofa.

"You're called a Shadow *Walker*. In order to get what I need, you're going to have to walk in the Shadowland. That's where the crawlers really are."

I leaned back and watched him through squinted eyes. What if I hadn't finally found answers? What if I'd actually found someone crazier than myself? That could be a very bad thing. I leaned back slightly and let out a long breath. "I've never walked in any *Shadowland*."

I wouldn't say he was looking down his nose at me, but his chin was slightly raised. "I. Know."

I tilted my head back a bit, matching his angle. "How do *you* know that?" Unless he'd been tailing me from birth, he had no idea what I'd done in my life. He might think he was all knowing, but he was the only one in this room with that notion.

"Because you're alive. Odds are, if you had wandered into one alone, you wouldn't be here."

I froze. Was I walking into my death tonight? I thought I had a death wish. Now that I was being shown the door, I wasn't so sure. "You said if I'd gone into one, I wouldn't still be here. Why in the world would I go into this place?"

"Because I'm going to help you. I'm an anchor."

"Anchor?" More words that had completely new meanings.

"To this world. I'm what will keep you alive."

Every word he said sounded like he'd said it at least fifty other times, and I was already getting tired of being stuck in his bad rerun. "If you can keep Shadow Walkers from dying, how come everyone else has died off? How come we're called paper dolls?"

He rested a forearm on the wall near the door and leaned against it. "I didn't say it was going to be easy."

There was a long pause where a normal person would be inserting reassurances. After all, that was what people did. They reassured you everything would be okay, whether they had a clue about it or not, and at the moment, I was feeling pretty bitter about it.

He leaned.

I waited.

"Are you not going to say anything about it being okay?"

"No." He shrugged. "You might not be."

"And this works on people?"

He straightened and opened the door. "No one's keeping you here."

I leaned forward, one foot on the floor, one still tucked under me, and stared at the door. I should get up, tell him to go fuck himself, and never look back.

But where would I go? Would I ever get rid of the crawlers? What life would I have if I did that?

He let the door fall shut. "And that's why it works."

I didn't argue. I tucked my leg back underneath me. "You've seen a lot of people try and do this. Do you think I'll make it?" At least I knew he'd give me an honest answer.

He put his hands in his pockets as he stood there across the room, our stares locked.

"I think you're my best shot so far."

"Why? Because I'm broken?" I asked, repeating his statement from the other day on a hunch.

"You say that as if it were a bad thing."

"Isn't that the way you meant it when you said it? In my experience, 'broken' tends to have a negative connotation."

"That's because your experience is gravely lacking. It only means you're in the belly of the beast. It's only bad if you can't figure out how to climb out." Hand on the door, he said, "Meet me down in my office when you're ready."

* * *

Not ten minutes after Kane left, I heard my door opening again. Did no one here know about knocking? I walked out of the bathroom, where I'd resumed the cleaning of my only set of underwear, to find Isabella standing in the middle of my living room with a large man behind her. The lack of notice was more irritating this time around, and I wasn't sure if it was her or the unfortunate position of being the second person to barge in.

"Kane said you needed clothes. I tried to round up a couple of things in the limited time I have available." She pointed to a spot in the middle of the living room floor. "Dump them there." The bulky guy behind her let go of two large garbage bags.

There was a definite difference in her when Kane wasn't present. Isabella alone sort of reminded me of an espresso without cream and sugar—straight bitter brew.

"Thanks." I offered it up more to get her moving than from feeling inspired by the garbage bags of clothing.

"I hope you won't be needing anything else. I can't be running errands for someone who's not…" She let her words drift off as if she really had to think about them. "Going to be part of the team for long."

"I can take care of myself, but thank you for the concern." *Now can you please get the hell out?*

She looked down at the bag of clothes, then around the apartment. "That's good. Nobody likes a needy girl."

"Well, good thing he's got you, then."

She smiled. Worst part about it was I couldn't tell if it was sincere or snide. I didn't bother contemplating it, either, and was simply relieved she turned and left.

* * *

I dug through the bags after she left and found lots of yoga pants and sweatshirts. Not altogether horrible, except for the coloring, but they all appeared clean. Clean was a step up right now. I picked out a purple sweatshirt, which was a tad bright, and black striped yoga pants. It would do.

After another five minutes, I made my way downstairs. The second I stepped onto the main floor, I knew something had changed. Where I'd gotten quick glances before, now I was getting hard stares—mostly from the vampires. I knew they were the vampires because their fangs all dropped as they watched me.

I took a few more steps toward the stairs that led to Kane's office, ignoring the hissing noise they made as I passed by. I would've made it there, too, if one of them hadn't shot in front of me, blocking the path.

"You're going to get it, paper doll." He was close enough that I could feel his breath and see the surface of his fangs, before he ducked his head uncomfortably close to my jugular.

I stood still, as if daring him to make good on his threat, and hoped he couldn't smell the fear on me. "You mean kill me? Your breath is already doing a pretty good job of it. You eat a corpse for dinner or something?"

"Back off, Mic. You know you can't touch her," Butch said from where he was stepping around him. "You, walk," he said to me, pointing to the same booth he'd been sitting in yesterday, which Leon was already occupying.

Mic didn't step back, but he did lift his head.

I spared a look up at Kane's closed office door. "I'm meeting Kane."

"He had to step out for a minute." Butch tilted his head back to his booth.

With a last look to the vampire, I held my hand up over my mouth, did a little test breath, and made a sour face. "You should stop feeding on road kill. It's going to kill you one of these days."

He hissed as I walked away, ignoring the fangs that dropped down as I passed some more vampires.

I slid into the booth where Leon already was, and Butch slid in after me so I was cocooned. "Really?"

"Yes," Butch said. "They all know about the vamp you killed at the mall. Word started spreading this afternoon when the girl he was occasionally…dating was found with bite marks. Didn't take much for them to piece it together after that and ID you." He tilted his head back. "Gargoyle."

"For the record, he was *killing* her." My stomach rumbled. "Order me a cheeseburger, well done?"

"He must've been *killing* her for a few weeks, then," Leon said, then turned toward the gargoyle who'd appeared. "Steak, rare, side of mashed, a salad with oil and vinegar and a very dead cheeseburger."

"You didn't see her struggling," I said, talking over Butch as he ordered his dinner.

"Which she wouldn't have remembered," Leon said.

Butch and Leon continued on with how wrong I'd been as my cheeseburger showed up. All I cared about was that I'd missed my chance at getting ketchup. This condiment issue was becoming a real problem.

Butch and Leon were still arguing about something or other, and I'd gotten through half my cheeseburger, when the crawlers scattered. Kane was halfway toward the table when I spotted him, as he passed by various vampires, all with their fangs put away.

He looked at me and then kept walking toward a different door, which I'd never used.

"Does he ever use words when he summons people?"

Leon scooted out. "No."

I made my way over, feeling the vampires eyeing me the whole way, but no one hissed or dropped fangs this time.

As I neared where Kane was waiting by the door in his crisp collared shirt and slacks, his eyes ran the length of my outfit.

"You look like you're trying out for the circus." His expression didn't give me the impression he was a fan of the tent show.

"I do a mean flame toss." It hadn't looked so bad when Isabella had the things dropped off, but then again, they'd been clean, so that alone was a step up. Either way, I wasn't here to impress him.

"I guess it's clothing," he said, more to himself than me, as he pushed open the door and a chilling gust of wind felt like it was burning my cheeks.

"Where we going?"

"To fix your mess," he said as the lights of a white Mercedes truck flashed. "Get in."

The truck was warm inside, and whoever had been in the passenger seat last had left the seat warmer on.

"Where would that be, exactly?"

"To the vampires."

"Why? Run out of blood sacrifices?" I was only half kidding and not feeling the least bit funny. He didn't seem to be feeling funny either, so neither of us laughed at my joke. All I could think of was what they'd said about all the paper dolls before me. Maybe all the deaths had nothing to do with the crawlers? Maybe it was all the other creatures around this place that ended up killing us.

"That's a good sign," he said.

"What's a good sign?" I asked, deciding I could use some good news of any variety, even from him.

He was leaning back, his left hand resting on the wheel. "Shadow Walkers who have a sense of humor tend to last longer, relatively speaking."

He really wasn't kidding. We really were going to see the vampires. He might be able to keep the ones that owed him in line, but I wasn't ready to walk into an unknown coven.

"Is this a good idea?"

"Yes. We're handling this now so that some random jackass doesn't kill you while you're walking down the street alone and screw up my plans." He drove along as if we were doing nothing more important than stopping by the mall.

I leaned over slightly to check out the speedometer. We were moving along at about fifty. Would a leap out of the truck at fifty kill me? If I hit the ground in a roll, it might give me better odds than the vampires. I looked at the door. I didn't really want to do either, though. "If they want to kill me, how are you stopping them?"

"Don't worry about that. Don't speak and I'll handle it."

"If you're going to handle everything and I'm not supposed to speak, then why am I going?"

He was quiet, like a teacher about to screw you up with a pop quiz or something.

"It was on the way to the place we're going afterward."

"Seriously?"

The man had the nerve to smile. "I didn't want to have to come this way twice."

"To save yourself a car ride, you're bringing me to meet a bunch of vampires who might want to kill me?"

"For someone who acts as if they don't value their life, you've got an awful lot of restrictions on how you endanger it."

"Because, like any sane person, I care about how I die."

"And you feel like you fall into that sane category?"

"When you get *your* sane card punched by Dr. Freud, then you can start throwing those stones."

After the handful of times I'd dealt with him, it was becoming clearer to me that I was never going to be able to be near him without wanting to push him down a flight of stairs. His one saving grace was that he scared the crawlers away, and I was starting to think that just came down to the crawlers having higher standards than me.

The truck bounced around as we pulled off the paved road and down a gravel drive. It was another ten minutes before we pulled up to a stately home. The brick building appeared to be draped in history so thick that I expected the lady and lord of the manor to walk out the door in between the large columns. That wasn't even close to what appeared.

"Stay nearby," Kane said as he got out of the truck and then started walking away, not concerned if I was near or not. I would've let the gap grow, except that vampires were not on my approved list of ways to die.

A man and two women stepped out onto the porch before we got within twenty feet of the door. All three seemed to be embracing their gothic reputation. From the fangs and the hissing, it seemed like I was going to get about the same reception as I'd gotten back at the Underground.

"After you're finished with your theatrics, tell Alexandria I'm here."

The male vampire, who even in the night practically glowed with his fair skin and white-blond hair, was suddenly off the porch, but stopped ten feet shy of us.

"Back off, Nick. You know I'd win."

With another hiss, he was gone, perhaps off to find this Alexandria, or maybe not.

"The young ones are always a bit irritating, but they age out of it pretty well. Usually lose the weird clothing after about five years, too," Kane said as I stood beside him.

The front door swung open, and a girl who appeared to be all of sixteen stood there. I really hoped vampires mentally matured, because a lifetime in your teens was too cruel for anyone to bear.

"Alexandria said to come in." She stepped back and held the door open, but vanished before we stepped over the threshold.

Kane waved his hand forward and I proceeded into the house. There was parlor open to the hall on the left side, where a redhead sat on one of the matched chaises. She had the sort of presence only someone completely confident in her appearance could pull off, and it wasn't without merit.

"Have a seat," she said, her fangs in full sight.

I walked in, hiding any hesitation I might've been feeling, and sat directly across from her. If vamps were like dogs, I didn't want her to smell my fear.

"You've got balls for one so powerless," she said, eyeing me up.

Kane sat beside me and relaxed back as if he were an everyday Joe about to watch a football game on the television, with his arm slung along the back of the chaise behind me. Did nothing rattle this man? And if not, why? Was he crazy? Was there something I should know, or maybe should've known before I got in the car with him in the first place?

"She's powerless. I'm not. I'd make a note of that," Kane said, and then yawned. Wow, his arrogance was staggering, but it allowed him to screw with people in the most entertaining way.

"I'm guessing you're here to tell me why I shouldn't kill your new pet." She flipped her palm toward me, a single red nail extended that matched her silky red dress. It wasn't gothic, but she could've toned down the show a bit. Although I was in a circus outfit, so who was throwing stones now?

"You know you won't kill her," he said. "You're not stupid enough to do something like that—at least, I don't think you are."

Why would it be stupid for her to kill me? My head swiveled back to Alexandria.

"If you're not concerned, why bother coming to see me?" She made a small O with her lips, which, again, were bright red, because why break a streak?

"Unfortunately for your breed, some of your people aren't the brightest. They don't know the downfalls…or the benefits."

She smiled slightly, but any warmth it might've given her face was killed by the fangs she had hanging over her lower lip. Although that thing I'd heard about red lips making your teeth look whiter was doing fantastic things for her fangs.

"They might not realize what's to gain. And that's what you're telling me, isn't it? There's something to be gained here for everyone?"

"You know we've always worked well together."

"I know we used to."

Really? He used to bang the vampire queen? Or princess? Or whatever she was? From the look I saw in her eyes, she wasn't the one who'd declined the last invitation.

"When it works out, I won't forget you," he said, almost sounding kind. My head nearly spun when I thought I heard the sound of guilt or remorse or something other than the normal fare.

"You think she might be the one?" Her eyes were grazing over me again, but only briefly, as if she didn't see the same thing he did. "There hasn't been one that's managed to last in such a long time that I'm starting to wonder if it will ever happen."

"She's stronger than she appears," he said with a confidence I wish he'd given me. But he hadn't had to sell me on the plan. I was stuck, and he knew it.

"My people won't be happy."

"You'll handle it, I'm sure."

Now I had to glance over at him. He was smiling as if he had all the confidence in the world. So he did know how to be nice to people?

Kane stood, and I followed his lead because I certainly wasn't looking to extend this visit.

"I'll be expecting a gift soon," Alexandria said as she remained seated while we left.

He paused, allowing me to exit first, and it was the only indication I had that he might not be so sure she wouldn't at least try and attack me.

We stepped onto the porch, and he said, "Not now," as if he knew my head was packed full of questions.

It wasn't until we were back on the main road that he finally said, "Now ask."

I jumped all over him the second I knew it was clear. "What is she getting out of this?" The idea of giving her anything roiled my insides. Kane might've felt bad for her sad eyes, but I hadn't. She'd wanted to eat me.

"Shadow Walking is like treasure hunting. There's a lot of people that need things that are found in a place only few survive." He spoke calmly, like he always did, even as he described a situation that might be the death of me.

"I'm going to give that woman a spell? This wasn't part of the plan."

He turned slightly toward me. "Neither was you killing vampires. I told you not to get involved. You did. There's a price to be paid for that."

"And if I don't pay?"

"You'll pay one way or another. I negotiated you a cheaper price than your life, unless you want to be by my side every moment of the day. This is an easier solution."

I leaned my head back, letting it bounce on the headrest as I stared forward at the starry night. He was right. I'd rather get the vampire a spell.

His last words before we drove the rest of the way in silence were, "Very few people get through life without making compromises."

If I'd been a smarter person, I would've paid more attention to those words.

9

He parked the car in front of a mausoleum with tombstones to my left and my right. There was a reason I hated cemeteries. These places were always crammed full of crawlers. The crawlers always seemed more alive in them, too, which was a bit ironic, considering the setting. As I looked about the place, it was no different than usual.

Even the Kane buffer zone seemed diminished as he got out of the car.

Kane walked around to the passenger side and opened my door, making me wonder if he had a little bit of gentleman lingering deep down in the depths of his personal hell somewhere. "Stay close to me and don't talk to any of them until I say so."

I would've kept close to him even without the warning. Kane's buffer zone was one of his most redeeming qualities. "Why are we here?"

I stared at a particularly large crawler in the distance. Its shape was twisting and turning, but never losing touch with the mausoleum, as if it were pinned down to it. It shifted in my direction but fell way short of me within the buffer.

"What did you come here for?" it whispered.

I froze instinctively. I'd always hated the ones that spoke the most.

Kane stopped as if sensing the gap between us growing. "Don't speak to it."

"You hear them, too?" I wasn't sure why I'd assumed he only saw them.

He nodded, waiting as I closed the gap.

As I walked through the place, I knew this wasn't where I wanted my life to end. Some people didn't think there was any good way to die, but I did. Had a whole list of good ways. If I went, I wanted to go suddenly—nothing long or drawn out. But even the quick ways had exclusions. No matter how quick it happened, I didn't want to go out the way the rest of my family did, even if I deserved it.

If Kane noticed me hanging closer to him, he didn't remark upon it. We kept walking farther and farther until I couldn't see the car anymore, for the shadows that filled the space all stretched toward me. As we walked, I heard them whispering, as if they were talking to each other now. How I longed for my little morning Chihuahua.

The farther we walked, the louder they grew, urging me toward them, and chills ran through me as I remembered the last time this had happened, and what had followed.

By the time I stopped, I was only inches away from Kane, and keeping that distance was pretty impressive. If we stayed too much longer, I might leap onto his back.

He turned to me, taking hold of my arm as he did. "You're going to pick out the crawler that makes you feel the worst, and then ask it to take you into its world."

"Wait. Here and now?"

"Yes."

I could hear the crawlers all kicking up around me, eager for this. That was how I knew it was a bad idea. Whenever they had talked to me in the past, we'd usually wanted different things out of life.

"As long as you hold my hand, and don't let go, you'll be fine."

He had a whole day to come up with a pep talk, and the best I got was *you'll be fine*? Yes, it was better than *take it or leave it*, but a big leap from making me feel good about this. "What about all the others you guys talked about that *weren't* fine?"

"The others let go. *Don't* let go." He spoke to me like he was trying to burn this very basic instruction into my brain.

If I wasn't going to let go of him… "Are you going with me?"

"I can't go with you, but I'll be with you."

I shook my head. "That doesn't make any sense."

"You'll understand once you're in. Gain entrance for now. Don't walk in too far once you do, only a few steps. The farther you go from the entrance, the weaker our connection will be. Go in and make sure you pay close attention to where you entered. Take a step or two and come back. Once you get back to the exact spot you entered, pull at my hand, and it'll be like pulling yourself out of a swimming pool with a ladder." He let go of my arm and gripped my hand. "Never speak to them unless you're holding my hand."

"Why?"

His eyes narrowed, as if that were another stupid question. "Because I don't feel like blowing up."

"How come *you* can stop them from blowing stuff up?" He always thought he was so special.

"Not easy to explain and impossible to teach."

Gripping his hand tightly, I looked him square in the eye and said, "You're lucky I'm already broken. I'm not so sure you could work with a normal person."

"Then we've got no worries, do we?"

"And there you go again, heaping on that charm. I swear, I'm going to swoon if you don't stop."

"Don't worry. I've got you." His fingers tightened around mine, and I felt a warm sizzle. I would've pulled my hand back, but he held it.

"What is that?"

"That's me. You'll get used to it."

I might not know a lot of stuff about this new world, but I did know normal human beings didn't sizzle when you held their hand. Means to an end. That's all he was. Didn't matter if he could light up the tree at Rockefeller Center.

He looked around the cemetery. "Find the largest one you can. The larger, the stronger. You're going to need a big one to cross you over."

I looked about the place, but nothing was close enough with his buffer zone.

"You're going to have to call one to you," he said, seeing my problem.

I used my free hand to push the hair back out of my face as I realized I was about to do something as natural to me as sticking my head underwater and trying to breathe. I wanted to run from these things. Not call them closer. But that was exactly what I was going to do, because if I was going to be forced to live this life, the only way I could stomach it was if I knew there was a chance of getting rid of these creatures forever.

"You doing this or not?" he asked as I came to terms with this next step.

"I'm sorry, I wasn't aware you had dinner plans. I said I was doing it. I'm all in here." I was all in mostly because I couldn't think of an *all out*, but that didn't change anything.

There was one far off, all the way at the edge of the cemetery, but I knew it had to be larger, or I wouldn't have been able to see it at all. It was hugging the shadow cast by a huge mausoleum. Unlike the others that were trying to reach for me right outside the buffer zone, this one seemed to be waiting for me to come to it. And something else felt different about it, as if it were older somehow, and who knew where that notion was even coming from?

I bent forward, held out my free hand, and clucked my tongue. "Come here, come on." I added some more clucking.

I could feel Kane's stare without looking. "What?" I asked, keeping my eyes on the crawler.

"That's 'all in'?" The judgment was dripping from the words.

"What would you like me to do?"

"Tell it to come over in a firm voice."

"And why would it listen to me if I'm coming off abrasive right out of the gate?" Whatever Kane was, he didn't need to be psychic to know I might've been implying something. *Some* people might think arrogance and bossiness was the best way, but I wasn't among them.

"People respond to authority."

Was that his excuse for his behavior? We'd see about that.

I would've argued right then, but I wanted this done and over with.

I straightened and pointed my free hand toward the ground in front of me. "Come here." Damn if the thing didn't start moving toward me like it was a dog.

"See?"

Figured he'd have to get an *I told you so* in. "Shut. Up. Or I'm telling it to go away next."

The man had the nerve to laugh.

It stopped a few feet away from us, and Kane tugged on my hand slightly, as if I didn't know it were there waiting.

"Will you grant me entrance?" I asked.

It expanded, as if it was breathing deeply of me.

"Alone," it said, looking to where Kane stood beside me.

"No."

"It's asking for you to go alone," Kane said.

I nodded, not that it had been a question. I guessed this was pretty standard.

The creature expanded again, and I wondered what it was sensing from me.

"You are granted entrance." Right in front of me, the air shimmered, almost like a mirage on a hot day.

My fingers squeezed Kane's hand and then I forced them to relax. "It says I can go in. Now what?" I asked, although the answer was pretty obvious.

"Step into it."

"Step into it?"

"Yes. Step in, look around, and come out."

"That's it?"

"That's enough for the first time."

Sometimes I wondered why I'd done the things I'd done in life. Kane had implied it might be part stupidity. This moment was definitely testing that theory.

Kane's hand squeezed mine, and I took a step forward before I could think on it any longer and possibly realize this was a bad idea. I walked into the shimmer.

I was still in the cemetery, but not. The landscape looked the same, but even though it had been a chilly night in winter, now it felt like I'd die of frostbite if I stayed too long. There were swirls of mist in the air, and the colors didn't seem right, as if the spectrum only consisted of different shades of blue. I turned to where Kane should've been, and even though I could feel his hand, I couldn't see him anymore.

But that wasn't the worst of it. I realized that the creatures I saw shaded in the shadows of my world were full-blown beings here, as if I'd gone from a hazy picture of them to high-def with that single step. It wasn't just me seeing them; they moved toward me as if excited by my presence, chanting strange words.

"Shadow Walker," one of the crawlers said, and reached out to touch my hair. Oh yeah, this was definitely new territory on many fronts.

"Shadow Walker," another one repeated. Now I had a half-dozen of them all stepping forward, calling me, and reaching a hand out.

I took a step back and nearly stumbled on reentry into my own world, or would've if Kane hadn't still been holding my hand. He waited until I steadied myself before he released me.

It took a second to shake the chill off, and I'd never thought thirty degrees would feel so toasty. I rubbed my arms and looked in the direction of the truck. "Do you think the engine is still warm?" It hadn't been that long. I'd think it would still be able to pump out heat immediately. "That place doesn't shift time or anything weird, right?"

His eyes narrowed as he looked me over. "You're okay?"

"Cold, but other than that, I'm fine. We done for the night?" I said, taking a step toward the truck while still keeping myself within the buffer zone.

He nodded and started walking back with me, but I knew he was watching me. I could *feel* him watching me.

I slid into the front seat and had the vents adjusted before the truck was turned on. Then blessed heat was pouring out and soaking into me.

He put the truck in drive, but even as he took off, I knew he was watching me closely. What did he think happened in there? Was I missing something?

He didn't speak again until we'd been on the road for a while.

"How did it feel?"

I shrugged. "I don't know, creepy? Like I'd stepped into a horror flick and was the star about to get a limb chopped off."

He nodded, keeping his eyes forward. It was strange how he could do that, look forward and still make me feel as if I were being watched. It was like a special talent only the arrogant got.

"Would you like me to describe it for you?" I offered, more interested in his response than offering a description. Why was he acting so weird?

"No."

Had he heard from the other Shadow Walkers, or had he seen it himself? He didn't offer up any reason why he didn't need a description. Maybe he didn't want to tell me how he knew?

I turned toward him and stared. Why did he seem...maybe not happy—but not unhappy? Did he think the Shadowlands were worse than they were, or was I the one missing something?

I stopped staring at him and turned to stare out the window when a really bad thought entered my mind. I've had some scary thoughts before, but not like this. "When I go in there, I could happen upon one of the crawlers that..." Memories of both explosions filled my mind, and that horrible skip happened where I couldn't finish the sentence. I moved on, knowing Kane would fill in the blanks. "The crawlers don't die in the explosions, do they?"

"No, they don't die. I don't know if you'll see those crawlers again, but probably not soon."

"Why?" I asked, sitting on my hands like they were cold so I couldn't unconsciously fidget. Odds were he'd notice I was doing it before I caught it myself.

"Those crawlers were both strong. I won't take you to a place where the energy is that intense yet."

"Yet? We're going to one of those places?" I asked.

"Eventually, we'll have to."

Because of the spell he needed. Figured it would be a doozy. It would have to be. Everything about this man was extreme.

"When am I going to get your spell?"

"Typically, this is about all a Shadow Walker can handle the first time."

I looked out the window before I raised my eyebrows in a slightly sarcastic lift. Where was he getting these people? Had they been that weak? Or maybe it was going to get that bad.

10

I'd crashed after my first venture into the Shadowlands with only a vague memory of getting back to my room and finding more monsters than usual swarming around once I was alone. I'd woken in the dark a few times as if I sensed them nearby, but kept my eyes glued shut as I tried to pretend I was wrong.

Now, as I lay there wide awake, a scream that I refused to let loose stuck in my throat. I was thankful for living in an apartment for so long that had paper-thin walls and a very responsive police department. If it hadn't been for that training, I'd never have had the control to hold back now.

Knowing there was nothing to be done about it, I unfocused my eyes and took count. Five of varying sizes moved around my room, their attention fixed on me. Never, ever had I woken to more than three. Not a good sign, and a little too coincidental in timing.

Was it going into the Shadowlands that made the others kill themselves, or was it that every time you went, there were more when you got back?

Keeping my eyes up toward the ceiling, I managed to avoid knocking my shins into the bed, only to bounce my hip into the dresser as I grabbed the first pants and shirt I found from the bags of clothes Isabella had dumped off. I blindly meandered my way into the shower.

* * *

Butch, Leon, Flip, and Jerry were all sitting in the corner booth as I headed across the main floor. I didn't look over at the vampires, but I saw a couple of pairs of fangs hanging low in my peripheral. They weren't going to kill me, so I didn't really care if they left them hanging out all day. The only thing getting under my skin today were how many damn crawlers seemed to be hanging around.

"Can I scoot in the middle?" I asked as I got to the booth. Since most people preferred the ends, Leon stood up quickly to accommodate me.

Flip looked around as if she suspected something was up, but didn't say anything as she slid in farther.

"So, you're still alive," Leon said, nodding as if getting through the first day was an achievement.

"Still alive," Butch repeated

"Still alive," I said, nodding.

"Heard it went well." Butch was watching me as he went back to eating his soup, and I got a hint of the same feeling I'd gotten from Kane last night. What had they expected to happen?

"Not so bad." My stomach growled as I smelled the various plates of bacon and eggs nearby.

"Need a gargoyle?" Jerry asked.

"Thanks."

The same gargoyle that had shown yesterday appeared after Jerry called, and I ordered up a ham and egg on a croissant.

The gargoyle disappeared, leaving me staring right at Isabella where she was sitting with a table of witches. As she broke eye contact first, it was hard not to wonder why that woman hated me so much. I could read it in her eyes, and it seemed even worse this morning. And if the eyes didn't tell me all I needed to know about her feelings, the words that drifted from her table to ours confirmed them.

"Yes, he's got her up on the sixth floor, but I'm sure it's only because he knows she won't last long." She paused as the table laughed. "I can't tell you how many times I've heard him talk about what a nuisance it was to have to deal with such fragile creatures. How they always end up being the weakest of the weakest."

The gargoyle dropped off my sandwich, distracting me from whatever else Isabella might've been saying. "Shit," I said, looking down at my plate.

"Don't mind her," Butch said.

I heard Isabella chattering in the background, but I'd lost track of what she was saying in the face of a bigger issue. "It's not her. I forgot to order coffee."

"I'm not sitting here and listening to this crap. I'm sick of this bitch. Let me out of this booth," Flip said, surprising me out of my coffee issue.

"Flip, thanks, but I don't care what she says." What I cared about was coffee. Was it even safe to call a gargoyle back for a mis-order? I looked about the table, and Leon was pulling his coffee closer to him, as if he knew I was wondering if he'd share. His even appeared to have a cream of some sort added.

"Let me at her," Flip said, now trying to push me out of the booth, but only pushing me into Butch, who wasn't moving.

Flip, giving up on getting Butch and me out of the booth, stood on the seat and walked across the table. Jerry rolled his eyes. Leon shook his head, and Butch just kept eating.

"Flip!" It was a last-ditch effort that she ignored.

"You can't stop her now. Once the fuse is lit, don't bother," Jerry said, waving a piece of sausage as he offered his sage advice.

Flip jumped from the table, landing right beside Isabella's chair and then yanking it out. "You want to keep that blond hair on your head then you'll shut the fuck up."

"Why?" Isabella said, getting to her feet and towering over the petite Flip. "The new paper doll too fragile for the truth?"

Leon nudged me. "That's going to really piss her off."

"Why?" I asked. "She doesn't even know me."

"She's big on fighting for the underdog, and, well...she's big on fighting in general."

Isabella was on her feet, and Flip was on her tiptoes trying to get in Isabella's face—or shoulder, actually. "Let's see how well you fare the next time you leave this place alone."

"Kane is going to hear about this," Isabella said, taking off toward the office.

"I'll tell him myself," Flip yelled after her as they both headed toward Kane's office.

Or, as I now thought of it, the Crawler-Free Buffer Zone.

I'd taken a few bites of the best sandwich I'd ever had, even without the accompanying coffee, when my name came down like a clap of thunder from the office above.

If I wasn't so exhausted by damn monsters last night, I might've been upset I was getting called upstairs. But they had kept me up, and although I knew I was going to somehow catch the blame for Flip and Isabella, it was hard to tamp down the smile as I looked up to where Kane stood on the balcony.

He shifted his head toward his office, and I wanted to do a couple of cartwheels. Bingo, winner. Butch slid out and I grabbed my sandwich, determined not to skip into his office and the only monster-free zone I'd ever found. I needed to pretend this sucked, even if it didn't.

My pace was calm for the first few steps, and then it might've kicked up a hair. I was close to jogging by the time I got to the stairs.

I didn't care what any of the onlookers thought, either. First of all, they all did cartwheels on his command, so they really couldn't speak. Second, so would I right now if it got me some damn peace.

Ever since I'd stepped into the Shadowland last night, it was like every crawler in the immediate vicinity couldn't wait to come out and hover all over me like a drunk guy at a sleazy bar who didn't understand the meaning of personal space.

I took the stairs to his office two at a time, only slowing my pace as I walked in. The labored breathing might've given me away. Plus, the angle he was seated at gave him a fairly good view of the top of the stairs.

Raised eyebrows at my entrance confirmed my fear that he'd seen my rush to get here. Flip and Isabella were too busy staring down each other to bother noticing me at all.

Kane jarred them out of their standoff. "You two, leave and shut the door."

Flip turned and gave me a *hang tough* wink as she walked out. Isabella waited until Kane was at her back before she gave me a smug smile.

Both eyebrows were up now as he glanced at the door and then me.

"I like to get my workouts in where I can," I said, breathing deeply of the monster-free air, even if that air smelled of Kane and cardamom. Okay, I wasn't going to lie. He might be a jerk, but there was no denying he smelled good.

"Hence wearing clothes with...moth holes for ventilation?"

Definitely a jerk. I glanced down at my neon-green sweatpants. Dated? Okay. But they were the most comfortable pick in the bag Isabella had delivered. "You don't want to wear something you might ruin during a jog." I didn't add that the clothes had been supplied to me by his person. Right now, I didn't particularly want to say her name.

"Isabella said you're causing problems." He was looking at me as if I'd instigated the thing and then been one of the people involved, when I'd simply been a spectator.

I didn't mean to yawn...or follow it up with a nice, wide stretch in my monster-free zone. I pondered my next position. I should've been mad, but that would take actual caring. I didn't care that Isabella, and it was definitely her, was trying to make my situation with Kane difficult.

He had something I needed, and I had something he needed; personal like or dislike had no place in this relationship.

I yawned again, wondering if perhaps I'd care if I weren't so tired. Nah. Probably not.

Instead, the only thing I could seem to focus on was that couch over by the wall. It looked like it had been made for afternoon naps. Even had a throw pillow.

"Olivia," Kane said, as if he were a school teacher and I a delinquent student. Did I feel a lecture coming on? Oh boy, that would be the jackpot. No monsters, a comfy-looking couch, and the potential to drag this thing out for a while. And I'd thought it was going to be a bad day.

"I don't care if you were the only Shadow Walker to ever live. Don't stir up trouble."

I heard the words as I walked past his desk and sat down on the couch. Oh yes. Just as comfy as the visual promised.

"What are you doing?" He actually sounded surprised. He was the one that put the couch in here. Wasn't sure what was so shocking about someone sitting on it.

"I figured this might take a while." At least, I hoped it did. I pulled my legs up underneath me and then sank back deep enough that my head had a nice perch on the sofa's back, without appearing too obvious about it.

He stood up and walked around his desk, as if maybe him sitting was the issue with me not shaking in my boots.

He stopped right in front of where I was sitting. "Olivia, did you start the fight downstairs?"

What response would buy me the most time in here? "I think I might've. What did Isabella say?" If I was lucky, this could buy me a nice chunk of time. I shifted just slightly downward. It wasn't my fault. This couch practically cooed to you to curl into it. If Kane didn't like it, he shouldn't have put it here. He should've gotten a wooden bench instead.

Where did he buy his furniture? Maybe if I had a couch like this in my rooms, I could've slept last night in spite of the fact that those damn things hovered all over the place like they were gearing up for a rave.

"Olivia?"

My eyes popped open. Had I started falling asleep? I hadn't even realized I'd closed my lids. He was leaning over me, and if I weren't so tired, I might've been alarmed. This wasn't the type of person you pissed off. I was sure of it by the reverence he received when he walked through the Underground.

Difference was, they didn't have monsters hovering over them every second of the day. Nor had they lost everything. When you thought of it like that, it made sense that I wasn't alarmed by him. Like Einstein said, "It's all relative, baby. It's all relative."

"Were you just sleeping?"

"No—I don't know. Could you repeat what you were saying? I really want to hear this. I think you might need to explain all the rules here. I'm not sure I understand everything about what I should and shouldn't be doing."

"Didn't Butch explain the lay of the land to you?"

"Yeah, but I'd really like to hear it again."

The almighty Kane seemed stumped for a moment. "I don't have time. Ask Butch to explain it again."

"You explain things so much better." I waved my hand toward his desk. "If you've got stuff to handle, I can wait for you to finish up. It's not a problem."

I kept my eyes open—without a crawler in sight—while I waited to see if it would work. It was near heaven in here after last night and this morning. Even Kane's narrowed eyes didn't bother me. Let him think I was crazy. I'd spent twenty-plus years having people think that. No skin off my nose.

He appeared baffled as he stood there, as if he'd been handed an octagon when he'd ordered a square.

"Why are you trying to stay here?"

"I'm not. What I'm trying to do is be a diligent and responsible part of this community." I shook my head as if he were utterly delusional.

He could think whatever he wanted, but I was not admitting that I wanted to be near him. Right now, we were tit for tat in needing each other. He needed a spell and I needed the crawlers gone, even though he thought I needed the money. That's how I was keeping it, too. I wasn't giving him one more thing to try and renegotiate with.

Although I wasn't sure why it would be a surprise to him if I did want to hang around. I would've thought every Shadow Walker who'd crossed his path would've been all over him for a little chunk of peace.

Unless…well, he *was* pretty unpleasant.

This was going to need further investigation…after a nap on this couch.

I sank a little deeper, daring him to say something to me.

He cleared his throat and I let my lids lower, ignoring any looks of disapproval. Any second, he was going to start in on me about something, but as long as the words weren't "get out," I'd be good.

A vibrating sound came from his desk. He walked over and picked up his phone while giving me a look that said we weren't finished. He answered, "Hold on," and walked back toward me.

He let out a sigh long enough for both of us, and I might've been wrong, but I had a feeling I was about to get kicked out. As he stared at me, something shifted a little, and for a split second, he didn't look like the arrogant, cold bastard I knew him to be. It seemed like there was a flicker of something warm in there. It was an improvement either way.

He walked back over to his desk, grabbed a notepad and pen, and startled me as he tossed it on my lap. I grabbed the pen before it slid to the floor, and looked up at him.

"If you're going to be here, take notes." He took a couple of steps away, hit the speaker button on the phone, and then placed it on his desk.

"Tell me the details of the deal."

A man said, "With the building on Broadway, they say they'll take the offer, but they won't do all the changes. They'll remove the beams, replace the sheetrock on the interior walls that have damage, the roof is a no go…"

Real estate?

11

Kane strolled in and stopped just short of the television I was watching while lying on the couch in my suite. *The Matrix*, although a great movie, didn't do shit to scare away the crawlers from my rooms, but it did happen to be the only thing distracting me from the one sitting beside me, or the one who *had* been sitting beside me.

After Kane had left this morning, I'd been stuck all day with these damn crawlers, more than I'd ever had with me before, without a hope of losing them for a second.

Now here he was, dressed as if he'd come back from dinner, smelling of perfume. Nice. I'd been tormented by crawlers because I was trying to get what he needed, while he'd been amusing himself with a woman, maybe women. I wouldn't put it past him to be *that* type. I'd put money on it, in fact. Although I wasn't sure if looks were enough to pull that off, and he certainly didn't have the charm.

I looked up. "Do you know why God created doors?"

He crossed his arms as he looked down at where I was sprawled. "Actually, I think carpenters create doors, but go ahead, I'll play along."

"So that people have something to knock on."

"Interesting. I'll make sure to spread the word." He looked down at the small space between the couch and TV. "Is there a reason the couch is a foot from the television?" I looked at where his pants nearly brushed my arm.

"I'm nearsighted." How the lies rolled off my tongue these days was impressive. They do say evolve or die.

His head tilted and one eyebrow rose.

I countered with a shrug. He was perfectly welcome to call me out on the real reason, but if my hunch was correct, he wouldn't want to. If I were him, I wouldn't want to. An increase of crawlers might change the negotiations in my favor.

"Are you ready?" he asked, not calling me out on the fib, proving my hunch.

"Ready for what?"

"For work."

Well, there went my plan to see if the crawlers subsided in a day or two.

He must have read the look of disappointment on my face, because he said, "You didn't think you were getting free room and board to sit around every day, did you?"

Clearly, my face didn't lie as well as my tongue. I was going to have to work a little harder on my evolution.

He walked toward the door, and damn if I'd let him leave without me. I was like an addict chasing down my hit of peace as I grabbed my jacket and followed.

He stopped right at the door, his eyes running down the length of me, and not in a good way. "I'd ask if you need to change, but I'm pretty certain you're happy that way."

"I'm quite comfortable, thank you."

"Yes, you do look that."

He stepped out into the hall and waited by the elevator in his pristine pants and polished shoes while I shut the door to my rooms.

As I stepped into the box with him, I still couldn't get over the novelty of being able to ride in an elevator like a normal person.

It wasn't until we hit the main floor of the Underground that I yelled, "Where are we going?" over the music.

"Somewhere you can't do any harm." He opened the back door and there was a bike sitting there, all black matte so as to be nearly invisible in the night.

"We're taking that?" It was twenty degrees outside, and I wrapped my arms around myself, already imagining the wind blowing through the jacket I had as if I were wearing nothing. But even a good jacket would leave me with a nasty case of frostbite on a night like tonight.

"We'll take the car." He walked to the Maserati parked next to it, but my instincts told me the car had been an afterthought.

I was still watching him sort of sideways as we drove. Did he never get cold? What kind of person didn't get cold?

"Yes?" he asked.

"What?" I asked back, realizing my sideways looks must've been a little too obvious.

"You have a question."

"No, I don't." Not one I was ready to ask.

"Then you were staring at me because I'm so ridiculously handsome?"

The way he said it left no doubt he was kidding. I felt pressure in my cheeks. I didn't want to smile, or let out a half laugh, but I did anyway. He might be a jerk, but that was a tad funny.

"What's the deal for tonight?" I asked, bringing it back to business. No laughter and joking here. It could only lead to trouble.

"Tonight you're going to retrieve your first spell. You need to know some basics. After you ask for it, if they know it, they'll tell you. But don't repeat it. If you say a spell, you cast a spell."

I'd been secretly enjoying his scent before he laid that information on me. "If I can't practice it, what if I say it wrong?"

He glanced over at me. "Hence the long drive. I don't want you blowing anything up near my building."

"I could blow something up?"

"Yes."

I was going to be able to blow stuff up. Did I want to? No, not really. Still didn't diminish the fact that I could.

"Stop looking so pleased with yourself before I come to my senses and realize this might be a bad idea."

Did he make another joke? No, couldn't be. It was shocking enough that he'd already done it once tonight.

But a spell… I was going to do magic. There were more questions that I could think of. "Once I cast a spell, is it gone or does it keep working?"

"It depends. Some will work perfectly over and over again, until one day they won't. Some get weaker and weaker until they sputter out. Some are one-shot deals."

He'd barely finished speaking before I jumped in with the next question. "How will I know what type it is when I get it?"

"You won't," he answered flatly.

It was really irritating to discover something new like this with a person who had the excitement of going for a teeth cleaning.

Didn't matter. I leaned back, thinking about how I was going to ask these crawlers for something really cool. Least they could do for tormenting me all these years.

* * *

"You want me to go in and ask for butterflies?" We were standing in a field not that far outside of Boston, a place that was fairly screaming and hopping with crawlers. I was shivering constantly, as they dropped the temperature around them by a good ten degrees, even keeping their distance. The magic was so thick that I felt it brewing and stirring under the surface, as if it were only looking for the merest excuse to burst into life, and here I was, someone who didn't know what they were doing. I stood on the edge of all this power, and what did he want? Butterflies?

Feet shoulder width apart, with his hands resting in his pockets like he was watching a horse race on a sunny day, he said, "Yes. Butterflies."

I took the entire picture of Kane in. No debating that he was a handsome man. His crisp white collar slightly open, his tie long gone, he'd clearly been gifted physically in an utterly masculine nature. Which all brought me back to—*butterflies*?

"Would you like a rainbow and a unicorn with those? We could shoot for a package deal, perhaps? Hey, maybe even winter wonderland as our theme?"

He tilted his head forward. "Stick to the butterflies. It's the only thing I trust you to not fuck up."

I measured the tit for tat. It seemed fairly balanced on the scale of verbal jabbing.

Butterflies. I shook my head and resigned myself to it. It was still a spell. "So what do I do?"

"You're going to go in like last time. After you get in, ask the first crawler you see for a spell to create butterflies. Even the smallest should have that ability."

"That's it? I don't have to say some weird verbiage or Latin verse?"

"Why would you have to speak Latin? Where do you people get this stuff?"

I didn't think he expected an answer, but I gave him one anyway. "I don't know. It's a really old language. You're telling me the crawlers all speak English and that's not odd?"

"I'm saying it doesn't matter what language they speak. You'll be able to remember and say the words."

I was the one rolling my eyes and popping up my brows now. "How am I going to remember words I don't understand?" There didn't seem to be a need to tell him I'd barely passed Spanish class and that I might've been linguistically challenged.

"*Because* you are a Shadow Walker. That's how it works."

"None of this sounds logical to me."

"It doesn't have to. It's magic."

"That's not a strong argument. For the record, I don't feel like you're trying to explain it." I didn't care if he'd done this countless times before, or how short his patience was. My patience with him was about as thin as a frozen pond in March. One of these times, and soon, I was going to crack, and bad.

"And that would be because I am not trying to explain it. Let's get a little further along before we sign you up for a master's program."

Get a little further as in "let's see how long you live." Man, that was really starting to make me burn. Every time he or one of his people treated me like I was a goner, it only made me want to live a little bit more, just to prove everyone wrong. We'd see how long I lasted.

I held out my hand, done speaking to him. I'd figure this world out on my own, and then let's see who was a goner.

He clasped my hand. "Go in. Ask for the spell. Memorize it. Bring it back." He leaned in closer, nailing me with an all-business stare. "Don't let go."

"I've got it."

"It's going to be harder to exit with the spell because magic doesn't like to cross planes, but it'll be fine. You'll get better at it as you go. If it's ever too tough, you can let the spell out on that side and get out."

"I've got it," I repeated, my temper about to take a knife to my nose at any second.

There was a large crawler not far from us, and I called it over to me. The more confident I appeared, the quicker the crawler seemed to do what I wanted, and the air shimmered in front of me.

I stepped through, debating whether I should act traumatized when I stepped out so I could up my price. Worth a thought. Anybody forced to work with Kane surely deserved extra for hostile work environment.

"Shadow Walker," a few crawlers murmured as I entered their land and eyed up my options. There was a huge one in the distance, but Kane had said even the smallest would be able to give me this spell, so I went for a little one that looked kind of like a housecat, if they were able to walk on two feet.

It didn't seem to have any interest in me, but I called to it anyway and it nearly stumbled its way over, closing the five-foot gap. Did it have to come to me if I called it in this land? It seemed like I'd forced it.

It stopped in front of me, and I mustered up my most authoritative voice, the one I used on the kids who used to mess with the candy in front of my cash register. "I want to make butterflies."

It made screeching noises that didn't sound that different from a cat. "Butterflies. I want to make butterflies," I repeated.

There was another screech before a litany of sounds flowed out of the creature that sounded nothing like any cat I'd ever heard. It was sort of melodic, and as I tried to commit it to memory, I found that it settled into my brain with ease, like a song I'd enjoyed and heard many times before. The strange words filled me with a sense of beauty and lightness, as if I could take to the skies and fly away myself. How could anyone call this dark magic?

The creature scurried off as soon as it was done, and I turned to exit the place. The crawlers had gathered around the place I'd entered, and as I faced them, they started a chant of my name.

Then they started moving toward me. Oh shit. I looked at the spot I had to get to, and then them. When Kane had said it might be difficult to leave with the spell, he could've been more specific.

I counted four in between me and the spot I'd entered. I bent over slightly and geared up to plow through them. I felt them grazing me as I passed full steam ahead, but they felt weaker than me.

My shoulder drove into Kane on my way out, and then he grabbed my shoulders and straightened me up.

Kane didn't have to say anything; the question was clear on his face.

"I got it," I said, the little chatter of my teeth making the last word sound more like "i-t-t-t." I looked for the car, heading that way without checking to see if he was in tow. I was halfway there when I felt his jacket settling on my shoulders, layering over my own.

"Thanks," I said, keeping my eyes on the car.

He didn't reply, as if he hadn't done something nice. He probably just wanted to keep me healthy so I could keep doing this spell stuff. Still, it was warm, and smelled nice too, so I didn't give it back, even after I was in the car with the heat running.

He eyed me from head to toe after we were both in the car, as if he'd expected me to look different. "How difficult was it?"

Leaning forward with my hands in front of the heating vents, I answered, "Not pleasant. Did you know they'd try and stop me?" I angled toward him, no lack of accusation in my tone or my stare.

He was still looking me over, and he hadn't taken the car out of park yet. "It's common."

My hands finally thawed, I sat back to absorb the heat from the seats better. "That might've been something you should've told me?"

He put the car in drive, finally done with his perusal. "Every other time I warned a Shadow Walker, it did more harm than good."

I glanced over his way and then turned. If this was going to take a while, and I was beginning to think it would, there were going to need to be some changes. "I'm not a number. Stop treating me like I'm a statistic. If you know something is coming, tell me."

"You might not like what you hear."

"But you'll trust me to handle it."

He didn't answer, and I let the silence expand as I thought of what might be coming. And for all my talk, I didn't ask because I was certain I wouldn't like the answers and I was still regrouping.

He pulled the car over near an empty park about fifteen minutes later.

He got out of the car and I followed him. "Where are we?"

"Getting a little distance from the initial site before you cast the spell. Remember that in the future. Otherwise you can create a magical hot spot. Funny things can happen around those, things you don't want to imagine."

I nodded. Had he just explained something to me without having to ask? Little late, but I tucked away the knowledge.

We walked a couple of feet, and I stopped when he did by the edge of a frozen lake.

"You ready to cast your first spell?"

Was I? I didn't have any clue. Any excitement I had was tarnished by the possibility that instead of creating butterflies, I might be blowing something up.

"Yes." Do or die time.

"Do you remember the words you heard?"

I nodded. I could remember them clearly, which was strange, since it was a language I didn't know.

"Say them."

"That's it?"

"As long as you say them correctly, yes."

I locked my arms in front of me as I tilted my head back and looked up at the stars for a moment. "And if I don't say them correctly?"

He looked up at the same stars. "Could get ugly, but that's why we're starting off with butterflies."

"Okay."

I took a deep breath, and found myself turning toward Kane, who was already facing me. He didn't look arrogant or impatient right now. "Let it flow from you. It'll be fine."

Kane being nice—now that was a dangerous thing. "Be careful. You're sounding almost human," I said, and I wasn't sure if that joke was more for him or me. Arrogant Kane made me want to be violent. This Kane was much more dangerous.

He made a fake shiver and then said, "Please don't insult me like that."

He turned his head forward, but I could see the smirk on his face.

It was definitely time to get this show on the road. I took a deep breath and then, as he suggested, let the words flow from me. They filled the air with a beautiful tinkling sound, and then, as I watched, glittering butterflies started to materialize in the sky. They were every color imaginable, and seemed to emanate light. They fluttered up and around in a circle that grew larger and larger until they spanned the entire area we stood, creating a halo of perfection as they shimmered on the air.

"Wow, I did this?" It seemed inconceivable that words taken from such a dark space could spawn this kind of beauty. And I'd had a hand in it.

"Yes. You did."

As I watched them flutter around, as much as I enjoyed this, I knew I wasn't going into the Shadowlands for butterfly spells. This had been my first baby step into casting magic, but I was afraid what it might become later on.

A cold wind blew, scattering the butterflies as dark thoughts filled me. I knew I wasn't wrong about one thing: Kane wasn't a man seeking butterflies. "I won't be getting too many more of these, will I?"

He stood relaxed beside me, watching the show as well. "You still sure you want the truth?"

I didn't want it, but I needed it. "Yes."

The last of the butterflies were carried away by a strong bitter gust, disappearing into the dark as he said, "No, you won't."

12

My bedroom was getting crowded as I dug through the bags of clothes with my eyes closed. The chill of crawlers hovered near my shoulders, as if they had a stake in the clothes I wore. Sweatpants or sweatshirts and more sweats. I pushed my hand deeper until my fingers grazed denim. I dragged them to the top and squinted an eye open. No holes, stains, or strange colors? Must've landed in the bag by mistake.

Probably not going to be quite as comfortable as the sweats and yoga pants, but I put them on anyway. Wouldn't kill me to make a little bit of an effort with my appearance. Somebody had to represent the Shadow Walkers in a good light, and I had cast my first spell.

I threw on the sweater I'd worn here that the gargoyles had laundered, and took a brief look at myself in the mirror. I toyed with a couple of odd hairs poking out here and there.

By the time I was walking onto the main floor of the Underground, I looked a little like I had before I'd given up on the world.

I'd cast a spell last night, and I still couldn't quite believe it. Was this how the witches felt when they'd started practicing? If I was going to be casting spells, it might help to have some witch friends. They hadn't seemed very friendly, but I hadn't tried, either.

I glanced over at the tables where the witches tended to congregate. They didn't seem too bad as they chatted and one pleasant-looking blonde giggled.

Butch and Leon were watching me. With a friendly wave in their direction, I made up my mind and took a step toward that table of witches, ignoring the red head shaking or the grimace on Leon's face. The witches were the closest people here to what I was. It only made sense for us to be on friendly terms. They'd like me.

Before this place, back in my previous life, I'd never have approached a group of people in an effort to make friends. But this was a new day, and I was, for the first time in my life—at least among these people—sane. I didn't have any secret monsters I had to hide.

"Be assertive, confident—people respond to those qualities," was what my dad had always said. I stopped by an empty seat at one of the tables.

"Hi, how are you all? I thought I'd come introduce myself." They stared at me. "My name is Ollie." They kept staring, with slightly less open eyes. "I'm not exactly a witch, but I figured since I cast spells, I'm pretty close. We probably have a lot in common."

The blonde that had seemed so pleasant before looked like a snarling dog now. "You can't sit with us."

"I do spells. I'm kind of like a witch now, or sort of."

"We've got butterflies covered," a brunette sitting beside her said.

I shot back with the only lame thing that came to mind: "Fine, but don't be asking me for any of my stuff when I get really cool spells." My face brightened; I knew exactly how stupid I sounded without having to hear their laughter to validate my opinion.

I turned, keeping my pace to a walk instead of a run.

"Yeah, paper doll, so scram before we punch some holes in you," one of the witches said as I walked away.

I turned and didn't make it three steps before I tripped on something that wasn't there and landed into a shifter. I ended up face first in his omelet.

The whole table laughed, and there were a couple of comments suggesting I wouldn't last that long anyway.

I got to my feet and turned on the witches, even as the shifter was still cursing me. "That was not nice."

"We didn't do anything. No one was even near you. You're a klutz," the blonde said.

I wiped the egg from my shirt as I said, "You better *hope* I stick to butterflies."

Leon came to my side to grab my arm and tug me away from the disgruntled shifter and witches. "Let it go," he said. "Come on, I'll order you up some breakfast."

I looked at the table of witches, generous with their smirks and giggles, and knew it was a losing battle right now. They were right. What was I going to do? Sic my pretty butterflies on them? I couldn't take on a gang of experienced witches. Not yet, anyway.

"Thanks," I said, turning away from them but committing each smirk and giggle to memory. They'd better hope I died.

I slid into the booth beside Butch. A body on each side, I had a monster buffer for breakfast, which was sorely needed.

Leon patted my shoulder. "Don't feel bad. That never goes well. And even though you might not have any witch friends, you're still alive."

"Yep, still alive," I repeated in the same singsong voice he'd used. It was becoming my own little anthem.

Leon called a gargoyle, and a gasp caught in my throat as it appeared. I might be here a year before I got used to the sight of them. I put in an order, making sure to specify how I wanted my coffee.

"In case you were wondering, butterflies are the normal first spell for the occasional Shadow Walker who makes it that far." Leon took another bite of his breakfast.

Butch sipped some sort of green brew that I thought might be tea. "Kane used to do the butterflies closer to the building, but had to stop."

Leon groaned. "What a mess. Took a month to get rid of them."

"Sometimes I forget about that idiot." Butch turned back to me. "This stupid moron somehow made attack butterflies. They were these beautiful things fluttering around, until you got close, and then they swarmed on you like a killer hive, stingers and all. They invaded the building and wouldn't die."

Leon was looking over his coffee mug at me.

"What?" I ran a hand over my mouth, wondering if I'd left some toothpaste smeared across it.

"Nothing. You look…"

"I look?" I waved a hand at him.

"Normal," Butch said. "He's trying to tell you that you look normal."

"Oh. You could've just said that."

The gargoyle delivered my food, and I ate as slowly as possible. Kane had said we weren't working until tonight. I'd be spending my day flipping channels, sitting nearly on top of the TV so the crawlers couldn't get in the way, and I seemed to have an endless supply today.

"Where are you guys going today? Need any help?" Maybe if I could ride in the front of the Caddy, with one of them on either side?

Butch took the last bite of his breakfast. "Nah, not today. Not a good day."

"Oh, yeah. Okay. Just figured I'd offer. I've got stuff to do anyway, so no big deal." Damn. I'd been going for chill, but that had come out closer to desperate. Nah. It couldn't have been that bad.

"Now you made her feel bad," Leon told Butch.

Nope. I had sounded that pathetic.

"We can't take her," Butch said. "We're going to be gone too long."

"She might not have that…" Leon glanced over at me and then back at Butch. "She might not want to hang around here that long. Can't we do that other thing later?"

I looked from Butch to Leon. "Do what thing?"

Butch was staring at Leon. "We can't. Checked the schedule. The others will be all over her, and she's too far away."

"Who?" The more they talked over me, the more I couldn't take the mystery anymore. The others would be all over her? "Another Shadow Walker?" I leaned back on the booth. I'd known there were quite a few of us. It wasn't like they'd made that a secret, but…

I didn't know how to feel about it. Had this other Shadow Walker's life been as destroyed as mine? Did the crawlers stalk her all day too? I'd never had anyone else to ask about this stuff. "How did you find her?"

"The usual way," Leon said, not offering any other details.

"You know…" Butch's neck seemed to shrink as he continued. "Like your event. Mass casualty, single survivor…" He rolled his hand in front of him as his eyes got bigger, a silent plea to not have to continue.

I nodded, feeling numb and suddenly wondering if being alone with the crawlers might be better. I didn't have to speak to them or pretend to be anything near normal.

My brain tripped over the mental scar as I lost my words, which seemed to speed Butch and Leon from the booth.

"We've got to run. We'll see you in a little bit?" Leon asked.

I forced a smile on my face and waved as if it were no big deal. "Sure. Good luck."

I hadn't had the chance to get out of the booth when a vampire was sliding in opposite me. Even though his fangs weren't down, I'd seen the group he'd headed over from.

Hopefully his boss had spread the word that he couldn't eat me. Considering there hadn't been any Kane sightings, and Butch and Leon had just left, the potential that I was going to be this vampire's lunch was looking alarmingly close. I didn't think a horde of sparkling butterflies were going to help me out.

Then he smiled and said hello in a way that seemed like he was looking for something a little more ancient than lunch. He was a good-looking—man? I'd noticed the vampires tended to be more attractive. Wasn't sure if that was how they were chosen or if the blood did something to them, but I had enough balls in the air.

"Hello," I said like a girl would to a guy she wasn't into, when she hoped he'd go away.

Flip made her way over and slid in beside me. "Go away, Casio. She's not sleeping with you."

Or you could be like Flip and tell them outright.

"Little premature, no?" Casio responded in a way that spoke of a comfort level.

"Yes, I have heard that about you, Casio." She then laughed at her own joke. If I didn't already have so much bad blood with the vampires, I might've laughed.

"Why must you be like that? I told you I would sleep with you, too."

Flip scrunched up her face, but her attention was focused on me, not Casio. "The witches got to you."

"I wouldn't say they got to me." I could've simply fell. I didn't think I had, but it could've happened.

Flip's eyes were trained on me, squinting as she looked closer at my shirt. It was the nicest thing I'd worn since I'd gotten here, except that there were egg stains on it now.

"What?"

Flip's lips curled back and she shook her head. "You're going to have to get out of here really soon."

"Why?"

"'Cause witches be bitches," Casio said, as he shrugged off his jacket. "We've been warning everyone for decades, but no one *ever* listens."

"Casio, not the time to climb up onto your soapbox about how the vampires are the saints of the world." Flip held out her hand, and he gave her the jacket. "You know you aren't getting this back, right?"

"Tick tock, tick tock, you're running out of time," he said, looking at my shirt.

"What's going on?" I looked down at my shirt and realized my clothes were literally decaying as I sat there.

Flip threw the jacket over my shoulders and tugged me forward out of the booth. She continued to pull me toward the back hall, and I let her. "What's happening to my clothes?"

She tugged me toward the elevator. "Where's your room?"

"Sixth," I said, pulling toward the stairs.

She showed how strong she was by nearly dragging me back toward the elevator. "No time for the stairs."

The elevator doors were sliding open as my jeans were falling, the hip area threadbare at this point. I gave up on trying to hold them up, and focused on keeping Casio's jacket, which came just to the top of my thighs, closed. I was shedding clothes all around me as the crawlers sniffed them. "Those damn witches."

"So this is what the sixth floor looks like." Flip stepped into the hallway and paused, turning her head this way and that. I had to jostle her to the side to find my way out and get away from all the crawlers stuck in the elevator with me.

"I'm the door on the right."

She followed me in but stopped right inside the door again. "Interesting. Very"—she took a moment to take it all in—"hotel chic."

My hands busy keeping what remained of my clothes in place, I made my way into the bedroom. "I don't understand. How did my clothes fall apart?" I yelled to her.

"It's a decaying spell. They probably had the gargoyles slip it into your breakfast. Those stony-faced bastards can be bought pretty easily. You're going to need to avoid cotton for a while." She walked in the bedroom and opened my closet to find it bare.

I pointed toward the garbage bags on the floor.

She kneeled in front of them and started tossing stuff out as she dug. "Looks like it's going to be pretty hard to do. This is your stuff?"

"Well, the stuff Isabella got me."

She let out something in between a guffaw and a chuckle. "Now it makes sense. She's never met a female she didn't dislike, especially ones within ten feet of Kane." She let out a sigh as she sized me up.

"How long is this going to last?" Casio's jacket was starting to shed threads.

"Depends on which witch did it. If it's one of the weaker witches, it might only be a few days."

"And if it's not? If it's one of the stronger witches?"

She puffed out her cheeks. "A few months?" Her voice rose as she spoke.

My shredded clothing and me sank back onto the bed as visions of being holed up in these rooms with only the crawlers indefinitely occurred to me. But I couldn't hide. I had to work. How was that going to go?

"Grab a sheet. I'm going to do you a solid, so remember you owe me."

"What can you do?"

She smiled and held out a finger as she dug her phone out of her pocket and dialed. "Have a 911. Need some magic-proof clothing in small." There was a pause. "I don't know. Active wear, maybe a couple of evening outfits, the basic spectrum. Shoes, too. Don't forget those."

She pointed to my feet.

"Seven," I said.

"Size seven."

She nodded, as if the person on the other side of the phone could see her. "Okay, up on sixth, door to the right. We'll be here waiting." She slid her phone in the back pocket of her jeans.

"Who was that?"

"That was you being saved from having to wear a shower curtain all week."

As she said it, the seam on the shoulder of Casio's jacket started to fall down, and I tugged the sheet up higher. "Oh shit. How long do I have?" I asked, doing a mental count of the towels.

"The sheet will hold. The spell only works on clothing. I've seen it enough to know. This is how the witches like to welcome Shadow Walkers who make it past a couple of days."

I wondered if I could belt this sheet up and use it as a dress of sorts if the clothes coming didn't work out. "Hey, I thought there was a rule that there wasn't any magic use in the building?"

"Obviously, this wasn't explained to you thoroughly. There is no magic used *that comes to Kane's attention* in the building. There's also no magic in the building according to Butch, Leon, or Jerry, except for an occasional slip-up that they think they let go because they're such nice guys. Reality? As long as you don't get caught, it's game on."

She took a seat on the bed, resting against the tufted headboard. "I wouldn't bring this to Kane's attention unless you want to be the new target. You're not doing so hot on getting along with people now. You add being a tattletale to the list?" She rolled her eyes and whistled. "You could end up indebted to your eyebrows."

"Indebted?"

"Yeah—"

A knock at the door interrupted her. It was the first time I'd heard that sound since I'd been here.

"Come on in," Flip yelled. "Don't make a face. They're dwarves," she whispered quickly as she got up and headed toward the living room.

I followed her in just as five men came walking in. None of them stood over three and a half feet tall, but they were all broad of shoulder, and every single one of them looked grumpy. But they were well dressed in suits that could've been Armani.

They wheeled in a rack with covered garment bags hanging from it, and the last man was carrying boxes. They wheeled the rack until it was in front of where I'd taken a seat on the couch, and placed the boxes on the coffee table. "You owe us. Do you acknowledge this debt?"

The only clothing I had was falling off me in threads. If it weren't for the sheet, I'd be naked. There were times in life you could negotiate, and there was this moment. "Yes. These won't fall apart?" I asked.

A dwarf with a black suit, silk purple shirt, and perfectly coiffed dark hair stepped forward.

"Of course they won't. They resist magic. We made them. We don't make junk."

"No offense."

They seemed offended anyway as they turned to leave.

"What's the cost?" I asked as they were walking out. The same dwarf answered, "We'll let you know," before he shut the door.

I immediately started rummaging through the clothes. "Where did they come from?"

Flip had moved to the shoes. "They've been here. You know the empty booth on the floor that no one ever sits in?"

"Yeah, I do, now that you mention it."

"They sit there every day. Dwarves are only seen when they want to be, and they've got a weird thing about people watching them eat."

She was oohing over a pair of black boots when I asked her, "How much do you think they're going to want?"

"They brought you a lot of clothes."

In other words, I didn't want to know.

I pulled out a pair of dark jeans, examining them. There was a label on the back with a zigzag line that looked like a mountain outline, and then, in silver embroidery, *D. Ware.* "These seem really nice."

"Those are the shit. I've got a pair of those jeans handed down to me. Can't afford new ones. They're, like, a year of pay."

I fell back on my ass on the floor, from where I'd been kneeling as I tried to count up how many garment bags I saw.

Flip shuffled through some more bags, pulling out and holding up a little black dress. "They really hooked you up. They must think they're going to get paid back in spades."

Looked like I'd already sold my soul. Might as well get the most out of it. I grabbed the jeans and a light sweater, and noticed they'd even included bras and panties. Standing with a hand clenched on the sheet, I took them to the bedroom.

The clothes fit as if they'd known my measurements down to the centimeter, nothing pulling or pinching. No awkward bagging. They were perfection. I stepped around a crawler to go into the bathroom, looking at the larger mirror there. I hadn't even known I could look this good. If the monsters hadn't been staring in the mirror with me, I might've kept looking.

Flip eyed me up as I walked back into the room. "Damn, I didn't realize what you were packing under all those ugly rags."

"Neither did I."

"Something wrong with your eyesight? Why do you keep staring at the ceiling?" she asked as I bumped into the wall on my way back to the living room.

I forced my eyes to her face. "I thought I saw a bug." Even though she knew about the crawlers, old habits die hard, and it was easier to slip back into lying about their existence than explaining that they were everywhere right now.

"Is it the crawlers?" she asked as if I hadn't handed her an easy out. "It's kind of cold in here."

"Yeah, pretty much." I bit my lip, hoping I wasn't going to have to get into the weeds explaining how bad it had gotten. Living with them was bad enough.

"Well, having done my good deed and assisting in selling your soul to the devil, I've got things to go handle today." She smiled and headed toward the door, putting any fears I had to rest.

Or most of them. "Wait, I didn't really sell my soul, right?" Who knew how this place worked?

"No," she said, walking out my door as I followed her. "Not your soul. I can't guarantee they won't come looking for your firstborn." She laughed and then shook her head.

I wasn't feeling so giddy about it myself.

The elevator doors slid open and Kane stepped forward. He paused, his eyes narrowing slightly in my direction. I waited, expecting to hear him say something rude about what I was wearing.

He didn't comment about the clothing. "Be ready at eight." He walked to his apartment and shut the door.

Flip flopped back against the wall beside the elevator, waving her hand over her face. "Holy shit, did you see that? Or feel it?" she asked, nearly breathless and with a sheen on her skin.

I looked over at Kane's now-closed door and then the rest of the hallway. "What?"

"It was near boiling levels. You didn't feel that?"

"Boiling levels of what?"

She looked at the door, at me, and then the elevator. "Um…"

"What are you talking about?"

She pushed off the wall and started backing into the elevator, a crawler following her in. "You know, I think I'm coming down with a flu or something."

No way was I stepping into the elevator with her, not even for an answer.

"Thanks for the help with the clothing," I yelled as the doors began to shut.

I heard a muffled "You got it, kid."

13

It was a record low that evening as Kane and I stood before a building with knocked-out windows and a partially caved-in roof. There were charred places here and there, and I doubted it had been occupied in the last decade. "What is this place?"

Kane stepped slightly closer to me, blocking the wind some. "It's an old school. It burned down after a mysterious explosion."

"How bad of an explosion?"

He stood beside me as if it were as warm as a summer day. "Crawler bad."

"Why do you want me to Shadow Walk here?" There was an obvious connection, but I wasn't taking for granted that I knew anything in this world.

"The crawlers tend to be stronger in places they've destroyed."

Or maybe I had a better handle on things than I realized. "How much worse does it get?"

He shifted slightly backward, blocking a little more wind from me, as if he were doing it on purpose. "Are we still doing that honest thing?"

The words "honest thing" pretty much said it all. "Yes, we're still doing that thing."

"It'll get pretty hard as the spells get harder. The crawlers might give you the magic, but not because they like it." He took a step toward the building.

I let a little gap grow in between us, losing my wind blocker. I had started down this road to find a way to be normal, and yet things seemed to be getting worse. There were more crawlers than ever. Still, when he paused and looked back to see if I was coming, I moved forward. He stopped inside the threshold and held out his hand.

I took it. "What should I ask for?"

"Nothing too difficult. You'll work up to something more difficult."

"How do I know what's difficult?"

"If you think it might be, it probably is."

With that great information, I called over the ugliest crawler in sight and entered the Shadowlands.

The first thing I noticed was it was colder here, but I felt Kane's warm grip.

The words "Shadow Walker" carried with the air as the crawlers started to edge their way over to me.

I sized them up. The more time I spent here, the more I was beginning to sense different levels of power emanating from them. It might have been my own delusion, but it felt true.

I walked along a few more feet farther, feeling Kane's warm hand around mine. It was strange how I could wander this world and yet he'd remain in the same place in our world. Although that was another thing: what made my world any more real than here?

As I passed by crawlers in varying shapes and sizes, I ignored them as they called to me until I found one that felt right. It was smaller, maybe four feet tall, with shaggy, long hair and the freakiest red eyes I'd ever seen.

More crawlers were already heading near, so I didn't waste any time in calling it over.

"I need a spell to protect me," I said.

It didn't hesitate, singing its song of magic and proving my hunch correct. It took off as soon as it was done, and I turned, seeing the rest of the crawlers starting to gather right where I needed to go. I counted eight, with four more on their way.

This might get a little ugly, and I couldn't afford to waste time worrying. I needed to go, and now.

And then the ones on their way over stopped. Another moment and the ones that had been blocking my way were moving away from me.

Frigid air blew against my back. All my senses lit up as I tried to figure out where the strong source of power was coming from. I didn't know what it was, but I knew it was close. Too close.

If I ran, could I make it?

"Hello, Ollie."

I stopped breathing as my hands trembled, and not from the cold. I turned around, afraid of what I might find.

He looked human as he stood in front of me. Dark featured, dressed in jeans, I could've seen him on the street in my world, except for the waves of magic rolling off him.

"Who are you?"

He moved forward, and I backed up a step.

He looked down to where I held an invisible hand, but shifted his eyes quickly. "Who? Or what?"

I flexed my fingers around Kane's hand and felt a tightening in response. As long as I felt him, I'd be able to get out. That was what I told myself, anyway. "I guess I mean what."

"My name is Asher. I'm one of them," he said, motioning to the other crawlers that seemed to keep their distance from both of us now.

I glanced around, and then stated the obvious: "Why don't you look like them?"

He stared in an unearthly way that was definitely not human. "They don't look alike either."

But they all looked like monsters. I was torn between running and being afraid that movement might set off some sort of attack. "How do you know me?"

"I've known you for a long time."

"How?"

"Those on this side can feel the presence of Shadow Walkers. The ones that can partially walk your world bring stories back." He twisted his head in an awkward angle, as he continued to take in all of me, but didn't step forward again. "May I show you something?"

I shook my head. "I have to leave."

"I'll give you a gift if you let me show you. It's safe. I won't let anything bad happen while you're with me, and I'll escort you safely out afterward." He smiled and then turned, as if I'd already agreed.

I didn't move forward, but the crawlers did, in my direction.

"Where is it? How far?" I called.

He stopped and waited for me. "Just around the bend."

I walked forward, slowing down when he did so to maintain a pace behind him.

The farther I walked, the colder I got, and the less I felt Kane's hand. I gripped him tighter and felt the responding squeeze and what felt like a tug. He knew I was going farther, and he was warning me.

My steps faltered, and I was about to tell this person I wouldn't go any farther when we made a turn. There was a lake, and on it, beautiful black swans glittered upon the water as if they were made from crystals. "This world has beauty if you are willing to see it. Not all that lives here is bad."

I watched the beauty, but the knowledge of how many Shadow Walkers had died before me was the equivalent of a warning flag repeatedly flashing in front of my frontal lobe. "I need to go back now."

"I'll take you back, but I've got one last gift for you—and a warning as well."

* * *

I nearly fell as I stepped into my world, but not because I'd been running toward the entrance. Asher had done what he'd said and escorted me back. The second I stepped to exit, I was yanked forward. Kane with his hands on either arm stopped me when I would've face-planted.

"What the fuck, Ollie? Why were you gone so long? What were you doing?"

I wrapped my arms around myself as a chill hit me like I'd just stepped into the North Pole. "Why am I so much colder than last time? The temperature must've dropped forty degrees since I went in there."

"Because you went too far." He pulled off the wool sweater he was wearing, leaving himself in nothing but a snug white T-shirt, and tugged the sweater over my head without asking. It was one of those bulky knit ones, and his heat was still clinging to it, so I didn't protest, just found the armholes with my hands.

"Aren't you cold?" *And more importantly, what the hell are you that you don't feel it like the rest of us?*

"It's an aftereffect of Shadow Walking," he said, and started herding me toward the car, while I was blowing warm air into my hands.

I must've been moving too slow for him, because his arm wrapped around my waist, urging me there quicker. "Why didn't you follow my orders?"

I didn't bother answering. I was too cold to argue with him. He opened the car door for me and shoved me into the interior. Quicker than I would've believed possible, he was seated beside me with the car started and the heat cranking.

I was leaning back on the heated seat, my hands positioned in front of the vents, when he grabbed my legs. He pulled off my new dwarf boots and proceeded to rub my feet and calves.

He was so close that all I could smell was him, could feel the heat pouring off him. He lifted his shirt and tucked my feet and legs under his shirt as his hands worked higher, grazing my knees and then the tops of my thighs. Maybe it was the heat of his touch after the stark, cold Shadowlands, but the warmth of his fingers spread inside me with a tingling feeling.

I leaned forward, my tongue darting out and licking lips that suddenly felt dry. I looked up and saw him watching me.

"Don't make an offer you aren't willing to follow through on."

I jerked, realizing what he'd thought. "You're warm, is all. Don't flatter yourself," I said, pulling my legs back, my face growing hot at what he'd implied. I curled them up on the heated seat. It wasn't as warm as him, but it would have to do.

He was handsome, but he was also the worst person I knew. It might've looked like I was looking for something from him, but that was not what I was doing. If he wasn't so arrogant, he would've known that. Instead, now I was feeling defensive. No wonder my heart was racing.

He put the car in drive. "Why were you in there so long?"

After what Asher had said, I wasn't sure if this was the time to be completely honest. He knew everything about me and I knew next to nothing about him. But a partial story might help me mine for some more information.

"There was a person in there. Well, not a person. He said he was a crawler, but I've never seen one look human, not in all my years."

I waited and watched as he absorbed my words without even a flicker of emotion. It wasn't like other times where he'd been clearly uninterested. This was a purposeful mask, meant to keep me out.

"Do you know anything about that? Is it normal for them to look human in there sometimes?" I asked, following a hunch that it wasn't.

"There are some."

I had nothing but my gut to go on, but it was screaming that he was lying to me.

"Did you speak to him?" he asked, keeping the calm in place.

"Briefly."

"About what?"

"Just that he knew of me from the other crawlers."

"That's all?"

"And he showed me a lake with beautiful birds swimming. It was strange, because he didn't call me Shadow Walker like the others. He called me Ollie."

"He?" He turned, hardness in his eye. "You mean 'it.' He's not human."

"You're right," I said, and he turned his full attention back to the road. I didn't know what Asher was, but I wouldn't be debating it with Kane, not after that.

"Did you get a spell?"

"No. I didn't want to stay any longer," I lied without hint of shame.

He nodded, as if I'd finally done something he agreed with. "Don't talk to him again. It's too dangerous."

I nodded. I knew he took that as me agreeing to not speak to this person again. Didn't matter if he misunderstood that it was me finally realizing I had no idea where I really stood with this man.

I thought of the warning the shadow man had said to me as we drove.

"He's not what you think."
"Who?"
"Him." His eyes went to my hand.
"I don't know what he is. Do you?"
"Don't trust him."
"I can trust you?" I asked without hiding the doubt I felt from my voice.
He looked down and stood there quietly for a moment. When he looked up, he said softly, *"If you were smart, you wouldn't trust anyone."*

We weren't partners in any sense of the word. We weren't friends. All I could hope for now was that I hadn't been wrong about everything, because I didn't want this man as my enemy. That I knew.

But full disclosure? Those days were over. At least until I knew what he was hiding. And I knew he was hiding something. I was someone who'd been hiding for years, and you couldn't fool a pro.

14

I strode through the room, heading toward the table with my shoulders back, as if the witches hadn't done a thing to me and the vamps didn't want to kill me, as if the empty booth in the corner didn't hold a bunch of dwarves that might take my eyeteeth for the debt I owed them. I acted like I knew Kane had my back and that strange man in the Shadowlands hadn't said anything to me.

Most importantly, I walked like I hadn't woken up and cried when I saw how many crawlers were in my room this morning. That I didn't have huge bruises on both legs from when I'd stumbled around trying to get dressed with my eyes closed.

No one knew any of that, though. If you saw me strutting through the Underground, all you saw was someone who had a handle on things. Because I was realizing one thing about this new world I'd been thrust upon: they fed on the weak like hungry vultures picking over a carcass. I'd be damned if I was going to be someone's dinner.

I scanned the room, head high, as I neared the booth, of which I was starting to feel partial ownership. Even if she hadn't been sitting next to Butch and Leon, just as I had my first day, I would've known she was the new Shadow Walker.

She pushed the food around on her plate with her fork and spent more time peeking out from behind her dark bangs and watching everyone else than actually eating. Where I was a bit shorter and filled out, she appeared willowy and long. Her eyes, the same color as mine, froze on me as I stopped in front of the booth.

Butch looked over at Leon. "We've never had overlap before."

"I say we take it as a gift from the shadow gods and run." Leon grabbed his bagel, and they slid out of the booth like they'd been told that a genie granting their every wish was in the next room.

I ignored them. So did the newcomer.

"Hi," I said, sliding into the booth. I reached out my hand and tried to appear as friendly as I could. I knew how the people in this place could be to newcomers. "I'm Ollie."

She shook my hand and returned my smile, as she eyed up my entourage, which was growing by the day. "I'm Penelope. People call me Penny."

Her eyes shifted briefly to the crawlers and then back to me.

"Is this normal for you?" she asked, staring at me with more concentration than necessary, as if she were afraid if she relaxed even a hair, she might accidentally let her eyes wander toward them again.

"It wasn't, but it is now. Seems to be getting worse."

"He wants me to talk to them." She tilted her head toward Kane's office, as if she were afraid to say his name or look there.

"I know. It was the same with me."

She nodded, looking slightly better, but far from leaps and bounds of progress. It was understandable. It wasn't like I'd offered any great reassurance other than sitting next to her, alive and breathing. I hated to agree with Kane about anything, but maybe she needed this to be soft-pedaled a bit.

"The people here seem kind of scary," she whispered, so low that if I hadn't been watching her lips, I wouldn't have been able to decipher what she was saying.

"They're not as tough as they look," I offered, hoping she hadn't killed anything on her way here. "Most of them leave me alone, but…I wouldn't bother trying to reach out. They tend to keep to themselves." I'd spoon-feed her the rest of the reality as we went. If I told her any more now, I was afraid she'd bolt out of the place.

Was this really what most Shadow Walkers were like? Did most of us seem this fragile? They did call us paper dolls.

It didn't matter. I'd toughen her up. I'd get her through. I'd get us both through, and any other Shadow Walkers who showed up.

She took a bite the size of my pinky nail. "They say most of the Shadow Walkers don't make it. That you're the first who's made it past a couple of days in a long time. Is it that bad, what we have to do?"

I shouldn't criticize her lack of appetite, since I didn't have the urge to order anything. "It's scary, but it's not all that bad." I leaned back, thinking of the best way to describe it that was accurate but not terrifying. "I've never been to Antarctica, but it's what I'd imagine it to look like in its dark season. The crawlers can get a little friendly, but as long as you get in and out, you'll be fine."

The line of her shoulders softened as she tilted her head a little. "That doesn't sound so horrible."

"It's not. When you do it, Kane is going to hold your hand and keep you linked to him the whole time. Don't let go of Kane's hand and you'll be fine."

She leaned an elbow on the table and rested the side of her head on her hand as she turned toward me. "He said I didn't have to do it. But he offered me a lot of money and said he could get rid of *them* if I did."

"Yeah, I get it. Same here." Was it always the same? I knew what living with the crawlers had done to me, and there was no doubt I was holding up better than her.

"I want them gone." Her skin grew redder as she continued. "The money would be good, too. I've had problems holding down jobs."

I held back the sigh that wanted to drift out. "It's not just you. It's hard to maintain a normal life when you're running away from imaginary monsters all the time." I held back specific questions, afraid of how many similarities there might be. If I let loose the way I wanted, I'd be afraid we'd turn into a pity party for two, and I didn't want to put her in a worse mood before she went in for the first time. That would be a downer. We'd have time to share our scars after.

She toyed with her full plate of eggs.

"You'll be fine. Do you know when you start?"

She chewed on a cracked lip for a minute as her eyes kept flitting to Kane's office and back to me. "I think tonight." She dropped her fork loaded with eggs onto the booth, where it bounced down to the floor.

I handed her one left behind from Butch or Leon that looked unused as I tried to think of anything that might pep her up a little.

"Then you'll be free tomorrow afternoon and we can hang out. We'll have lunch and I'll show you around the area a bit. I know a great source to get some new clothes. It'll be a lot of fun." And it would be, for her, anyway. I might have to nail the dwarves down to a firm price, and figure out how many children I'd have to birth for them, but I'd get it worked out.

A crawler standing over her shoulder shifted, and I caught sight of the gargoyle that had been bringing me my food the last few days.

"Hey, I hate to leave you to fend for yourself, but I've got to run and handle something." I slid out of the booth, calling back to her, "Find me later."

She nodded, and I took off toward the gargoyle, who was walking into the back hall.

He looked over his shoulder as I approached, and picked up his pace. I broke into a run and grabbed his arm before he disappeared into thin air. "Hey, you served me breakfast yesterday and the day before."

"So?" he asked, shaking off my hand.

"You know who I am?"

"Another paper doll."

Wrong words. I'd already been ready to lay into him for his part in the witches' scheme. Now I wanted to rip him open, too. "Except this paper doll is going to live to a ripe old age, and if you do anyone else's dirty work and fuck with my food again, I'm going to make it my life's mission to find a spell in that dark place only Shadow Walkers go to make your existence a living hell."

If I got any closer, I was going to step on his toes. "Next time someone tells you to do something, remember my face and think about whether you want to be on my bad side. 'Cause this doll"—I hooked a thumb toward my chest—"is made of something a lot tougher than paper." I took my finger and jabbed it into his shoulder. Or tried. This sucker really was made of cement. How was that possible?

Stop. Don't get distracted. Finish your threat, because you're a big, bad Shadow Walker who messes with the darkest magic around. "Tell all your friends that they can be added to my shit list, too. This is the only warning you'll get." How was I going to find him if I had to follow through on my threats? "What the hell's your name?"

He rolled his eyes, which also appeared to be some sort of cement. "Zee. Name's Zee," he said with no hesitation.

He didn't seem convinced or even intimidated. Actually, he didn't look different at all, so maybe the scowl was permanent? Wait, was that a slight softening above one brow, or did he need some patchwork? Could've been a chip.

"Now you listen to me," he said. "I'll make you a deal. I'll keep the witches, vamps, and werewolves out of your stuff. I'll even do you one better: I'll let you know if I hear about someone screwing with you, but you're going to owe me."

My mouth dropped open. How had this gone wrong? I'd threatened him thoroughly. He was supposed to be scared of me. Was it possible to get up in the morning and make it to bed in this place without another debt being added to the pile?

Worst was, he had a better offer on the table. I took a step back as I debated the situation. The gargoyles did handle all the food, the clothing, my rooms—my entire domestic life was at their whim. Basically, they could totally screw with me in any way they saw fit, and there wasn't a damn thing I could do about it. "How much is this going to cost?"

He seemed to become more fluid suddenly, his hands moving about. "Moderate. I'm not trying to rip you off or anything. I'm an honest gargoyle just trying to eke out a living. You give a little"—his shoulders raised a hair— "I give a little, and we're all happy." A nod here and a wave of his hand there, and I was suddenly realizing this wasn't his first sales pitch. Wouldn't have been shocked if he tried to whip out an extended warranty on the tires or an underbelly rust coating.

"What do you think? We have a deal?"

I did a mental count: Kane, dwarves, vampires…couldn't forget Flip, and Casio would probably want his pound of flesh because he'd given me his jacket. "Why not. I owe everyone else. What's another debt?"

His held up a finger as he tucked his chin low. "Wait up a sec, how far down on the list am I? I don't want to be last."

"You haven't even told me what you want yet, and you're already complaining about where on the list you are?" Actually, it might've been a valid concern. How much of me could I spread around?

The gargoyle scowled deeper, proving again that his face wasn't frozen when he didn't want it to be. "I don't want to be last."

"You won't be last. Don't worry about it. You'll get your fair share of my blood."

When his lower lip jutted out, I knew I had to get out of there. "Not the last couple drops, though."

"There will be no whining over who gets the last piece of me. Are we good or not?"

He pouted slightly but then relented. "Fine."

Fine wasn't *good*, but I took it and headed back into the crowded main floor, hoping to find Penny still there.

The booth was empty.

"Olivia." I turned to see Kane at the top of the stairs, and I knew that look. Heaven forbid he actually said, *Come into my office*. No, he just looked at you and walked back in without saying anything, expecting whoever it was he'd summoned to do as commanded. And a please? That *really* wasn't happening.

As much as the unspoken order chafed me raw, I wasn't going to turn down a chance to get within the crawler-free buffer zone. I managed a calm pace up the stairs this time, strolled over to the couch, and collapsed.

He tracked me from where he sat behind the desk. "What's with the new clothes?"

It had been clear he'd noticed yesterday, but he sure took his time mentioning it. I ran a hand over the black jeggings, which felt almost like silk, and the softest sweater ever, which hung to perfection. All the dwarf clothes fit like that.

He was still waiting for an answer. I wasn't going to tell on the witches. Nope, not going to tattle. Rather, bide my time and hit them back myself.

Why was my wardrobe always Kane's business, anyway? It wasn't like I asked him where he got all his shirts and pants. He had enough fingers in my day-to-day.

"Did you call me up here to question me about my clothing choices?"

He leaned back and stared at me in that way I'd seen him do before. I wasn't sure if it was designed to make me squirm or if it was his relaxation pose and he'd been gifted with an innate ability to put someone on edge simply by being him. Either was possible.

"You're off tonight. That's all." He went back to whatever it was he did. I remained seated. *I* wasn't ready to be dismissed yet.

When I didn't move, he glanced at me with an *I'm too busy for you* look. Sometimes I swore he was insulting on purpose. You couldn't have that many looks without a little practice. No one was that good.

"Why am I off?"

"Because you're not on." He looked away again and cleared his throat.

I remained seated. I wasn't in any particular rush to leave the only buffer zone I'd known. "Are you teaching Penny to go in the shadows tonight?"

He kept his attention on the things on his desk as he asked in a flat tone, "Does it matter?"

"She'll be okay." I leaned my head back and wondered if that had come out like the question it was becoming in my mind. I'd told her it wasn't a big deal. It didn't seem like it was. But then, why would everyone call us paper dolls? Why did none of us last?

He didn't answer my non-question, and kept about his business.

"She will be okay, right?" Now it was definitely a question.

"I don't know."

He answered like I'd asked him if he'd be interested in having waffles for breakfast tomorrow, or some other equally mundane thing. That was not reassuring at all.

Forget him. I'd give myself my own pep talk, since he was so lousy at them. "Well, why wouldn't she be? It's not that big of a deal. It's like taking a walk in a sort of dim-looking park with an unfriendly pack of dogs that want to check you out."

I still had my head leaned back, looking at the ceiling just for the novelty of it, when Kane exhaled as if resigning himself to unwanted companionship.

If I liked him, I might've felt funny about imposing myself on him in this way. There was a certain freedom when you didn't give a shit what someone thought of you.

"That's how it is for you. Not how it is for everyone."

"How is that?"

"It means you seem to be less fazed than almost all of your predecessors."

No. She'd be okay, at least the first time.

I kicked my feet up on his couch and settled in. I desperately needed a nap, and hoped he didn't have any appointments coming up, and if he did, that they were quiet.

* * *

The door to Kane's apartment had shut twenty minutes ago. It wasn't that he was that loud that I could hear it from inside my suite so much as I'd been sitting beside my door, maybe with my ear against it, listening. Well, me and my ten closest crawler buddies, that was.

I leaned back, rubbing the feeling into the lobe as I gave it five minutes more, to make sure he didn't come back before me and my entourage walked next door and knocked, not expecting an answer. "Kane? You in there? I'm out of toothpaste."

Nothing. Of course there was no answer. He was out initiating Penny into the dark world of the Shadowlands.

I pulled down my sleeve and used that to test the doorknob. Then I used my bare hand. If Kane thought I'd checked his rooms, he probably wouldn't be concerned with proving it by dusting for prints.

It was open. Was that a good sign or bad sign? Either he didn't have anything to hide or didn't leave anything to find. Either way, I'd gone this far. Had to follow through.

His place wasn't what I'd expected. That was when I realized I'd assumed it would look like my suite. It wasn't anything like it. Where my rooms were generic, this place had serious personality. It was Kane's but not what I would've expected of the man I knew. Cold and sleek, contemporary or industrial? This place wasn't any of those things.

The place was huge compared to mine, with warm black maple floors throughout. The couch was a worn leather chesterfield, situated in front of a stone fireplace that had a mantel halfway up the two-story ceiling.

I moved into his bedroom, having no delusions about the morality of what I was doing. If I were going to survive this new world, I needed to know who I was dealing with. No more trusting the food or taking people at their word alone. It was time for something more tangible.

I paused by the bed and ran a hand over the navy-blue spread before walking over to his drawers, feeling innately wrong as I opened each one. This wasn't me, or it hadn't been in the world I'd thought I'd lived in. But that world didn't really exist, and I couldn't be that girl.

Other than noticing that gargoyles folded his things a little nicer, there was nothing out of the ordinary.

His closet was a walk-in affair, with no need to open drawers. Everything was shelved on perfect display.

I searched the kitchen, the living room, and every surface in the place, and yet there was nothing. It was his place, it had his smell and his energy, but that was it. Not a bill or an old ID. No pictures, even.

I left, more convinced than ever that he was hiding something big.

15

The second I hit the main floor of the Underground the next morning, my eyes went immediately to Butch and Leon's table. No dark head bent over food. I'd crashed after my first time, so it wasn't surprising that she was sleeping in.

I made my way across the floor, trying to focus my eye enough to see where I was going but still keep the crawlers sort of hazy. When I used this trick, I could pretend that they were only shadows.

I slid in next to Butch, calling for a gargoyle as I did, and placed an order for an omelet and coffee before turning to Butch and Leon.

"Where's Penelope? What time did her and Kane finish up? I can't believe I fell asleep so early last night." Actually, what I really couldn't believe was how strong that NyQuil I got from the gargoyles was.

Butch choked on the lox he was eating. Leon glanced over at him before answering, "Pretty late, I think."

I nodded, having figured as much, since we'd never finished before midnight.

I scanned the crowd, shifting in my seat. She'd held it together yesterday but had been nervous. "What room is she in? Maybe I should bring her some breakfast. She might be leery about coming down here on her own." I glanced at the clock. It was nine a.m., so I'd give her a couple of hours before I tried to find her.

Leon cleared his throat and then took another bite instead of answering while he stared at Butch. Butch stared back at Leon, as if there were some sort of silent debate going on. Butch finally said, "She's gone."

I leaned back. I'd known something was wrong. "Shit. She went back home?" It wasn't like I didn't understand it. I'd done it myself. This world was overwhelming, and signing up for what Kane wanted? Of course she'd get cold feet. Any sane person would.

Leon put his fork on his plate and then shoved it away before leaning back on his seat. "She died last night," he blurted.

My vision blurred and my fingers felt numb as the word "died" seemed to rob everything from me. The music perpetually playing became a buzz in the background. I didn't know if Butch and Leon were speaking or eating anymore. I vaguely noticed Zee, the gargoyle, clearing plates from the table.

It couldn't be. All she had to do was step into the Shadowlands and step out. How? Had he made her do more? It didn't make sense.

"Who says she's dead?"

Butch and Leon were looking at each other as if stumped.

"Who?" I asked, leaning toward them.

"Kane. Who else would tell us?" Butch asked, as if maybe I knew something he didn't.

"How did he say it happened?"

Leon had more pity in his eyes than impatience. "She went in and she couldn't handle it."

"Couldn't handle what?" There had to be more. He'd asked her to do more. It was the only thing that made sense.

Butch reached out like he was going to touch my arm, but stopped. "We don't know. Neither of us know what that place is like. It's just what we were told."

I'd told her it wasn't that bad. I'd told her it would be okay. I'd acted as if it weren't a big deal.

Paper dolls, that was what they called us— but the name hadn't hit home like it was now.

Or how often one of us was led to our death.

"How many times has this happened and you people keep doing it anyway?"

Leon looked up from where he'd been staring intently at his eggs. "We didn't know she was going to die."

Butch looked over at him. "But suspected it would, because they almost always do."

Leon shrugged, defenseless against his friend's admission. "We just follow orders."

"I hope those orders help you sleep at night."

Neither of them said anything, and our booth grew quiet. As far as I was concerned, every single one of us had blood on our hands.

It had to stop, and there was only one way. I looked up at the light coming from Kane's office.

"Ollie..." Leon started. He must've picked up on my target as I got out of the booth with single-minded determination.

"Let them work it out," Butch said.

He wouldn't have been able to stop me as I headed toward Kane's office.

I took the steps at a run and opened the door, without bothering to knock. Kane glanced up at where I stood right inside his door, ready to do battle.

He laid his pen down. "Isabella."

Isabella straightened and then left with a grace that wasn't natural. She must've practiced that for years. I practiced not ripping her hair from her head as she walked past me. How many Shadow Walkers had she seen come and go? Did she enjoy it?

I waited until the door shut behind her. I'd only known Penelope for a day, but she'd been the only person I'd ever known who'd walked in my path, as dark and scary as that was. Now Penelope was gone, and I didn't want someone like Isabella saying her name or pointing out she was a paper doll.

I focused all my attention on Kane, who was, for once, returning the favor.

"Does she know?"

He remained seated. "She knows Penelope is gone, but that's all."

It was a measly salve, but it was something.

"What happened to her?" The demand was clear in the firmness in my voice. If he wanted any peace, he was going to have to tell me. There had to be something else.

"I told her to hold on to me. She let go." His voice was soft, but I saw the tension in his neck.

"No," I said, shaking my head and taking a couple steps toward him. "Why didn't you hold on to her? What aren't you telling me?"

"She let go." He leaned back in his chair, but I wasn't lulled into believing the posture. He didn't care for this line of questioning. If I wasn't on the verge of trying to strangle him, I might've wondered why he answered at all.

"No, I don't believe you. I've felt your grip."

"It's different. I can keep a stronger grip on you. Every Shadow Walker is different." He stood, right as I was about to call him out again. "Would you like to sit down, or would you like to keep calling me a liar?"

"I've got a newsflash for you. If you keep recruiting Shadow Walkers and they keep dying? You're a murderer."

He was gone and then he was by the door, locking it, and I'd barely seen him move. He walked slowly back toward me. He closed the distance and didn't stop until I either had to step back or get stepped on. I stepped back and then held my position, refusing to relinquish any more space to him, whatever he was. He wasn't human, though. No way. Who had I gotten myself involved with?

He spoke softly, but he was close enough that he could've spoken in the softest whisper and I would've heard him. "If I wanted to kill her, or anyone else, I don't need to put in that much effort."

I didn't blink as I stared right back at him. Human, not human, I didn't care. "You should've known she couldn't make it, or pulled her back the second she walked in."

His eyes narrowed, and then he let loose words that felt like a gut punch. "You knew the pitfalls and you sat there with her yourself, telling her it was going to be okay. I know because she was clinging to that even as I was telling her it might not be. Don't lay your guilt at my doorstep."

We were like two fighters squaring off in the twelfth round, neither of us sure if we had any blows left. I wasn't sure who stepped away first, him or I, but I ended up on the couch as he settled behind his desk, our distance safely in place again.

"Would it have been better if I'd left you alone, never telling you what you were? You would've left destruction in your wake, over and over again. How many do you think would've died before you figured it out? I gave her a choice and gave her the truth, just as I gave you."

I ran both hands through my hair, leaving my head down as I asked, "Where's her body?"

"With her family. We faked an accident late last night to explain it."

I wanted to vomit. Probably would've if I'd eaten anything.

"If it doesn't work, and so many of us end up dying, why do you keep recruiting us?" I slumped back into the couch as I thought of the deaths before me. "Why have us go into that world over and over again? What's the point?"

He leaned back as we watched each other from a safe vantage point. "To find a Shadow Walker like you."

"Why? So you can obtain some obscure spell, for what? You want more money? More power?" I didn't know what this was for, and that might've been the worst.

"Don't presume to know my business. If you can't handle this world, you're free to leave. Nobody is keeping you here."

It was too late to leave now. I hadn't been willing to leave when there had been a fraction of the crawlers around me. Now it was getting to the point that I didn't want to open my eyes in the morning, and I was swigging NyQuil to get to sleep.

There was no leaving. I was in this for the long haul, or however long it took him to get what he needed. But I could limit the damage to anyone else. "Don't recruit another Shadow Walker. If you find one, you send them a frigging letter. That's it. No more."

He appeared calm, but I wasn't fooled by the act. "I don't take orders."

"And I won't take yours if you bring another one here. You lose one more Shadow Walker and I won't do it again. Damn everything. I might be new to this world, but that doesn't change who I am. I'm telling you, you recruit another one, and I will go down in flames before I help you again."

He rested an elbow on either chair arm and linked his fingers in front of him. "I'll make you a deal."

"Which is?"

"As long as you stay alive, I won't bring another one on." He'd already picked up his pen as if he were done with the conversation. "If you care that much, I suggest you stay alive as long as you can."

"And I want someone else to anchor me." It was a long shot, but I had to try. He couldn't be the only one capable of it.

He lifted his head up. "Well now, that's too bad for you."

"Why is that?"

"Because I'm the only one strong enough to do it. You want to keep the other Shadow Walkers alive? You're stuck with me, just as I'm stuck with you."

He thought he knew it all. "You think you're invincible. That you'd never be on the other side of this."

"Not invincible, Olivia, but very close."

I headed toward the door, choosing the crawlers over him today.

My hand was on the knob when he said, "By the way, did you find anything interesting last night?"

He knew. I'd half expected him to from the moment I'd decided to go in. Odds were he'd have that place secured somehow.

I turned and looked him square in the eye. "No, but I'm sure you already knew that, too."

He smiled.

I left.

One of these days, I was going to have the upper hand. It might be a long way off, but I would.

16

It was eight o'clock and we still hadn't left. Kane had sent me a message to be ready at seven, and yet I was still sitting here waiting. Not that I'd ever been described as super punctual, but come on already. An hour?

If I could chill out on the couch like a normal person, maybe it wouldn't be that bad. But I'd been avoiding Kane all day like a person dodging a pink slip in their locker after budget cuts.

After a day of monsters to the max, I'd had to rethink my position on Kane, or at least my proximity to him, if I wanted to keep all my marbles in my head.

I'd also had one, two—maybe twelve hours too many to dwell on what I'd said to Penelope and how it might add up to my culpability, if there were actually a court of law in this messed-up world.

If I hadn't told her it would be okay, would she have been more cautious? That question was the key to the manslaughter charge I was prosecuting myself for. When I couldn't stand being in my own head another second, I went in search of the other person who had blood on his hands and was also currently guilty of being late and leaving me to the hell of wall-to-wall crawlers.

I took the stairs down to the ground level only to have to climb another flight up to his office on the second floor. Who had been the architect of this place, and had he been running a budget special?

Happiness and good will was walking out as I approached. "Isabella."

"He's in a private meeting." She pulled the door shut as I stood there.

"Let her in," Kane said from inside, right before the door clicked into place.

I smiled, all friendly crocodile teeth, as I walked past her.

She sneered.

Kane, who was relaxing behind his desk, watched as I walked in. So did the man standing in the room with him.

He was large, in a thick-boned sort of way, with a hell of a brow ridge. There was a sharpness to his stare, even though he would've blended right in with the Neanderthal display at the Museum of Natural History.

"You need to share," Caveman said to Kane in a voice that matched the face, while he was still sizing me up.

"Come now, Collin, you know I'm not the sharing type," Kane said in his *I'm going to screw with you for a while because I can* voice. Boy, did I know that tone. Luckily, it wasn't directed at me this time, because I was too tired to be aggravated.

Collin turned his full attention back to Kane. Wasn't sure if I was digging the vibes I was getting off Collin. I gave him a wide berth as I made my way to my couch. Yes, that's right. I'd officially claimed it—secretly, that was.

"She's the first Shadow Walker to live more than a few days since I can remember. You can't keep her all to yourself." Collin's voice was a getting a little rumbly.

Kane kicked his feet up on his desk and crossed his ankles. "Who says I can't?"

I should take a nap, but this was becoming mildly amusing. I compromised and lay on my side, facing them and letting my eyes drift slightly closed.

"I know you worked a deal with that vampire bitch."

Hmmm, hated vampires, and I'd seen that brow ridge before, many times, actually, as I passed the werewolves in the Underground. Actually, before then, come to think of it. The first two men to show up and try and talk to me had been especially hairy, with a bit of a pronounced brow ridge. Now it was all clicking into place.

And where did that throw pillow go? Did someone steal my pillow? No reason I couldn't rest while watching the show.

"That has nothing to do with you." Kane stretched out his arms and yawned. Damn, that man deserved an Oscar.

"I want a piece."

"Come up with a better offer."

Right when I'd started to enjoy the show. Why? Why did he have to keep negotiating over my abilities as if I were an asset he owned?

I laid my head down on my arm. It didn't matter what they decided, anyway. I'd do what I wanted, for who I wanted. Kane could play pretend all *he* wanted. Meant nothing if I didn't go along with the program.

That was the thing about Shadow Walking. I was, for all intents and purposes, alone. That meant I could do whatever I wanted in there and he wouldn't know a thing about it. I needed to keep that in mind next time I went in.

"She's not yours," Collin nearly growled. Did I have the pleasure of napping in front of *the* head werewolf, or at least one higher up in the pack? Had to be, because you needed to be a decent chunk of alpha if you were going to growl at Kane.

"I've got a contract." Kane's voice was even.

I'd signed a nondisclosure, not a contract, but I wasn't getting in the middle of this conversation to correct Kane.

More importantly, had Kane missed the growl? See, if we were friends, or even friendly, I'd be giving Kane a nudge right now instead of plodding forth on my nap efforts. Collin was a little too close to the line of unacceptable behavior in civilized company—or even Kane's company.

"There's a way to void that contract." The growl was still underlying the voice.

There was no contract. Unless Kane had scammed me? Definitely possible. This magic stuff was tricky. In the human world, they had to tell you the bad stuff, maybe in really tiny print, but it was there if you were the one in a thousand who read it. This place? Good luck getting anything in writing.

If there were a contract, how did that get voided? Bye-bye, nap. Now I had to pay attention. Why weren't they speaking, anyway? I pushed back up and caught the look on Collin's face as he stared at me, and was glad I was on the far side of the room.

I was young, no debate there, but I'd seen that stare enough times to know exactly what type of man I was dealing with, and exactly what he was saying he wanted from me. It made me want to cross my arms in front of my chest and pull a big blanket over myself.

I met his stare and gave him a silent *fuck you*.

"Never going to happen," I said.

"I wouldn't be so sure about that."

Before I could react, Kane spoke from where he sat behind the desk. "Yes, she can be, and so can you." Kane didn't scream, but his tone alone sent warning flares across my skin.

Collin might put on a good show, but I caught the dry swallow before he puffed up his chest.

As much as I appreciated the backup from Kane, I wasn't delusional enough to think it came from someplace noble. Kane didn't want competition for my resources. I'd live with the motivations, since they were currently benefiting me.

"You can't keep the only Shadow Walker who's made it this long to yourself." It was a halfhearted argument with no heat in it, and everyone in the room knew it.

"Can't I?" Kane asked, taunting the man.

"They'll all turn on you if you do this."

I was new to the politics of this place, but I'd thought he'd come up with something better than *no one else is going to like you.* I wanted to hang my head and sigh in embarrassment for him. How long had he known Kane? Did he know him so little that he thought that was going to work?

"Let them." And there it was, right on time. This poor slob needed to go back to the werewolves, where he could get away with only growling. Kane was medaling in the breaststroke while Collin was still doggy paddling in the baby pool.

Kane put his feet on the ground and stood, sucking all the air out of the room with that one move. "We're done here." Or, as I'd translate it, *Get the hell out before you can't.*

Collin didn't look done, but when everyone knows you don't have any bullets, it's sort of pointless to wave the gun around. He turned, and I watched him leave, wondering if when he reloaded, which I thought he might go do, the next bullet might be aimed at someone's back.

I waited a few minutes before I spoke, not knowing what kind of hearing the guy might have, and if he'd linger around just for that purpose.

I propped one knee up, for the sole purpose of an armrest. "I owe everyone else. Maybe we should've played nice with him?"

"Can't. Not with him."

"He's going to be a problem," I said.

Kane was staring at me in a way I didn't particularly like.

"Do you have anything…" He waved his hand toward my clothing.

I looked down at my dwarf sweats and t-shirt and back to him. I had a feeling they'd been meant to sleep in, but I'd had a rough night and wanted to be ready for any napping opportunities provided. "Anything what?"

"The opposite of that?"

I thought about what was in my closet. Almost all my clothes were the opposite of what I was wearing, but just to spite him, I said, "No. I'm a big fan of comfort."

"I'll have Isabella send something up."

Did he truly have no clue about that woman? "I'm sure that's not necessary. I'll find something."

"I think it's better if she does it."

"Tell me where we're going and I'll go pick something up." This was where if we were in a movie, I would've inserted a long, awkward pause as I waited. "You think I can't dress myself?"

"Do you even own a cocktail dress?"

I thought back to the clothes the dwarves had given me, and remembered the little black number Flip had held up. "I have a dress. Why?"

"We've got to stop by a party tonight."

"A party?"

"It's business."

17

Five minutes after I got back to my rooms, there was a knock at the door. A single knock before it opened. I knew it wasn't Kane, because he wouldn't have knocked at all.

Flip strolled in and flopped onto the couch. "What's going on?" I asked.

"Kane." She smiled all big and fake.

I put a hand to my hip. "And why would that be?"

She lay there, leg over the couch arm, obviously thinking this over. "You figured out I'm not tactful, right?"

I nodded.

"Then maybe you shouldn't ask me that. I've got a hard enough time keeping friends."

"You're probably right." I already knew what Kane thought, and Flip wasn't capable of softening what he'd said to her. "I'll be right back. Going to change."

It took her a total of two minutes to call out, "What's taking you so long?" She didn't wait for a reply, as the door was yanked open. "I *knew* that was going to look good."

"I don't know. It's not really me," I said, pulling the hem down and then realizing all I was doing was lowering the bodice.

"*Much* better." She dumped the contents of the small bag she had in her hand onto the dresser and started poking at my face with her makeup.

After a few minutes of brushing and drawing, she stepped back. She came close again and started messing with my hair, fluffing it with her fingers before stepping back and admiring her work.

She dug out a pair of spiky black heels the dwarves had supplied.

I slipped them on as she nodded approvingly.

"Now you look like someone Kane would date when you go to this party. Gotta make it believable, because most people know he won't mess around with Shadow Walkers."

"Why? What's wrong with Shadow Walkers?"

Her mouth dropped open a minute before she remembered to close it. "I don't know. Just something I thought I'd heard so long ago I don't even remember if I did hear it."

Flip lied as well as she kept her temper in check.

Before I could interrogate her, the crawlers scattered and Kane stepped into the doorway, phone still to his ear. His eyes met mine; they didn't stay there long, but ran the length of me.

He held the phone to his chest and said, "Let's go," before he turned and left.

I wasn't sure where we were going, but I was positive that this was *not* a date.

* * *

I followed him out to the car, waiting the whole time for him to remark on how I looked. Even Butch, Leon and Jerry, who we'd seen on our way out, had all made appreciative comments on how nice I looked.

Not Kane. He didn't talk until we were about to pull up to a valet.

"Act like you're with me," he said right before my door was opened.

Kane walked around the car and wrapped an arm around my waist as we walked inside what looked like an upscale restaurant that didn't have a name. I couldn't help the little shiver it set off, or how I couldn't seem to think of anything other than the heat of his hand as it touched the bare skin of my back.

"Why?" Okay, that might've been a little snappish, but he couldn't say, *Hey, you look nice*? Would it kill him to pay me a compliment?

"Later," he said as he ushered me inside, and now I knew why he hadn't spoken on the way over. It was easier than answering questions.

The more I Shadow Walked, the more I seemed to sense magic around, and this place was jam-packed with the stuff. It was darkly lit, and the décor was mostly in dark reds.

Kane took two glasses of champagne off a passing waitress and handed me one before putting a hand at the small of my back.

An elegant woman in her forties walked over with a nod to Kane, and smiled at me. I tried to not stare at her ears, but it was difficult. I'd never seen pointy ones.

"Marissa, nice to see you." Kane tilted his head toward me. "This is Olivia."

She nodded as she stared at me curiously. After another ten introductions, I leaned closer to Kane. "Why are they all staring at me like that?"

"They're trying to figure out why you're still alive."

I smiled widely. "Nice."

I vaguely remembered being introduced to some more people, but it became a blur, as there were more drive-bys.

I felt an older gentleman's eyes on us.

"Who is that staring?"

The arm that was wrapped around my back, the one I was so conscious of, was pulling me closer and upward. His cheek grazed mine as he whispered in my ear, "That's the head of the vampires in the area."

"What about Alexandria?"

"She's his enforcer. He doesn't like to be bothered with minor squabbles at this point." His lips grazed my ear, and I knew he felt the shiver it caused. "If she had caused us an issue, we would've gone to him next."

He was simply whispering into my ear, his hand cupping my head as if it should be there, and yet my breathing was shallow and my nipples had hardened.

When his lips shifted to mine, I didn't think of moving. I met them.

I wasn't a virgin. I'd gone through one phase where I thought having a man in my bed would save me from the monsters. I'd tried it a few different times with a few different men, and it hadn't worked.

Maybe I would've kept "dating" if I'd known it could feel like this.

But I'd never melted. Ever. I'd expected to, but it hadn't happened, until now. The room and the people in it ceased to exist as his hand curled back around my waist, pulling me snug to him as his tongue delved into my mouth and tangled with mine. Then I was exploring his, my free hand curling into his hair. I couldn't even feel my feet touch the ground.

Until a man called Kane's name and he pulled back from me.

Kane turned fluidly to greet the vampire who'd approached us.

"Forgive the intrusion, but I wanted to say my hellos before I left." He smiled, and I didn't believe for a second that he felt bad over intruding.

"So this is the promising new Shadow Walker?"

"Ollie, meet Fredrickson."

I smiled, still a bit flustered from the kiss.

"Well played," he said, his eyes going to Kane's hand sitting at my waist. My feet hit the ground—hard.

Kane and Fredrickson were still talking, and my participation didn't seem to be required, luckily, as the truth hit me. *Act like you're with me.* That was what Kane had said. He'd been putting on a show while I'd been ready to jump into bed with him behind closed doors. What was wrong with me? I didn't even like him.

I made it through another twenty minutes of mindless hellos and a room tour while I tried to decide how I was going to spin this so I didn't look like a fool.

We were in the car for ten minutes before I asked, "Why did you do that?" I'd kept my voice calm, but my insides were churning like the Atlantic before a hurricane.

He glanced over at me, and in that second, I knew whatever he said was surely going to make it worse. "There's only one way for them to try and pursue you at this point, and that's if you become *involved* with one of them. I shut the door on that possibility tonight. I didn't tell you because I was concerned you'd overreact."

I loved how he explained it, so businesslike and matter-of-fact, even handling my emotional instabilities for me. It was as if he knew I was mad, and that was making him mad. As if he had a right?

We didn't talk for the rest of the drive. I had no idea where we were going, but I wasn't breaking the silence. Nope. I'd rather be surprised than talk to him right now. If I did talk, he'd really see some overreaction. The fact that I'd nearly melted in the arms of this arrogant…

Wasn't going to think about that now—or later, hopefully.

About five minutes later, he pulled the car around a large, new building and into its back parking lot and cut the engine.

He got out.

I didn't.

I was still trying to calm down my inner hurricane. This was business, and I needed to be as cold and calculating as he was. That was the way through this mess. Maybe the only way.

He came around, opened my door, and stood there, waiting.

I let out a long breath. As much as I was trying to calm the waters, I had a feeling he was going to churn them back up.

"You planning on getting out of the car, or are you too upset about a simple kiss to work? It was good business, and you didn't seem to mind at the time." He left me sitting there, door open, and walked toward the building.

Count backward. One hundred, ninety-nine, ninety— Fuck this.

I got out and caught up to him in under a second. He turned, clearly expecting something, and I was going to give it to him.

"You should've told me what you were going to do. I'm sick of you and your high-handed ways."

"So you *are* too emotional to work?"

His body was relaxed but his jaw tensed.

"I'm angry, not emotional. You shouldn't have done that." My voice echoed off the large building as we stood in the empty parking lot.

"Stop acting like an injured foal. It benefited you as well as me. You were leery of Collin the second you met him—which actually showed some sound judgment on your part. I made both of our lives easier, and you know it."

That was all the kiss had been. Simplify his life. Make it easier on him so he didn't have to be bothered all the time. I'd just gone from a category three to a five. "I don't want to work with you anymore. I want someone else."

"You can't get another anchor. I'm your best shot. Your people die off like—"

I crossed my arms. "Paper dolls. I'm aware. I want a new one anyway. If Collin thought he could work with me, there must be other people out there that can anchor me."

"Really? You think you'd fare better with Collin?" He crossed his arms as well, and we faced off two feet away from each other.

"Maybe." I watched his whole body tense now. No hiding it. He *really* didn't like this Collin guy. I'd have to remember that.

"We're not working tonight. Get back in the car." He walked back to where he'd parked, fifteen feet away, without waiting to see if I'd follow or not.

I stood rooted to my spot. "No. I think I'll go find Collin tonight." Where had that come from? Shit. What if he took me up on it and I got left here? Then I remembered how mad I was again, and decided I'd walk back if I had to.

He didn't bother turning back as he said, "Even if he were delusional enough to try and anchor you, he won't do it after tonight. He's surely heard already." He stopped by the passenger side of the car and opened the door.

I took a few steps toward him to make sure he could hear me. "When I tell him it was a lie?"

"Too many people saw the way you kissed me. Everyone will know by now, and Collin doesn't have the balls to tread on what's mine. You were pretty convincing back there, no matter how put out you might be at the moment."

My skin burned like I had a hot poker to it.

He walked around to the driver's side. "Unless you plan on sleeping out here, I'd get in."

I might be angry, but I wasn't stupid. Walking back with nothing but crawlers beside me was not how I wanted the already bad night to end.

Not that I was so sure he'd leave. He was still resting his arms on the car as he waited.

But I was making one thing very clear before I went. "I would've acted like that with any man who was halfway decent and a passable kisser. It wasn't you."

He raised his eyebrows. "So you do that a lot, then?"

"No. I'm not saying that. I'm saying I would've."

He nodded as if he were thinking over something way more complicated than the facts I'd just laid out. "Okay."

"And another thing. One day, I'm going to be so powerful you won't be able to boss me around anymore." I ducked to get in the car and then popped back up. "Not that I'm going to be here that long. But if I was, I would be and you couldn't."

I went to get in the car.

"Ollie."

I straightened again. "What?" I asked, but it was more of a bark.

"One day, you might become powerful, but I'm still going to boss you around until you can figure out how to stop me."

I ignored him and got in the car. He was laughing as he got behind the steering wheel.

"Anyone ever tell you what a jerk you are?"

"Not normally to my face," he said, and laughed harder.

Didn't know what he was in such a good humor over, but it made me even angrier.

18

I walked into Kane's office and saw Butch and Leon making coffee, and Kane sitting behind his desk. Kane glanced at me briefly and down at his desk again. It was hard to tell what he was thinking, but I was definitely feeling some miscellaneous weirdness after last night.

I threw my hands up to the heavens. "Still alive!" I proclaimed, as if I were doing a wave at a football game.

"Still alive," Butch and Leon mimicked, and I laughed. Being alive shouldn't have been as funny as it was. Maybe it wouldn't have been if I wasn't so uncomfortable over the fact I'd yet again been forced by the crawlers to seek out Kane's company.

Still, Butch and Leon both laughed. The only person who seemed to not have a smile was Kane.

"That's supposed to be a joke?" Kane asked, and I could tell he wasn't in the best of moods. Still, a bad-mood Kane was better than a horde of crawlers.

Fighting with Kane I could handle. It was the other weird feelings I didn't know what to do with. When Butch and Leon didn't say anything, I spoke up. "We think it's funny. You know, for a paper doll, I've lived a long time."

"It's not funny," Kane stated as fact.

"I swear, you can't manage to be likable for more than two minutes."

"Then why are you constantly around?" he asked.

Well, I'd walked right into that one, and there was no way I was telling him the truth. And damn it all, now I was going to have to storm out or look like I wanted to be around him. Shit and double shit.

"I don't know what you're talking about. I was looking for Butch and Leon. I told them I would help them today."

There was a choking noise, but I wasn't sure if it came from Butch or Leon. I wasn't going to know either, as all I saw were their backs as they hightailed it out there.

"The two that ran out the door? Those two?" Kane leaned back, kicked his feet up on his desk, and waited. Times like this, I would've sworn he knew I was using him.

I lifted my head and walked toward the door. So much for a morning respite. Now I was going to have to eat my eggs while staring at monsters.

"Where are you going?" Kane asked as I was about to open the door.

"Going to eat my breakfast."

"We might start early today, so you might as well stay here so I don't have to go track you down."

I dropped my shoulders and groaned as I turned. "You always make me wait around."

"What do you want for breakfast? This might take a while. I've got to make a couple of calls before we go." He waved his hand toward my couch as if he wanted me out of the way.

I stopped halfway across the room as I thought about it. I didn't feel like eggs today. "Order me a grilled chicken over romaine, some roasted peppers—"

"You want your lunch order?" he asked.

I shook my head. "I don't always get that for lunch."

He dropped his chin and raised a brow. "You've gotten it every day this week."

I thought back for a second. "Fine. I want my lunch order."

"Some of those magazines you like just came in too," he said, right before he called a gargoyle.

I sat down on the couch and settled in beside the stack. "Nice."

* * *

"What was that?" Kane asked, looking at me where I sat on his couch.

It was the first time he'd spoken to me in hours, besides asking me what I wanted for lunch.

"Nothing." Oh shit. I must've groaned out loud or something. Damn him. Ever since last night I hadn't been able to stop thinking about sex. And him. Together. Then, on top of it all, I'd dreamed about it. Now I was thinking about that dream.

It was ridiculous, since I was still angry with him. I wouldn't have been sitting in his office at all if the crawlers weren't making me crazier than he did.

It wasn't like I wanted to talk to him. He didn't seem to want to talk to me, either, was content ignoring me as I sat on my couch and flipped through the batch of new magazines.

"Come on. Let's go." He tossed some papers down onto a pile and stood.

"We actually going to do something this time?" Whether he admitted it or not, yesterday had been all his fault.

"As long as you don't get your feathers in a bunch."

Was he teasing me? I could feel my feathers bunching even as he spoke, but I shrugged. I needed to get this spell stuff working before I killed him. This place was getting way too complicated for me.

By the time we left and got to the field, I was ready for work.

"Why don't we go to the same place more than once? Why is it always new places?"

"Two reasons," he said as he stopped beside me. "We don't want to create a hot spot where the crawlers might be able to come through on their own. Second, different places here correspond to different crawlers there."

Hmmm. That seemed reasonable enough.

"We're going to up the game. Do you think you're ready?" he asked.

He was acting nonchalant, but for the first time, I felt like I was hearing some nerves on his part. Which was strange, since I was the one going in.

"I'm ready." There was only one way to finish, and if this was what it took, I'd get through it.

"Ask for a reversal spell."

"For what?" Was this it? The spell he needed?

"It can be used to undo magical incidents."

That was the spell he needed? It didn't seem like it should be that big of a deal. Kind of useful, though, considering what the witches did to me. Did he know about that? Was this for him or me? "Who needs it?"

"Alexandria, the vampire you met. Her longtime lover was turned into a werewolf."

"That sucks. Can't she find a new boyfriend?" I asked, right before Kane said something that blew my mind.

"Said like someone who's never loved."

"I've loved." Maybe not a man, but plenty of people.

"You wouldn't have said that if you had."

"And you have?"

"Yes."

"Okay, Mr. Love, let's get this show on the road."

I grabbed his hand before I got any more details. All this did was make me think of last night, and the combined feelings had me close to strangling him again. If he was so serious about love, he shouldn't be so loose with his kisses.

I felt like an old hand at luring a large crawler over, and then I froze.

Every time I Shadow Walked, I might end up like Penny. Or all the other ones who'd died before me. Now that it wasn't an abstract idea, it seemed a lot scarier.

I felt the heat of Kane's presence as he stepped slightly closer to me. "You're tougher than they were."

It was easy for him to say that when he wasn't the one who had to go in there.

"What happened with Penny?" I'd already asked, but I still didn't understand.

"I told you. She let go."

"It doesn't make sense."

"I don't see what happens once you go in." His hand tightened around mine. "But I know that as soon as she went in, my grip on her felt weak, nothing like when I'm anchoring you."

This could all be bullshit. He needed me to go in. Still, I felt compelled to thank him, and I did.

"Don't. I'm merely helping you accomplish our mutual goals."

I'd never realized how rejected you could feel from someone declining a thank-you. Or why would someone bother? It was such a simple gesture. It was as if he needed to maintain a distance between us or the world would cease to exist.

"Are you ready?"

I nodded. I might still be next to him in some manner in the Shadowland, but at least I wouldn't be able to see him.

I asked for entrance and was in the Shadowlands.

I didn't waste any time, feeling my impending death like never before. I found the biggest crawler in the place and called it over as quickly as possible.

"I want the spell of reversal."

He growled, and I got the feeling it meant no.

"What do you have? Give me something that'll do the same thing."

He started chanting the words, and I locked them away in my brain. I was realizing it didn't matter how complex the words were or that I couldn't understand any of them. There was this place in my brain that opened, as if it were made solely for this purpose, and it stored every nuance.

It was a good thing, too, because this one wasn't ending. It went on and on. By the time it was done, my brain was near buzzing with what it had accepted.

I squeezed Kane's hand. He squeezed back. Somehow that had become our signal I was coming back through. I might've squeezed a little harder than normal. Kane had said the stronger the spell, the more difficult the exit. The way this one was buzzing around, I was downright scared.

I took a couple of rapid breaths, not knowing what I was getting myself into, and I turned around.

There was the exit; there was the horde. They were waiting for me to make the first move. Could I make it past them, or was I going to die?

I stepped a couple of feet back to get a better running start, hunching over into what I was coming to think of as my linebacker position.

Claws scraped me as I pushed through the group of them, but I still managed. Feeling their bodies against me was worse.

As I stepped out of the Shadowlands, I realized I'd lost one of my shoes, but I wasn't in the worst of shape. This time. How many more could I handle before I wouldn't be able to make it back?

"That was fast," Kane said, looking me over.

"Thanks." I wasn't sure if that had been a compliment, but I felt like my efficiency was definitely a plus. I needed to keep that in mind.

Less time for them to gather to try and stop me.

He looked me over and then ran his thumb over a tender spot on my cheek, where one of them must've caught me with a claw. His hand dropped quickly as if he suddenly realized what he was doing.

"You got the spell of reversal?" he asked, all business now.

"Something like that."

"What do you mean, something like that? What did you get?"

"*Something* like that."

He went to the car and pulled out the pad. "Write it down."

He held out the pen to me, but the words were gone.

"Why aren't you taking the pen?" he asked.

"It's not in my head anymore."

He was staring at me as if he were trying to assess the problem but couldn't believe it. "You forgot it already?"

"Uh, no. Something different."

"Ollie, what did you do?"

I thought back over it, confused as to what had happened. I'd had it in my head, and then...

I held out my hand and opened it, afraid of what I'd find myself. Now that I did look, it wasn't so scary. It looked like a perfectly formed Tahitian pearl, like the ones I'd admired in the jeweler's window down the street from my old apartment.

Kane seemed more distant, colder, than normal. "Tell me exactly what happened."

I recited the events as I recalled them.

"You had the spell in your head, and when you passed through, it became this?"

"Yes. Why are you acting so weird about this?" He was staring at me again as if we'd only met for the first time. "And why are you looking at me like that?"

"Because if you can do this, you're almost ready."

"Ready?"

"For my spell."

For some reason, I thought that would make him happier than he seemed.

As I stood there, I closed my hand over the pearl.

"What are you doing? Give it to me?"

"It's not in my head anymore. What if I need it?"

"But you don't need it."

I didn't tattle on the damn witches, and now I was screwed, with no reason to need the thing. I handed it over...slowly.

19

Every room, every corner—there was no escaping them today. I took another bite of my bagel as I eyed Kane's closed office door. He was in there. I'd seen him go in not even an hour ago.

What a joke of fate. The man that got my ire up quicker than anyone I'd ever met also happened to be my only sanctuary.

I wasn't going to run to him, not again. I could do this.

Forcing myself to look somewhere else, I turned toward Butch just as a crawler climbed behind the booth and loomed. I jerked back.

Butch's eyes narrowed, and he looked over his shoulder before turning back to me. "What? Is one of those things sitting on my shoulder or something? Knew I felt a draft. It's getting to be that I need a sweater when I get around you."

"It's not on your shoulder. It's hovering behind you. How'd you know about the draft?"

"Remember, this place has been a revolving door of Shadow Walkers," he said, scooting closer. "This is creepy."

"Tell me about it. At least you can pretend they aren't there." I took another bite as I watched the door, praying Kane would call me for something so I wouldn't have to make up a lame excuse to go up there. It was starting to appear like I was stalking him.

"Sorry I freaked on you guys the other day."

Leon shrugged, and Butch waved his hand. "Not a big deal."

They blew it off in a way that made me think it bothered them more than they wanted to let on.

"Hey, at least you're still alive," Butch said.

"Still alive," I repeated. It was my anthem now, and I knew how they meant it as well. If I was still alive, all could be fixed. Death couldn't.

I'd just begun to warm slightly, a smile emerging, when I heard it.

"He wants to use you," the crawler whispered.

I jumped up, banging my legs on the table. Leon and Butch both looked underneath the table, as if trying to figure out what had happened.

"Leg spasm," I told them, and they went back to eating.

"He wants to use you. He's going to take all your powers and spells for himself."

I put the bagel down, losing my appetite and afraid I'd drop it from a trembling hand. They never spoke to me unless I spoke to them, and I hadn't since the last explosion. Something was changing, and not in a good way.

"Shadow Walker, I can help you do things you never imagined. I can get rid of all your problems."

My eyes shifted toward the witches, and then I pulled them away quickly.

"I can make it so they'll never bother you again."

I kept my eyes forward, afraid to even glance at the crawler talking to me.

"You okay?" Butch asked.

I nodded, afraid to answer because I'd be talking in its direction. What if it thought I was talking to it instead of Butch?

It wouldn't stop, though. *"I can help you. You'll never get sick or old; you could live forever, have everything you ever wanted."*

Now I knew it was lying. I'd never have everything I'd ever want, not since they'd robbed me of that with the explosion.

"I can help you find the one who did this to you," it whispered, and it felt like I could feel its words graze my skin, but I held my tongue.

My crawler problem kept getting worse, and there was only one thing that had changed in my life that could possibly have caused this. The more I went into that place, the more they haunted me in this world.

I had to get away from them. I had to, and there was only one place.

"Where you going?"

"I forgot I had something I wanted to talk to Kane about." I'd exited the booth, and didn't turn to look at Butch as I gave him my explanation.

I took the stairs two at a time until I got to Kane's office and opened the door without a knock.

Kane sat behind his desk, Isabella up close and personal, as always.

"Come in." I didn't miss the sarcasm dripping from his tongue, but I didn't care. No crawlers, and I took the first easy breath since I'd awoken.

Kane stared at me in that way he had, like he knew something about me even I hadn't figured out yet. I wanted to tell him to stop, but that wouldn't keep me in his office.

Now what? I looked back over my shoulder at the door, knowing they were waiting out there for me.

"I had a couple of ideas I wanted to run by you." Ideas? Great, now I had to come up with even more bull. Good work. I should've picked a fight with him. That would've been way easier. "I'm afraid I'll forget if we wait, and I think they're *really good* theories." I nodded as I said it, and raised my eyebrows like the worst salesperson ever.

He was staring at me, and I knew he wasn't buying my sales pitch. What was I going to do next? Try and tell him I was really good at paperwork? Yeah, that might have to be my next pitch, because I wasn't leaving this room. I needed a break, even if it was just for fifteen minutes.

"Let me finish up here and I'll find you when I'm ready." He looked back down at the papers he was going over. Isabella looked like the kid who got the biggest piece of cake.

I didn't move right away, and tried to think of some fighting words. I should've opted for the fight right out of the gate. Bad move on my part.

And then I got a miracle. He turned to Isabella and lifted the files. "Take these with you, too."

He'd been talking to her, not me.

She nodded, forcing a smile because she'd thought the same thing I had, that he'd been kicking me out.

"Sure." She took the files, and as she walked past me toward the door, I couldn't resist the urge to say, "Now who's got the bigger piece?"

She might not have known what I was talking about, but she knew it was a poke in the eye.

Kane's eyes shifted to the seat in front of the desk and then back to me.

I took the invite, happy to be anywhere near him. That was something I hadn't imagined happening when I'd first met him, like, ever.

He leaned forward. "I'm all yours. What are these theories that are so fantastic that you don't think you'll remember?"

Had he let me stay to mock me? Now I really had to come up with something good.

I glanced over at the couch. Damn, it looked good. I crossed the room.

He cleared his throat. "I thought you had ideas you wanted to talk about?"

"I do. It might take a minute for them all to come back. I think best when I'm lying down with my eyes closed."

The fact that I didn't have to close my eyes to not see the crawlers made it hard to keep them open. Now, if I could just get Kane to give me some peace, I'd be in heaven.

I waited for him to start talking, and he didn't. If he wasn't talking, I wasn't going to either.

* * *

I woke to the door opening, but didn't budge. "Be quiet. She's sleeping," Kane said.

"You want me to move her up to her rooms?" Butch asked.

There was a pause, and I waited to see how many minutes of peace I had left. Then Kane said, "No. Let her be. She's fine."

"What about that thing?"

"You can handle it. Bring Leon. Don't slam the door on your way out."

* * *

The witches laughed and looked over at me again. It was the third time since I'd sat down in the booth with no one but the crawlers on either side. This wasn't me being paranoid. I did another clothing check, but nothing was falling apart, as promised by the dwarves, but the witches kept laughing.

I turned my head, trying to ignore the sound, and saw Flip walking into the Underground and heading toward me. She slowed beside the witches' table, as they were in the throes of laughing yet again, long enough to throw them a nasty stare. They barely paused before starting up again.

Flip slid into the booth beside me, only pausing when her shiny green vinyl skirt wouldn't glide over the leather seat.

"Do you know why they're laughing?"

"Huh? What are you talking about?" She looked about the place, everywhere but the witches.

Flip lied like a cat swam.

"I saw the look you gave them. They keep looking my way. I don't want you to get involved, but I deserve to know why."

"Not sure what you mean." She suddenly was fixated on the hem of her skirt, then a chip in her lavender nail polish, as I watched her.

"Flip, tell me what you know."

She bit her lip. "I'm not sure if this is something that you *should* know."

"Tell me."

She bounced around in her seat, and then the witches broke into a new round of laughter. She glanced over at them like someone would look down at their shoe after they stepped in a pile of poo. "Okay. I heard the witches had a showing last night."

"A showing?" I put my fork down, having lost my appetite already. "What's that?"

The witches kept laughing, and I knew it was turning up Flip's temper to full blast. "They've got a place a couple of blocks away. It's one of their hangouts when they want to do stuff that they can't get away with here. They have their 'showings' there. One of them must've lifted a couple of hairs from you, because from what I'm hearing, you were the feature last night."

"Flip, I'm new to this world. You've got to break it down a little better for me." Because if it was what I thought…

I pushed my plate away.

"It's like a highlight reel of someone's worst moments. They played yours last night for anyone who wanted to see."

The Underground had been slow last night. I'd noticed but hadn't thought much of it…until now. I scanned the room, really paying attention to the people there for the first time today. Some weren't looking at me. Some *kept* looking at me.

A cold sweat broke out on my skin, like an ice cube abandoned in the sun. A wave of nausea swept through right behind it.

Maybe it wasn't that? They might've only seen goofy scenes of me running from my third-grade class or something. "Do you know which ones?"

"From what I heard, there were quite a few—"

I leaned forward. "Did you hear which ones specifically?"

She was back to biting her lip. "Might've included some scenes when you were a kid, screaming about monsters."

Compared to other times, that was nothing. I could get past that. I waved my hand, hurrying her along. "What else?" I swung my leg under the table. Maybe it wasn't as bad as I'd feared.

Her voice got softer as she said, "They showed you and your family at the gallery, and, you know, the explosion and you kind of falling apart..."

There are bumps and scrapes you get along the way as you live life. Then there's the gaping wounds that hurt so badly you aren't sure you'll make it through. You don't know if you want to, because it means living with a pain that brings you to your knees and doesn't seem to end. You begin to wonder if you'll ever get on your feet again. That's what that night was to me.

Flip leaned in closer, her hand out, as if she didn't know if she were supposed to pat me or hug me.

"I'm fine," I told her before she asked.

"You sure? You don't look it. You don't want to, like, talk or anything, right? I mean, you can if you need to, but I'm not the best at heart-to-hearts. I'm better at screaming. Do you want me to go scream at them?" She glanced back over at the witches. "I'm really good at that."

"No. I don't want you to get banned from here, even for a few days."

She nodded, but I had a feeling it wasn't the end of it. "What about hugging? You humans do that a lot. It's been centuries for me. Even then, not something I was really fond of. I mean, if you need to hug it out, I will."

"Don't worry. Not a hugger."

A couple of the witches looked over and started laughing, the rest of the table quickly following suit. They knew Flip had told me, and it seemed to increase their amusement.

"Do you know why they hate you?" Flip asked.

"Not a clue," I said softly. If the way she was staring at them was any indicator, she was gearing up to spill some secrets.

"I'm not supposed to talk about it because fairies frown on getting mixed up in the squabbles of others, but I'll tell you anyway." She edged closer. "They're jealous. Witches can work magic fine, but most of the time they

stumble onto new spells out of luck. They don't
create them. The majority of the spells they do
have were handed down over the years from
ones they got from Shadow Walkers. They can
say that your magic is 'dark,' but so is theirs.
The stuff they have that's left. The simple tricks
tend to last the longest, which is why they've
got plenty of the paltry stuff. Even though
Shadow Walkers don't come to magic as easily
as witches, when they do come into their own,
they're spectacular. There's not a witch here
that'll be able to hold their ground against
you...you know, if you stay alive, that is."

"How do you know all of this?"

"Fairies have long lives and even longer
memories, and we like to gossip amongst our
own. Plus, I've known a few Shadow Walkers
that stuck around for a while.

"It was a rough beginning, but after they
got the knack, they kicked some serious ass.
Made the witches look like preschoolers. The
witches know it, too."

All I'd ever heard about was how fragile we
were, and the paper doll comments. I couldn't
believe I'd never asked about any that had
made it. "Do you know of any that are still
alive?"

"Only a rumor of one who might still be
around. She's been in retirement for some
time, from what I've heard."

I nearly startled her as I leaned close and
grabbed her arm. "Can you find out where she
is?" If she was retired, she'd learned to live

with the crawlers somehow. A crawler that had slid into the booth next to Flip hissed in her direction, as if it knew what we were discussing and didn't care for it.

"I know someone who used to talk to her. I'll see if they're still in touch."

Another loud burst of laughter from the witches, and Flip looked like she was going to jump out of the booth.

I squeezed her forearm. "I'm okay. I'm going to handle it."

Her eyes widened. "Can you? Handle it, that is?"

I chewed on my lower lip. "I think so."

She nodded, looking intrigued but not asking for any information that might incriminate her later on in the court of Kane.

"I'll see you later," I said as I slid out of the booth slowly, trying to avoid touching the many crawlers. "Have to take care of some things."

I walked out of the building, keeping to the rules, before I remembered the words of the spell Asher had given me. His gift.

The witches had finally crossed a line I wasn't willing to ignore.

20

My old apartment building stood in ruins with tape running around the perimeter, warning people to keep their distance.

It had been my last stop today, the last piece of my old life violently ripped from my hands.

Whether I wanted to embrace the new one that had been thrust on me or not remained to be decided. But I didn't see any alternatives right now, so I was going to make the best of it.

I had a limitless supply of magic awaiting me, and I was going to start making the most of it.

I turned and started walking home. Tonight I was going Shadow Walking.

* * *

There were puddles everywhere as I entered the Underground. Must've had a pipe break or something. You'd think with all the witches around, someone would manage a quick plug.

Strange how the ceilings didn't have any water damage. Then I noticed the looks directed my way and stopped in my tracks. What had I said when I used the "gift" right after I'd left the building?

The words hadn't meant anything, but I remembered the impression of storm clouds gathering as I thought of making the witches have an endless span of dreary days. I looked over at the table the witches used most and found the worst of the flooding, some gargoyles in the process of mopping up.

Instead of marching right into Kane's office and telling him to make sure he was around tonight, a detour might be in order. Not that I definitely was to blame. Maybe someone else had caused the rain clouds to open up inside the building. Who knew? I certainly wasn't an expert on this place.

I kept my pace relaxed as I strolled over toward the booth where Butch and Leon were sitting. It wasn't soaked, but it had some puddles in front of it.

"I'm alive!" My words lacked the normal festiveness.

"Not for long," Butch said, shaking his head.

I slid in, keeping my act up until I was sure there was enough evidence to convict. "Why's it so wet in here?"

Leon's eyes rolled, and his head moved with them.

Butch ran a hand over his wet hair. "You couldn't drizzle on them? You had to hit them with a monsoon? I couldn't even eat my pizza. There wasn't a single spot to hide from the windblown rain."

"Wind?" So much for hoping it hadn't been too bad.

"Yes," Leon nearly shouted. "The wind that came with the storm you set on them—which, in case you wanted to know, lasted three damn hours because they refused to leave. Luckily, it went with them."

I slumped in the booth.

"I wouldn't get too comfortable," Butch said.

I glanced up at Kane's door. "How mad?"

They didn't have to answer.

"Olivia." My name rang out over the room.

Kane was at the top of the stairs. He didn't move an inch, keeping his gaze on me before turning and walking back into his office. He left the door open.

I turned back to the guys in the booth and, with a fake smile and two thumbs up, said, "And hoping to still be alive tomorrow."

There was a grunt and a half nod.

"As always, thanks for the pep talk." I turned and walked up the stairs. I had to slow my pace or people might realize I wasn't dreading going into his office. If they knew I was actually eager to get in there, they might start asking questions.

The bottom line was that I shouldn't have been eager to get in that office, but I'd take a pissed-off Kane sans monsters any day over no-Kane monster slumber party.

I entered the office and shut the door. I might not care that he was pissed, but I didn't want the entire building to hear us screaming, either.

Kane was standing by the window. "Come here."

I took a step and then paused. The window was open. Was he going to push me out of it? I wasn't afraid of him, but that didn't mean I shouldn't be.

"I'm not going to kill you. I still need you, remember?"

He could've said it a little nicer, but it was a valid point. I walked over, reminding myself that he was too perceptive by half.

He pointed out the window. "See that?"

The building next door had char marks on its brick, near the top. A peek through the windows showed construction going on.

He leaned in closer. "That used to house some of the people who live here. That is why there aren't many rooms left. That is why I don't allow magic in this building."

I nodded, taking it all in as if listening to a school lecture. "What happened? I mean specifically?"

"One of the witches thought it might be funny to wake her friend up with a dragon in the morning. Nearly gutted the whole building."

He stopped looking at the building and turned his attention on me. That was when I realized that he might be acting calm, but he was seething down deep. "You were told that there was no magic in the building."

"I know."

"Then why did you do magic in my building?"

Wow, he was pissed. Was it the death wish that was stopping me from being worried? I thought I'd started to lose my death wish, though. Then why was I so sure that he wasn't going to hurt me?

"Olivia, why did you do it?" he asked, maybe even more annoyed since my attention had wandered.

"I didn't know I was doing magic in your building. I tried to do it in the alleyway." Even as I said it, it sounded lame. Yes, technically, it *was* outside. It had seemed so much more removed before I really thought about how close the alleyway was.

"You're telling me where. I asked why. I'm giving you a chance to explain why you aren't responsible for my building looking like it was in the middle of a hurricane. Give me something so that the rest of the people who live here understand why I'm not throwing you out."

Throw me out? Where would I go? He was asking for the one thing I wouldn't tell him. "I can't. Can you dock my money for the repairs?"

"You don't have any money yet and may never have it if you don't get my spell. And more importantly, I don't care about the money. I want to know why you did this."

"Did you ask the witches?" I immediately crossed my arms. That sounded awfully stupid too. Why was I so bad at this?

"I'm asking the person who caused the damage."

I'd had Kane all wrong on this count. When I'd walked in, I thought we might end this screaming at each other. He wasn't a screamer.

A lot of people don't realize it, but that's much worse. Screamers get all the anger out of their system and then there's only a sputter left over to actually do anything about the problem they were mad about.

People like Kane, on the other hand, didn't waste their energy with needless things like putting on a show. The non-screamers were the ones you had to watch out for.

This wasn't going to end well. If he hadn't heard about the "feature," I wasn't telling him. It was bad enough that it had happened. There was no way I was talking about the memories they'd ripped from me and put on display.

I wasn't sure what he'd do if I didn't tell him, but he wouldn't kill me. I was fairly certain of that, so it was better than telling him.

I shifted my shoulders up and said, "Are you kicking me out?" I stared at him and could feel my eyes start to burn. No. God no. Of all times to start crying, this was not it.

I took a couple of steps away from him, any excuse to give him my back. I got myself under control before I turned back around.

"No. I'm not. You're going to give me an answer."

The way he was staring at me, I knew I wasn't getting out of this room until I did.

I thought about the door at my back and considered making a run for it. I also knew how fast he moved and knew I didn't have a shot. I wasn't getting into a race that I was sure to lose.

The thing that was so strange in this moment was that I felt relieved. I'd had nowhere left to go, no money. I could sit in this office all day and it would be an upgrade on my previous situation. I walked over to my couch and made myself comfortable, not saying a damn thing as I did.

"Wrong choice," he said as he sat down behind his desk, staring at me across the room. "When we're finished here, we'll be going to get another reversal spell."

I crossed my arms and stared back. I wouldn't be getting them anything. No. Not for them. Not ever. Let them walk around drenched until it eventually faded away.

"I had to evict them from the building. You will be fixing this."

I crossed my legs. He was a bright man. He'd hear my answer.

"You can't win."

I smiled. We'd see about this. I'd spent a month lying on a couch, with crawlers everywhere, before I got here. It was like I'd been overtraining for this marathon. We'd see who caved first.

"You'll never outlast me."

"We'll see." I kicked my feet up on the table in front of me, crossing my ankles now.

He kicked his feet up onto his desk, crossing his arms.

The game was on.

* * *

Leon walked in an hour later, glanced at Kane then myself, and tried to back out of the door quicker than he'd walked in. "Sorry, thought you'd called me."

"Get in here," Kane said.

"Yeah?"

"You're aware of the flood that happened because of a certain monsoon?"

I snorted and then rolled my eyes. Obviously Leon was aware, since, as of an hour ago, there still wasn't a dry place to sit, and everyone's pant legs were soggy from walking through puddles.

Leon made a choking noise before grunting out, "Yes."

Kane stared at me as he directed Leon. "I want you to find out what caused the fight in the first place."

Leon threw his hands up. "The witches aren't here, and last time I saw one—"

Kane tapped a pen on his desk. "Find them. Follow the puddles if you must."

I took a breath, focusing on keeping it shallow so my nerves didn't show. The witches wouldn't talk. Not after the stuff they pulled. They couldn't.

Leon turned his back on Kane right before he walked out, and used that moment to roll his eyes at me.

I got the message. Leon might be pissed he was getting dragged into someone else's mess, but there was no way I was folding.

And then it was just the two of us again.

We'd been sitting there for another ten minutes when my eyes wandered over to where he was reading a paper, his feet up on his desk and his profile on display. He was wearing the same shirt he'd worn the night we went to the party. I could tell by the cut of his collar and the slight white-on-white stripe. I ran a knuckle over my lower lip. I'd never admit it to another living soul, but I still thought of that kiss.

He turned quickly, catching me staring, and his expression changed from one of anger and determination to something else that made my skin warmer.

No way he knew. He had some crazy skills, but he couldn't read minds, or we wouldn't be here right now.

But the cues of arousal weren't super hard to read. My skin burned slightly as I broke eye contact first. I'd rather show weakness than what else was going through my mind.

"You feeling okay? You're looking a bit flushed."

Oh yeah, he'd picked up on it.

"Just thinking of a memory, is all." Technically, it was a memory. Let him think it was anything but what it was.

A knock sounded at the door, and somehow I knew it was Isabella before she even stepped into the room. If it were possible, the knock itself had sounded annoyed.

She pursed her lips as she looked my way. She'd already known I was in here with him.

"Kane, you've got that meeting in an hour."

"Cancel it."

Her face couldn't have screwed up any tighter if she'd been chewing on a bag of lemons.

"Are you sure you want to do that?"

"Yes."

I saw her hands clench tightly around the stack of papers she was holding. "Shall we work on these, then?"

I wanted to roll over laughing as she continued. Even if there were a hundred other things I could be doing, I'd sit here for a week to watch her scramble. It was driving her nuts that Kane and I were locked up here alone.

"No. Take the night off."

Was it that he didn't notice how prickly she got, or did he not care? He had no idea how she felt about him. He was way too perceptive to not know, unless he chose ignorance.

It was another hour later when Butch walked in. The second he glanced over at me, my stomach sank. Someone had told him. I knew it had been a lost cause. Too many people knew.

I widened my eyes. He knew why I was sitting here and what that meant. Butch stopped in front of Kane's desk and then kept walking to the Keurig machine.

"Butch?" Kane said, but we all knew what he was really asking.

Butch glanced over at me again as he picked out a little cup. "Got nothing. The gargoyles said they didn't have vanilla."

Kane's eyes narrowed on Butch, and he was thinking the same thing I was. Butch had just lied for me.

Isabella strolled in as Butch was leaving. "Kane, I've got something of interest for you." She nodded toward the door.

She stared at me as she waited for him to get up and join her. She knew. Figured it would be her. She was friends with the witches.

I sank a little deeper into the couch, wishing I could sink right through the cushions and through the floor as I watched him exit with her, shutting the door behind them.

Kane walked back in by himself five minutes later. "You can leave."

I made a huffing noise, as if I'd expected more from him. "That's it? I flooded your building and now you're going to just let me stroll out?" I rolled my eyes.

"Yes," he said, his voice calm in spite of my goading words. "We're done for the day."

"Why?" I shot off the couch and marched over to where he'd sat back down at the desk. "I don't need your pity, or want it."

He looked up, and I couldn't read a thing from his expression as he said, "It was a warranted action under the circumstances. The witches cast the first spell. That's all."

Watching him, I wasn't sure what I believed. But I still had a job to do, so I made the choice to believe what he said. If I didn't, I wouldn't be able to work with him every day.

Without saying another word about it, I left the office and found my target. She was standing over in the corner looking down at her phone with a grin on her face. She glanced up and then looked back down at her phone, as if I were of no concern to her.

"That's okay. You don't need to look at me. But listen good. Get involved in my business again and you'll be wishing you got off as light as the witches did."

The smile stayed on her face, but I saw the tremble in her hand. Message delivered.

21

Kane strolled in as I was lying on the couch in my living room the next evening.

He stopped right beside where my head was resting. "You do this an awful lot."

"Do what?" I asked, opening my eyes now that I knew for sure it was Kane.

"Watch TV with your eyes closed, or a foot from your face."

I stared up at him. "My eyes felt tired. Sometimes I like to listen to it instead."

He nodded—and not in a way that indicated any belief in the bullshit I'd just fed him.

"Get up. We've got somewhere to go."

I pushed off the couch, having no complaints there. The more time away from the crawlers, the better. "Where are we going?"

"Work."

* * *

It was another dilapidated building.

"Why do we always go to the most depressing places ever? Why is it never a park on a sunny day with butterflies sailing on the gentle breeze?" I lifted a hand and let it drift along an imaginary trail a pretty purple butterfly might take.

When the imaginary butterfly flew off, I looked over at Kane who stood there, eyebrows raised.

"Little too far into happy land for you?" I asked, feeling like we'd somehow reset since yesterday, and not complaining about it.

"Didn't realize you were a resident," he replied, confirming the reset.

I shrugged. "Some of us like to visit every now and then." It was good to be back to normal. That brief moment back in his office, when I hadn't been sure how he was feeling, if he'd been pitying me... This was better.

I looked about the place. The drearier the locale, the bigger the crawlers.

When I finished tonight, what was my tomorrow going to look like? When I'd started, I hadn't had the first clue as to why we were called paper dolls, but I was learning quickly now. If Shadow Walking didn't kill you, the insanity of being surrounded by more and more crawlers made you want to off yourself.

I needed to get him his spell and get out of this world before I became another link in the chain of deaths.

"I'm done playing in the sandbox. You said I was ready. Tell me what spell you're looking for and let's get this going." There wasn't an immediate response, as I would've expected. Didn't he want this?

"Well?" I asked, turning to him.

"Are you sure you're ready?"

Why didn't he seem happy about this? How bad was it going to be? "No. But if I can't do it, I'll dump it there, like you said." And hope that they let me through. "What's the spell you want?"

I held out my hand, waiting for my marching orders.

He took it. "Ask them for something to merge a soul and body."

"That's what you've been searching for?" Was he missing a soul? He had a bad attitude sometimes, and a major ego, but he wasn't soulless.

"Yes." It was said in a curt manner that made it very clear that was the only information I could expect. "If you can't get that, ask for the spell of immortality."

"Afraid the girls won't clamor if you get some silver at the temples?"

He didn't look annoyed by what I'd just said. He looked pleased. "So you find me attractive?"

"That's not what I said."

"No, that is *exactly* what you said."

How did this keep getting worse? Time to quit this topic before I dug in any deeper. "I get you a spell for immortality and we're done?"

Spell of immortality. That might be something interesting to keep in my back pocket. But would I want to live forever?

"No. That's the spell for the dwarves. Odds are you won't be able to get either of them here, but might as well try."

I looked down at my jeans and back up before he caught me. "Why do you think I owe the dwarves?"

He looked at my jeans and my sweater before his eyebrows rose. "I know dwarf clothing when I see it. You won't be able to walk away from this world clean until you pay all your debts. And at the rate you're going…"

I started making my cat calls to a larger crawler, not wanting to discuss any other debts.

He shook his head. "How you were the one to survive is beyond me."

"You better be nice if you want your spell."

"You're right," he said, so solemnly that I stopped clucking for a moment. "Your clucking noises are orchestra-worthy. I only criticize because I envy you from the depths of my soul."

I hated when he was funny. Now I had to pretend he wasn't, because I wouldn't contribute to his ego getting any bigger. Someone had to pretend he wasn't perfect.

I made another clucking noise, and the crawler came and opened up an entrance.

"See you in a few." Those were my last words to Kane before I stepped into the Shadowlands, and I hoped they were true.

As always, I was the center of attention in this place the second I stepped in. I wondered if it was the heat I threw off or them sensing something other than themselves.

Didn't matter. I took a few steps in and found the biggest crawler I could. Get in and get out before I drew too big of a crowd and they blocked the exit.

"I want a spell of…"

The monster stared, waiting for my request. If I got this spell, then what? I would wake to even more crawlers, because I did every single time.

And I still didn't have a choice. The only way out was through. "I need a spell to merge a soul and a body."

Something happened then that had never happened before. The shadow monster laughed at me. Then it swirled into a small typhoon and vanished in the air.

I looked for another one, but they had all scattered. No crawlers at my point of entry or anywhere else.

Without any other option, I was on the brink of leaving when I felt him.

He was here again. Asher. His energy drifted on the air toward me as he approached until it was palpable as he stood a few feet in front of me.

He briefly glanced at where my hand grasped Kane's invisible one, but didn't linger there.

He looked around and then smiled, although he didn't appear happy. "Seems you scared everyone away."

"They didn't like my request."

"No. They wouldn't. That's potent magic." His head turned this way and that, taking in my pants, my shoes, my hair, as if he'd never seen me before.

"You heard me?"

"I was nearby." He took another step closer. His eyes were back on my face, but he seemed to still be examining. "You're getting stronger."

"Stronger?" I leaned away. That was the last way I would've described myself.

"With magic." He held his hand out as if he wanted to touch me.

I stepped back again. Another few steps and I'd be out of here. "I can't stay."

"Just for a few minutes."

* * *

I walked through the Underground beside Kane and got on the elevator that would take us to the sixth floor. We stood shoulder to shoulder as the doors closed. Not that I wanted to go upstairs, but I'd use the excuse to milk a couple of more minutes of peace.

He rocked in place slightly. "Strange how long you stayed if they all scattered."

"I told you, I was hoping they'd come back." I knew he hadn't believed me. The whole ride back, I'd been waiting for him to say something.

The doors opened, and I stepped out.

"Be careful, Ollie," he said as I walked toward my rooms, and then he was gone, in his apartment.

The moment his door shut and I was in my rooms, there were crawlers everywhere. It was hard to walk in a straight line to the bedroom without walking into one. There was no doubting it now. They were getting worse every time I stepped into that place, and there didn't seem to be a plateau. Would it get to the point I couldn't take a step one way or another without stepping into the chill of their presence? Was there really no escape? Did all the paper dolls die from mistakes made in the Shadowland, or was it suicide?

No. There would be no suicide for me. I'd made a promise to my father years ago, and I'd live in insanity if that was what it took. But I wasn't going to have to. I could do this.

People—I needed lots and lots of people to create a buffer. Staring at the ceiling, I made my way out of the apartment.

I was halfway down the hall toward the stairs when the crawlers scattered.

"Where you going?" Kane asked.

What the heck? Was my door rigged for sound or something? "Getting kind of hungry. Figured I'd go see if there was anyone downstairs that wanted to get a bite to eat with me."

He looked at his watch and nodded.

I was aware it was nearly three in the morning. I nodded.

I wasn't sure what we were agreeing on with all this nodding.

He waved me over as he took a step toward the elevator. "Come to the office with me and I'll order you something. I need help with my paperwork."

He made it sound like an order, but I knew he was throwing me a lifeline. It was pity. He was pitying me. The question was, did I care anymore? Did I care enough to say no?

His office *was* a mess.

He pressed the button, and the doors opened, then stood aside, waiting for me. "Come on."

"This isn't…"

He walked onto the elevator and then said in a raised voice, "I've got outstanding debts from twenty years ago. At this rate, some of those people are going to be dead before I get around to collecting, if they aren't already."

I'd seen the paperwork. He was probably telling the truth. And if we could help each other…

I got on the elevator. The door shut.

"Ever think about hiring more help?"

"I have. Most supernaturals don't need the money. The vampires kept salivating over the humans and the wolves wouldn't stop sniffing their asses."

"Oh. What about the—"

"The gargoyles aren't good at paperwork. I found out the hard way that they sweat cement dust when they're taxed."

"What about the—"

"Ollie, please stop."

I nodded.

22

I woke to a grunt before I heard Butch say, "Why is it that every time I see you lately, Ollie's always sleeping somewhere nearby?"

Wake up and say hello or roll over and pull the pillow that had magically appeared while I slept over my head? I opted for the pillow.

"We were working," Kane answered.

"That's working?"

"Keep your voice down. What did you need?"

I repositioned the pillow, trying to get a little more soundproofing.

"Message came in today from Alexandria. She wants a meeting."

"Tell her to come."

"She doesn't want to come here. Says you need to see something out there."

"That's her problem, since she's the one that needs the meeting."

"Her messenger said she knew you'd say that, but that she really needs you to go there."

There was a pause. "You want me to tell them you're not coming?"

"No. I'll go. But she's going to have to wait a while."

* * *

Next time I woke up, I was in Kane's office alone, except for the crawlers. I pushed off a blanket I'd never seen before and banged my shins as I tried to make it out without opening my eyes.

I got to the stairs and looked around. It was lunchtime. Where was everybody? Keeping my eyes out of focus, I made it the best I could to the booth, only banging into a few shifters on the way.

"Gargoyle?" I was glad I had my eyes partially shielded when one popped up. The curly red hair sprouting out of his head and blue eye shadow was bad enough in low definition.

"What?"

At least he wasn't flirting with me. "Do you have chicken soup?" The crawlers trying to crowd in around me were causing a bad chill in the air.

"Wait." I looked at it closely, trying to confirm my assumption. Yep, definitely different than the one I'd spoken to about our agreement. "Zee is my usual gargoyle. You know the deal with my food, right? Your colleague spread the word, right?"

A glance over at the witches' table told me that he knew exactly what I was speaking of.

"I got the message." He was disappearing from sight as Flip's raised voice in the corner made me wince.

She was kicking a werewolf's chair. The werewolf in question happened to be twice her size, but that wouldn't bother Flip none. She was smiling again by the time she scooted into the booth opposite me. "Damn, I've got to start wearing a jacket around you."

"What was that about?" Flip didn't need a reason, but it was a better topic than how many monsters were hovering nearby.

"That big jackass over there scooted his chair right into me. You know what he said?" she asked, hitting me in the arm to keep my attention.

"No. What?" I asked, happy to listen as she scooted closer to tell me her story, forcing out a larger crawler in the process.

"That he didn't see me."

The gargoyle was back and putting down my soup as I said, "Oh."

As soon as I saw her face shift into confusion, I knew I'd messed up the response.

"You don't get it. He was taking a dig at my small size."

Flip only paused in her indignation to order food from the gargoyle. He gave a grunt and disappeared.

"Maybe he really didn't notice you? It is possible," I said.

"I mean, yeah, it is, but he still banged into me, and my leprechaun blood can't let something like that slide, you know?"

I nodded, trying to keep her happy so she wouldn't leave. "Why don't I ever see any leprechauns around here?"

"Full-bloods don't like others. They don't have my flair for socialization."

I would've laughed, but she wasn't kidding.

She rubbed the chill from her arms as she said, "I'm glad you're here, though. I've got news for you. I talked to some old-timers who said they knew where you might be able to locate that Shadow Walker."

"Where?" I asked, skipping to the important question and not asking what people around her called old-timers.

"Before I tell you, I have to warn you, the info wasn't free. The leprechauns are going to come looking for payment at some point."

This felt reminiscent of when I'd run up my credit cards when I was eighteen. Back then it had been to pay for a trip to Iceland, then Russia and Japan, all in an effort to find some place on this earth that didn't have monsters. I'd ended up with a whopping amount of debt and no progress. Hopefully this wouldn't end the same.

"How bad?"

"Bad, and you need to make sure you pay up. You don't mess with the leprechauns. This isn't like a Lucky Charms commercial. They're hardcore."

"I owe everyone at this point, so give me the details. I'll worry about the debt after I get out of this mess."

She dug her hand into her back pocket and handed me a folded piece of paper. "She's not too far."

I looked at the address. An hour's drive. I had a valid license, but I hadn't driven since the day after I'd gotten it.

"You need a ride?"

"I don't want to drag you into this."

Her eyes got huge. "No, not from me. I meant you could get one of the gargoyles to drive you. They do errands. Just make sure they don't talk, if you know what I mean. I don't think this person wants to be found."

I tucked the address in my pocket. "What's one more IOU?"

"Babe, that's how things work around here."

"Why can't anyone just be bought off with money, like the normal world?"

"Because most of the creatures around here have plenty of that. No one cares about money. Magic, that's the real currency in this place, and you, my girl, are going to be one rich bitch—I mean, you know, if you keep living. I've got faith in you. And by faith, I mean, I give you better than fifty/fifty."

"Thanks for the overwhelming pledge of support."

"You got it. I gotta go, though. When the gargoyle gets back, tell him to bring my food to my room? It's too damn cold here."

* * *

"Gargoyle?" I whispered right outside my door, after having no luck in my rooms.

Zee popped out of the air, hand on his hip. "What? Why do you keep calling? This is my busy time."

"You could hear me in there?" I motioned to my wide-open door.

"Of course I can."

Not the time for a fight when I needed something. "I've heard you can arrange transportation?"

"Where?"

I dug the crinkled paper out of my pocket and handed it to him. "I don't want anyone to know, either."

"This can be arranged, but—"

I held my hands up. "Yeah, yeah, it's going to cost me. I got that. When can you do it?" If Kane held true to form, he wouldn't be looking for me until after seven at the earliest. I had a solid six hours to get this done.

He scratched his jaw, letting some dust loose into the air as he did. "I could arrange this within the hour, but you're going to have to put up some spells. We don't like the debt to get too high...just in case."

I was getting a little sick and tired of everyone assuming I was going to die at any minute. "I don't have a spell for you." The only spell I had right now I was saving.

He shrugged. "I'm not sure what we can do for you then. I mean, we can only take so many IOUs."

It took a few minutes to digest that a gargoyle was telling me I didn't have any credit left. "You haven't asked me for anything yet."

He tilted his head back. "Well, now we are. We had a sit-down and we know what we want."

"What?" I didn't miss the way he scanned the hall, making sure we were still alone. My mind spun quicker the longer it took him to spit it out. I'd survive the crawlers, I'd manage to get Kane's spell, but these cement fuckers would end up being the death of me.

"We want a beauty potion," he whispered.

Don't laugh. That would be very mean and possibly screw me, because I needed them to keep my food clean of spells. I forced my lips to stay together until I was sure I had the urge under control. "Okay. Done."

"Tomorrow at eleven. We'll take you after we get it." He smiled—or that was the expression the pained look on his face most resembled—before he disappeared.

Damn gargoyles. Instead of thinking I had six hours to accomplish this, I had six hours to kill before I could do anything, stuck surrounded by crawlers.

23

I'd gone into the Shadowlands an hour ago with the best of intentions. I'd get them both: a beauty potion for the gargoyles and Kane's spell.

I made sure to ask for the beauty potion first. It had been the right choice. When I asked for Kane's, they all disappeared again. I strolled out as pristine as I'd gone in. I should've started asking for his spell right out of the gate. Made exiting a lot easier.

As far as the crawlers afterward, though...

Kane hadn't bailed me out this time, either. I saw him hesitate when we parted. I had this feeling that if I said something, he might change his plans. I hadn't.

I'd gone to my rooms and guzzled back NyQuil until I couldn't stay awake if I wanted. Then this morning, I'd gone down and had breakfast like everything was fine.

By five to ten, I was sitting in my apartment and waiting.

Zee appeared in my living room at exactly eleven and immediately asked, "Do you have it?"

"Yes."

"Really?" he asked, and for the first time since meeting him, his face smoothed over. He started waving his hands about as if he didn't know what to do with himself for a second. "Hold on. I've got to call them."

"Call them?"

"So you can do the spell on all of us."

I bit the inside of my cheek. I hadn't known I was supposed to be the one to cast the spell, on all of them, in Kane's building. Somehow testing it out on one gargoyle didn't seem so bad. Then again, it was a beauty potion. How bad could it be?

He wasn't waiting for me anyway. He disappeared, and when he popped back in, he was one of twelve.

"We're ready," he said, in the front of the group.

"I'm not supposed to do magic in the building. Maybe we should find somewhere—"

I heard multiple nos. The group became so disgruntled, so fast, that I was afraid they were going to hear us above the music on the ground floor if I suggested another delay.

"Okay! I'll do it now." Otherwise I'd have to come up with a reason my room was packed with gargoyles. "Maybe I should stand in the middle of everyone, so the spell spreads out evenly?"

If I was in the center surrounded by them, I wasn't surrounded by crawlers. Concentration didn't come easily with them around.

They made a hole in the center of them that I stepped into. They closed ranks on me, and it was bliss.

I opened up that door in my mind, the one that the spells seemed to go to rest, and let the words flow over my tongue and past my lips.

The spell felt like a kiss from a lover as it worked its magic, and a warm embrace seemed to envelop me. I tipped my head back as I spoke, and reveled in the feeling.

Seconds or minutes, I wasn't sure how much time had passed by the time I'd finished. Completely relaxed, I opened my eyes and focused on the group of gargoyles.

Holy mother of dark magic, what had I done? Something like a squeak came from my chest. I was a dead woman. It was true. I was going to die by gargoyle.

Except they weren't beating me. They were hugging each other.

"You're beautiful!"

"No, you're beautiful."

I heard another ten mentions of how beautiful they all were, mixed in with laughter and tears of joy.

Zee turned to me. "You made us beautiful!" He crushed me in a hug.

I was lightheaded by the time he put me down. I found the nearest seat as I listened to them make plans to show everyone how gorgeous they were.

Instead of using the door, they all started to vanish, presumably to "show everyone."

"Zee," I called before he disappeared with the others. "When can you take me?"

"Tomorrow morning at eight."

I nodded. I wasn't arguing about anything right now.

24

It was barely dawn, but maybe I could get food and get back to my room before anyone else showed up. I should've seen if the gargoyles did room service last night before they'd vanished, but I hadn't been thinking clearly.

The place was dead. I slid into our booth and called a gargoyle. Get in and get out.

The gargoyle showed, and it was a bad as I remembered. I ordered quickly and then prayed it would be quick. I'd have to deal with the crawlers on my own today. I'd show up later, after they'd all seen the new look and the dust had hopefully settled.

"Hey, you're down early. You eating?" Butch slid into the booth.

Leon, who'd walked in beside him, settled in on my other side.

I pushed on Butch. "Why don't we go out for breakfast today? Come on, all of us. It'll be fun."

Butch didn't budge. "Too hungry. I've got to get a snack, at least. We've been out all night."

"It won't take that long. Isn't there a place—"

"Gargoyle," Butch said, ignoring me.

I stared at my hands, the table, a stray piece of lint on Leon's left shoulder.

I was looking down, but I knew right when the gargoyle popped up by the gasps on either side.

If I didn't look, they'd know something was up. *Please, don't be the blonde. Anybody but the blonde.*

I locked down my expression and lifted my gaze. It was the blonde.

This gargoyle appeared to have a platinum wig sprouting out of its cement head, and red lipstick that came almost as high as its nose dropped down. And the eyebrows… There were no words in the human language to do those justice.

"Here is your scrambled eggs and coffee, light and sweet." It slid my plate and mug toward me.

"Thanks."

"You got it, sugar." Then it winked at me.

"Can I help you?" it said, turning to Butch and shifting a hip out of a silk negligee as he did.

"Can I have a, um…" Butch started scratching his red hair.

"Yes?" it asked, pouting its lips.

Was it flirting with Butch? I sank a little deeper into the seat.

"Yeah, um…a roast beef sandwich."

"You got it, big boy." It wagged its thigh back and forth.

I put a hand over my face. This was bad. So, so bad. *Please, let this end.*

But the best was yet to come. It reached a hand over and ran it halfway up the top of Leon's thigh. "And what about you? What can I help *you* with?"

Leon was moving so far into the booth that he was crushing me up against Butch. Butch wasn't budging a hair out of the booth to make room, either.

"My regular will be just fine."

It smiled and finally disappeared.

"What the hell happened to them?" Butch asked. "You think the witches?"

I started shoveling eggs into my mouth as I watched the crawlers disappear. I looked up as Kane was walking into his office.

"Why would the witches mess with the gargoyles?" Leon asked.

The eyes landed on me, and I stared at my eggs again.

"Ollie? Did you do something to the gargoyles?" Butch asked.

I didn't look up. "I did what they asked me to, and they are very happy with the outcome, so I don't think anyone else should judge." I shoveled more eggs into my mouth.

Butch shook his head, dazed. "You think this is a good—"

"Here you go, cupcake." The gargoyle placed Butch's sandwich down. He placed down Leon's next. "I made sure it had plenty of *hot* sauce for you." It made a weird shape with its mouth and a puff of air came out as it said "hot."

I launched into my defense as soon as the gargoyle was gone again.

"They like it. They're happy. That's all that matters. Don't be so judgmental."

They both fell silent. I wasn't sure if I'd won my case or if it was because Isabella approached our booth.

"Kane would like to see you." She smiled, genuinely this time.

He'd definitely seen the gargoyles.

Butch slid out, and I made my way across the floor as more and more people were arriving for breakfast.

Kane was leaning back in his chair behind the desk when I walked in. "Isabella said you were looking for me?"

"Have a seat. I ordered you a tea."

"Thanks." He had a Keurig machine in his office. There was no need to order me anything.

There was no way he hadn't noticed the difference in the gargoyles. It was hard to miss. I strolled over to the couch and relaxed back as if I had no idea what was going on.

I didn't cringe when the gargoyle appeared, but I wanted to.

It only had a tea, and put it on the table in front of the couch. It winked at me before it disappeared. Looked like I was becoming quite popular with at least one supernatural breed.

I sipped the tea, which had been fixed to perfection, while Kane stared at me.

I took a few more sips and then raised the cup to my nose, trying to figure out the blend. "This is the best tea I've ever had. Delicious."

"You don't want to say anything about…" Kane waved his hand toward where the gargoyle had been.

I'd never seen Kane speechless.

"Whatever is going on, they are in a very good mood, so I don't think we should question it." I gave a slow nod, encouraging him to agree with me, and then took another sip of tea.

He leaned his head to the side. "Try not to do too much more damage."

"They seem quite happy." I placed my tea down and glanced at the clock, trying to figure out a way to get out of his office without raising suspicion. Considering I usually tried to camp out there, this could get tricky.

Isabella walked in, glanced over at me, and then acted as if she hadn't seen me. She turned to Kane. "Here's the list you needed."

"Thanks," he said, taking it from her as I got up and started wandering in the direction of the door.

She hitched a hip on the corner of Kane's desk. "Several rooms down on two opened up now that the majority of witches can't come in the building. I was going to have someone move Olivia's—"

"Leave her on sixth." He flipped through papers, not looking up, and I edged closer to the door.

"I thought that Olivia might be more—"

"She'll be staying where she is."

"Should I keep it open in—"

"No. As I said before, and *keep* saying, she's not moving."

"What about—"

"Isabella, drop the subject."

I didn't know if she dropped the subject or not, since I was out of the room, grateful to Isabella for once.

25

The house was way outside of town, but this was the address on the paper.

Zee looked relieved as I opened the car door and slid out. When I'd slid in close to him, after a crawler climbed in next to me, he'd informed me he was straight and preferred men. That was when I realized that Zee was a she.

"Wait here?"

She rolled her eyes but put the car in park. I took a step toward the house and then back to Zee. "I need you to get out of the car and try to punch me."

I'd been sitting on a protection spell for days, not knowing if they wore off after a while. I'd used it right before I left with her this morning.

"Why?" she asked, flipping her red hair as if she'd been practicing that move in the mirror.

"Can you just do it?"

275

She got out of the car and I immediately stepped back.

"In the stomach area. I don't want a bruise. And not too hard."

She let out a little puff of air like I'd ruined her fun. She made an awkward fist with her long pink nails and then plowed into me.

I nearly doubled over with the pain. So much for not too hard. The protection spell was worthless.

Zee got back in the car and was checking her nails already, making sure she hadn't chipped anything.

What the hell? I took a step back toward the house. I hadn't come out here to walk away. Protection spell or not, this person might be the key to living with these monsters.

I left Zee and walked up to the cozy Cape Cod, with its perfectly manicured lawn and bristly welcome mat. I clanked the iron knocker before I could think too long on what I'd say.

When a woman my age answered the door, I knew I must've gotten the wrong information.

"Can I help you?"

But maybe? She had black hair like mine, and grey eyes.

"I… Are you…" All the words I could think of—*are you a Shadow Walker* and *^cast spells because I need some help getting rid of crawlers*—would be translated to *I'm a nut case who sees things* if this were the wrong place. This couldn't be the person I was looking for. "Sorry I bothered you. Someone gave me the wrong address."

With a halfhearted wave goodbye, I turned and started down the walk.

"Who were you looking for?"

"The person I came for is older," I called over my shoulder, as I kept walking.

"Maybe too old to even be living?"

I stopped walking and turned back. "Yeah, maybe."

"You're at the right house." She pushed the door wider and then waved for me to join her before she walked back inside.

I followed quickly.

"I'm in the kitchen," she called as my feet hit the marble in her entrance hall.

I headed toward her voice, past a decor that fit with the woman I'd just seen, but not the person I'd expected.

She was standing in front of a gas range, putting on a teakettle. "Would you like a cup? I keep a fairly large assortment."

"Sure, thanks." I took a seat at the counter that opened up into the great room. There was silence again as I debated what to say. I'd been so worried about finding a living, breathing Shadow Walker who'd made it that I hadn't considered too many details beyond the logistics. I didn't have to worry. She made no pretense of not knowing who or what I was.

"How's it going? It's hard in the beginning. The witches giving you a hard time at the Underground? They hate newcomers, and they really hate Shadow Walkers with all our dark magic." She added a little shudder at the end that made me laugh.

"A little bit." She was a Shadow Walker. It was true. But how was she so young?

She rolled her eyes. "I know what 'a little bit' means. I haven't been there in decades, but that group never changes."

Decades? Smooth facial skin that no creamer could achieve. Her hands were smooth, too, so it wasn't artful plastic surgery, but she'd definitely said decades. Had she gotten a spell of immortality?

The whistle on the teakettle blew, and I tried to eye up her neck. I'd heard of people having youthful hands, but the neck always told the true story.

Or maybe not.

She took a box out of the cabinet and I opted for an Earl Grey. This wasn't the time to be wowed by some exotic ginger peach tea. Had to concentrate here.

Tea in place and box pushed off to the side, she said, "A hundred and forty."

"A hundred and forty?"

"That's how old I am."

My tea splashed onto my hand, and I ignored the burn. "How?"

"There's lots of pluses to being a Shadow Walker if you can handle it. I happen to have found a spell for eternal youth."

Don't ask. That one I knew instinctively. Spells didn't last forever, and there was no way she was going to be willing to share that one. Even if I wasn't sure I wanted to live forever, it would be nice to know I was digging myself out of debt.

"You're not going to ask?" she said. "You might actually make it for a while." She took a sip of her tea. "It expired after one use, anyway. Don't ask for a spell of immortality. That's a harder find. It's easier to layer a youth and longevity."

I nodded, feeling like I should be taking notes.

"Casio still around?"

"Yeah."

"Don't sleep with him."

"Wasn't going to."

"Then you're smarter than me. Was that a mistake." She rolled her eyes. "From what I'm hearing, you're the first Shadow Walker in a long time that's survived past the first few days."

"Why is that?" I said, angling to the side when one of the many crawlers that had come with me stepped in between us.

"Is there one there?" She motioned to the area directly in front of me.

"You don't see it?"

"I was a Shadow Walker. I'm not anymore." She picked up her teacup and motioned me over to one of the couches.

I settled in opposite her. "So you don't see them anymore?"

"It's not as good as it seems. There's a way to get rid of them, but it also cuts you off from that world. It obliterates that part of you. They'll be gone, and so will your use of magic." She was watching me as she spoke, her eyes intent before her gaze switched toward a window, looking like a bird who'd had their wings clipped would look toward the sky.

She started speaking again, this time the sadness clear in her tone. "At first, there was nothing but relief. You know as well as I do what it's like to be surrounded by those creatures every moment of the day. There's a reason most of us don't last." She rested a bent arm on the back of the sofa and used it as a headrest. "The craziest part is, now I wake every day hoping I see them. It would mean I could still cast a spell."

Her voice had grown softer and softer, until it seemed she was talking to herself by the end.

I didn't ask her why she'd miss casting a spell. That part I already knew.

I sipped my tea, more confused than before. "Can you undo it?"

"There's a way to shut the door. But you don't really shut it; you blast it closed until there's no going back."

I took a couple of more sips of tea, finishing most of my cup as I got a handle on myself. This woman was starting to make me rethink everything I knew. I didn't want to live this way anymore. Even now, she was gazing out the window and I couldn't stop looking at the ceiling, trying to catch a moment of peace. She'd forgotten how bad it really was.

"I'd happily get rid of them, whatever the cost."

She nodded. "There's only one man I know of who can do it."

"So you made a deal with Kane?" When I'd come here, a part of me had hoped there were other options.

"He's the only one who knows how to do it." Her attention was back on me, her eyes narrowed slightly as she stared.

"Do you know what he is?" I looked across the room, trying to ignore the crawlers in my way to break the tension growing between us. It didn't work, and I found myself getting up and walking a pace away.

"No one knows what he his." She was still staring at me. "Do you have any spells on you now?" There was something in her look, as if she was starving and thought I was hiding a burger behind my back.

"No," I said quickly, even though I did.

"Maybe I could try to anchor you and you could go get some?" she asked, and I was starting to think she had known I was coming.

"You've done that before?" I took a few more steps away.

"No. But I've been anchored so many times in the past that I'm sure it won't be a problem. We could go somewhere right now." She stood. "Let me get my keys." She started patting her pockets and then looking about the room, while also trying to keep me in her sights.

I measured the distance to the door.

"Is that them?" I asked, pointing to a pile in the far corner of the kitchen.

She turned her back, and I ran.

26

It was after seven by the time I got back. The gargoyles might be used as drivers, but that didn't mean they had a good sense of direction. They were worse at taking instructions.

After the fifth wrong turn, Zee had seemed a bit defensive as she explained that gargoyles usually attached themselves to one building and stayed there. It was so bad that the crawler next to me disappeared halfway home.

The second I stepped onto the main floor, Kane stepped out of his office and headed toward me. I wasn't optimistic enough to believe it was a coincidence.

I didn't care what he said. This was a free world, and I could do all the investigating I wanted. There was no ban on me speaking to other Shadow Walkers.

He walked over with a determined pace. "We need to head out early tonight."

He headed toward the back door, expecting me to follow. For once, I was relieved by his no-word commands, because he either didn't know about the Shadow Walker or didn't care.

I glanced at the clock on the wall, making sure it wasn't my timing that was off. It was barely seven. "Why we leaving so soon?" I asked, following him.

He stopped by the back door, pulling his phone out of his pocket as he said, "It's farther away, and…" He paused and then looked at me. "Forget it. You're off tonight."

He walked out the door alone, with no further explanation.

* * *

I pushed the door to Kane's apartment open an hour later. It felt heavier this time, as if maybe the ramifications of what I was about to do seemed to weaken my resolve, and my strength along with it. I was going to use a spell I'd learned how to retrieve against the man who'd taught me how to retrieve it.

But was it really using it against him? My life was in his hands, literally one of his hands, every time I went into the Shadowlands. If he let go, I'd be gone. I'd stalled long enough, because when I did get his spell, I knew I might be fighting for my life to get out of the Shadowlands, if the other spells had been any indication.

I had a right to know who I was dealing with, just as he knew every ounce of who I was. He hadn't asked permission when his men had stalked me, confirming what I was by digging through my personal records, even medical.

My hands ran over the back of his leather couch as I smelled his scent in the air. What happened if I found out something I didn't like? Then what? Could I walk away from the hope of ever living a life without crawlers?

There was no good answer for that. Hopefully whatever I found out wouldn't be bad enough to force my hand. I had to know, either way.

I started chanting the spell I'd tucked deep away, specifically for this moment. As the words flowed into the air, I felt a heady tingle of magic surround me in a warm embrace. Every time I did a spell, the feeling of coming home grew stronger. The warmth became more comforting, as if the magic were trying to tell me that this was what I was meant for.

I continued, the strength of the magic and my voice hitting a crescendo until I knew instinctively it was fully unleashed.

The air shimmered and sizzled around me. Then it fell flat.

Had I said it wrong? No. It had felt right, and I'd done enough at this point to recognize the feeling.

I was wrapped so in my own thoughts that I'd actually become oblivious to the absence of the monsters until I heard his voice.

"Dark magic doesn't work on me, and it won't work in here."

There was only one word for my current situation. Fucked. But maybe a few variations, such as fuckity, fuck, fucker.

I waited for him to say something else that would let me know how deep the water I was standing in really was. Could I wade out of this, or would I drown as soon as I opened my mouth?

As the silence continued, there was only one option left. Own it like I was right. Well, technically, I could fall on my knees and beg for forgiveness too, but fuckity fuck that.

I started my turn with confidence and then sputtered as I saw him reclined against the couch.

I faked a righteousness that I didn't have a ton of confidence in. "I put my life in your hands over and over again. I need some reassurances on exactly who or what you are, because we both know you aren't human."

"Keeping you alive isn't enough?" His eyebrow rose. "Keeping the vampires from killing you means nothing?"

"You do that because you need me. What happens next month or next week after I get you your spell? What if you don't do the things you promised?"

"It's the best you're going to get," he said, like a man who thought he held the winning hand.

"It's not enough. I don't know who you are or what you're capable of."

He was reclined, but I saw the tension in his jaw. It was as if there were something churning under the waters.

"How long did it take you to give up?"

I knew what was to come was much more entertaining when he was doing it to someone else. I should walk out now, but I couldn't seem to make myself move. "Give up what?"

"On life. Was there a particular catalyst, or did you wake up one day and say fuck it, I'm not in the mood anymore?" He acted as if we were having a casual conversation, when it was anything but.

I swallowed and felt suddenly stiff, like a cardboard cutout of myself. I should've walked out.

He waved to where I stood. "Did I read this wrong? I thought we had gotten to the point where we dug around in each other's lives, invited or not. So, tell me, when did you give up?"

For the life of me, I had nothing to say. I didn't know myself when I'd begun to not care whether I lived or died. But I cared now. I knew I did, but I didn't say that. Maybe I was too ashamed to answer because I had given up for so long. I didn't know, but I kept standing there silently.

"You had the balls to come in here with your spell, but now you can't finish a sentence?"

His anger finally lit my fuse. I'd seen him mess with enough people. I wasn't falling prey. "You can taunt me all you want. I'm not running out of here. I want answers."

He didn't move or give any sign whether I was right, but I knew I was. This was his way of cutting off any more questions.

"Really? You won't run?"

"No. I want answers."

He was on the couch and then he was in front of me, my chest nearly brushing his. "So do I. How honest are you ready to be? So far, I'd say you haven't been very honest about a lot of things."

He was toying with me. All I needed to do was stand my ground.

He raised his hand slowly until his fingers were grazing the skin of my neck, reaching around until they were at the base of my skull. They pulled me forward until our fronts were flush, and I placed my hands on his chest, not sure if I was getting ready to push him away or move them upward and urge his lips to join mine.

There was a strange friction happening everywhere we touched. I'd been single most of my life, but I wasn't innocent. I'd never craved a man like this before, where it felt like it was out of my control. It was a wild craving inside me that was screaming I needed this the moment.

Was it a spell? I didn't even like him, and yet my body sang everywhere we touched and a need formed deep within for something I'd not needed until now.

Maybe I could get answers if I slept with him? Or maybe that was a rationalization and all I'd get was sucked in so deep I wouldn't be able to dig myself out. What kind of normal life would there be after a man like Kane? And that was if I could step away. Maybe he'd use me for everything I could give him and then leave me for dead.

My hands had his shirt bunched as I breathed deeply of him. God, the smell of him drove me crazy enough from a few feet away. Now it was nearly intoxicating.

He stood there, watching me, waiting to see if I'd crumble.

I pushed off him before I completely lost myself. His hand, still at the back of my head, didn't budge for a second, and then dropped.

He smiled, confirming it had been a test.

"Knew you'd run," he said as I stepped back and his hand dropped to his side.

He had been messing with me. But for a second there…

No. I wasn't thinking of that.

"I'm not running. I just have things I need to do," I said as I walked from his room without offering up any details or waiting for him to respond.

I made it all the way to my rooms without running, shutting the door and leaning against it.

I hadn't run.

27

I was sitting in the Underground alone, if you didn't count the multitude of crawlers. Butch and Leon had left a half-hour ago. Flip was probably sleeping, as she liked to get a solid thirteen hours a day. She blamed it on having some distant drop of relation to Rip Van Winkle in her bloodline. I was thinking it might've been a drop of lazy. Jerry was nowhere to be found, but Leon had said he was starting to take later hours because he was hot and heavy with some vampire chick.

I saw the flash of light as the door to Kane's office opened. Kane stepped out and looked about the floor, his eyes never landing on me as he scanned the crowd. After all these Shadow Walks I'd done, Kane only needed to step into the same room and his presence chased away even a whiff of the crawlers. Away from him? It was like a monster rave every night of the week. He walked back in his office and shut the door, and the crawlers returned.

I toyed with my stew, losing the little appetite I'd had. I pushed my bowl away.

I was crossing the floor to the stairs when the flash of light caught my eye again, but I didn't bother looking up this time.

"Ollie, get up here."

I froze, and a spark lit in my chest.

He was mad, and I got that. But at least he was talking to me. If I were him, I wasn't sure I would be.

Not that I thought he was right, either. After what he'd said, I wasn't sure I wanted to talk to him. I knew he had secrets, and now I was positive they weren't little molehills, more like the Appalachians.

But we were pretty well matched in our wrongs.

If it weren't for the crawlers, I might've stewed some more. Waking up in a packed room was the only thing that drove me up the stairs to his office.

I opened the door that he'd closed, and he didn't look up from his desk, just pushed a notepad toward me. "Isabella is backed up. Figured if you had nothing else to do…"

I took the pad. Determined to make the situation if not perfect, cordial enough that I wouldn't get booted physically from his office, I said, "Kane—"

"If you are going to apologize, it's unnecessary."

"I was probably—"

"I told you. Not necessary."

Didn't look like I was going to get an apology, but I guessed if I hadn't given one, we were again even. I nodded, taking the pad with me and settling into my couch.

"We need to get an aging spell for Alexandria's boyfriend."

"Why?" Alexandria, the vampire with the mostest—everything. How long ago had he slept with her?

"Seems your spell reversed her werewolf all the way to a toddler." A short laugh followed the statement.

Why did he think it was funny that her boyfriend was now a toddler? Did he still have a thing for her?

And what was wrong with me? Bigger issues. "Is that a problem—for me, I mean?"

He tapped the end of the pen in his hand on the desk. "No. I handled it last night."

Last night, as I'd been searching his room. Wonderful.

He got out of his chair and pointed to the open laptop on his desk. "I need you to get on the computer and find a building with approximately twenty thousand square feet that has somewhere for overflow. It's getting too tight here."

"We aren't working today? What about Alexandria?" Not that I cared.

"No. She can wait." He pointed again at his desk.

I settled into his chair without complaint, happy for the break.

* * *

"I like this one. It's got an indoor pool in the basement." I jotted the address down on the pad before he agreed.

"Why does it need a pool?" His words were punctuated by the sound of the ball he was bouncing off the wall where he lay on the couch. It was the most normal thing I'd ever seen him do, and somehow sexy. I kept stealing glances over trying to figure out why, too.

"I don't know. It might be nice to have somewhere to do laps." I'd always envisioned myself swimming laps in my perfect future. But that future didn't have anything to do with this place or Kane, so I wasn't sure why it mattered.

"You think a pool is a good idea?"

"I don't need a pool, but maybe…" I used the hand not taking notes to eat a truffle from the platter Kane had ordered, which I seemed to be eating alone.

"You want it to have a pool?" he asked, like a man who knew the answer but wanted to hear it anyway.

"I'm just saying, it's not a bad thing for the people who might end up living there." I shrugged. Seemed valid.

"If you lived there, you'd want it?"

Man, he was stubborn. I relented. "Yes." Then added a qualifier: "Hypothetically."

He made a little zigzag motion with his hand. "Put a star by that one."

I did, before *and* after it.

The door swung open and a flushed Isabella stepped in. I wasn't sure if she'd been running laps or just doing a mad dash to get here.

"Kane, I'm sorry I took so long."

As her eyes settled on me, I held up a truffle and silently offered her one, knowing she'd decline. Then I took a bite as she watched.

"It's fine. Ollie has been helping out." Kane hadn't budged from his spot, as he continued to bounce the ball.

The way Isabella was looking around the room, you would've thought she'd caught us getting out of bed.

She stepped in between Kane and I. "Well, I'm here now, so why don't you—"

"Isabella, take the rest of the night off. I told you, we've got it covered. You should be happy. Ollie might even be getting you a pool."

"What do you mean Ollie is getting me a pool?" she asked.

Kane answered as if he hadn't heard the edge in her tone when she said my nickname. "New building has a pool. I know you hate the noise here, so I thought I'd move you over to the new place once it's done."

"Moving me?"

Yeah, *her*? I didn't want her swimming in my pool.

"You could have a bigger space." Kane kept bouncing the ball.

And swim laps in *my* pool.

"Should she be picking out the building? She doesn't know what we need."

Isabella looked over at me, and for once, we were on the same page. Neither of us wanted her in the building I'd picked out.

Kane kept bouncing. "Whatever it doesn't have, I'll fix. That's why I'll send you over there to get it straightened out for a few weeks."

Fixing my building while swimming laps in my pool. I stood up. "You know, I really feel like working tonight."

28

I ran a hand across my mouth and wiped at the blood. I could feel my eye swelling. After I'd asked them for an aging spell, it had gotten pretty packed in there. I'd caught some real nasty crawlers on my way out of the Shadowlands.

"You okay?" Kane asked, assessing the damage.

"Yeah. My face took the worst of it."

He nodded, but I could see him still looking me over, as if he weren't convinced.

I held out my hand, since this one had transformed into another pearl. "I didn't get a chance to ask for yours, since it was getting a bit iffy in there."

I shuddered thinking of how they'd swarmed in so quickly after I'd gotten the first spell. I'd briefly toyed with the thought of asking them for Kane's spell, in the hopes it might drive them away. But if it didn't, I feared I wouldn't be able to get out.

He took a step back. I'd never seen shock on Kane's face. I didn't think it was an emotion he was familiar with.

"That's what they gave you?" He was looking at my hand.

"Yes. I told them I had to age something." Hmmm, I looked at the object in my hand more closely. It wasn't a pearl. It looked more like a piece of well-worn bone. "Well, isn't that interesting?" I held the little piece up and turned it this way and that, noticing the porous holes in it.

"We've got to put that back in there, tonight."

"Why?" It looked normal enough, but I heard his tone.

"Because that won't age someone—that will age everything in its vicinity into dust. We've got to get that out of here, and now."

"Take it," I said, holding my hand out and suddenly feeling like we were in a game of hot potato.

"No. The fewer connections to this world it touches, the better."

I wrapped my hand around it, trying to not think of the words that were playing in my head.

"I can't go in again, not here. I won't make it back out."

"Get in the car. We'll go somewhere else."

He didn't have to tell me to follow him this time, and I climbed in the car.

We got out at another place five minutes down the street. It was a small stretch of woods with nothing much interesting about it. "This place?"

"The place doesn't matter right now. Call one over, get in, leave it, and get out."

I called a small guy over and gained entrance. As soon as I crossed, I laid the small bone carefully on the ground in front of the closest monster, and every other monster in the vicinity took off.

"Uh, yeah, sorry about this, but I've got to make a return."

If I'd turned to leave a second earlier, I wouldn't have seen her.

But I did. And she saw me.

Penny was walking toward me.

I wasn't sure if I wanted to head toward her or run away. It couldn't really be her, could it? She was dead. They'd said she was dead. Had said they'd faked an accident and returned her body to her parents. Had they lied and left her here?

"Ollie," she called.

"Penny?" I moved forward.

"Ollie, you've got to get me out of here." She closed the gap and grabbed my arms, tears streaming down her cheeks.

"How are you here?"

"I've been here for…I don't know. But I'm cold, Ollie, and I want to go home."

I didn't tell her that everyone thought she was dead, and took her hand with my left one.

As soon as I did, I felt the presence of Kane's hand weaken where I held it on my right. Maybe he couldn't keep two people grounded. "Come on, we're going back right now."

She nodded, and gripped my free hand with both of hers. It was only a few steps away to exit, but she couldn't seem to step any closer.

"I can't move, Ollie." Her eyes held a desperation that tore me to pieces.

I could see her trying, the sheen of sweat breaking out on her forehead. I was struggling to move her, too. It felt like instead of air, I was trying to pull her through set cement.

"Penny, come on! Push," I yelled.

"I'm trying." She sobbed the words out, and I could see she was straining, trying to move.

I felt Kane's hand still on mine, but weaker. If I let go for one minute, long enough to get us closer to the exit, would it be that bad? I unwrapped my fingers from around Kane's, but he still held on. One tug and I'd have two hands with which to get her out, and we were so close.

I didn't have a chance to see if I could free the hand Kane was holding, as I was yanked back through the entrance.

I crashed into Kane's chest, two hands gripping my arms before I would've bounced off him. "What the hell? Why did you do that?"

"What happened in there? I felt you letting go." Kane's fingers dug into my shoulders.

"It was fine. I've got to go back in." I struggled against Kane's hold, tried to look over my shoulder and see if the air was still shimmering or if I'd have to call another crawler over. I couldn't get myself turned around.

"What happened?" Kane demanded again, his hands unrelenting when I didn't have the time to waste on him.

My hands were planted on his chest as I pushed. I wanted to scream, but maybe explaining was the quickest option. "I found Penny. She's alive and she's in there. I've got to go back."

He wasn't letting go.

"Do you hear me?" I pushed again. What was wrong with him? Did he want me to abandon her? "If you don't help me, I'll go back alone."

He moved his face close to mine and held me still. "You can't help her. She's not alive."

"You're wrong. I don't know what you thought, but she's in there and I almost had her out." I kicked his shins, trying to encourage him to let go. "Get off me."

"Ollie, listen to me. You can't help."

Penny was waiting for me, but he wouldn't budge. He wanted to leave her there. Maybe he knew she'd been there the whole time, and he'd forgotten in our rush to unload the other spell? What if I couldn't get back to her again after tonight?

No, I had to get in there. There was only one thing I could think to do. I opened my mouth, and the spell, the gift Asher had given me, started flowing off my tongue. I wasn't sure if it were something I could use twice, or for different things, but I had to try something, and it was all I had. I said the words as I conjured up a thought of Kane sleeping, hoping it didn't turn out like the drizzle and the monsoon.

I saw the magic shimmer in the air, and Kane's jaw clenched as he heard me, and he must've seen it, too. A lump formed in my throat while I waited for it to hit. Hopefully it would only make him sleep for a day or so and not longer. But boy was there going to be hell to pay when he woke up. He'd have to understand he'd given me no choice.

The shimmer in the air suddenly dimmed, and it smelled like a skunk had sprayed nearby.

Kane was still there, wide awake.

"You tried to spell me." His jaw locked in place, and I was afraid of what was going to happen after he unfroze.

"Why didn't that work?" Probably not a good question to ask him, but I was at a loss for something more appropriate for a moment like this.

"Because it won't work on me. I should let you go get lost in that damn world for trying that."

"Good. Let go." I pushed harder, but the man was unmovable. Until we were both moving.

"I should, but I won't. Have any more spells you'd like to try out?" Hands still on my arms, he lifted me off my feet and walked me backward to the car.

I didn't scream or carry on. I waited until he put me back on my feet and then tried to talk to him calmly. "Kane, I've got to go back."

He turned and looked in my eyes so intently that I thought he might be willing to listen.

"Go to sleep," he said.

His words confused me until I tasted the magic on the air and felt my legs growing weak.

"What did you do?" I asked, knowing my words were slurred. My legs were going out from underneath me, and my body felt like it weighed more than I could hold up.

"What you tried to do to me."

* * *

"What's going on?" Butch asked.

I kept my eyes closed as I lay on what felt like the couch in Kane's office. It took all the concentration I had to keep my breathing easy and my lids from fluttering. If he knew I was awake, he might put me right back out.

"I had to put her out after she saw Penny," Kane said.

"Shit." I heard Butch groan, and then the sound of him scratching his stubble. "Did you explain?"

"Tried. She didn't want to hear it."

"Did you explain it like I would, or did you give her a Kane explaination? Just so you know, there's a big difference," Butch said.

"Doesn't matter. She tried to spell me, so I spelled her."

Butch groaned again. "I'm not sure what happens when the two of you are alone together, but it's never good. Are you really sure this was the best way to handle it?"

"I didn't call you up here to get advice. I need you to keep an eye on her. I have somewhere I have to be."

If Kane left, I had a shot of getting out of here. Keeping still at that moment might've been the hardest thing I'd ever done.

"I would've watched her while she was still awake," Butch said, sounding like he was over by the desk now.

"You can't handle her awake," Kane said it as if it were fact.

"I think I—"

"You can't." Kane waited a moment before adding, "Not anymore."

"Fine." I heard the chair near the desk scrape across the floor as a door opened and shut.

And then there was Butch.

Shit. Was I going to have to try and spell him, or did I give up on Penny? Deep down, Butch was a softy. Maybe I could talk him into helping me?

A growl sounded from across the room. For a second I thought it was a crawler, before I heard Butch talking to himself. "Damn I'm hungry." The chair scraped again. "It's not like I won't see her leaving if she tries."

I heard him cross the room and leave. I looked out the window of the office that overlooked the main floor of the Underground and saw Butch settling into our booth and calling a gargoyle, his eyes trained on Kane's office door.

I didn't waste time. "I need a gargoyle."

"What?" Zee asked, as she popped in.

"I need a ride. And you've got to get me out of here without anyone seeing. Can you do that?"

Zee was transforming into her sales-pitch persona. "It's going to—"

"Stop. Whatever it costs is fine. Rake me over the coals, but we leave now. Can you get me out of here without anyone seeing?" I couldn't stop peeking out the window. I didn't have time for this.

"You're going to have to hug me."

"What?" Didn't he say he was a she and into men?

"I'm strictly dickly. It's the only way I can get you out of this office."

"Sorry," I said, fearing what my expression must've been.

* * *

The entire ride over, I debated if what I was doing was crazy. It was. But was it deadly? Maybe not. If I could open up an entrance and call to Penny, without going fully in, I could make it.

If I didn't try, I might regret it for the rest of my life. Should I have stayed and waited for Kane to maybe explain why it wasn't a good idea? He'd already told me she was dead. How could I believe anything he said? I still didn't know what he was.

Zee pulled up to the same stretch of woods where I'd seen Penny.

"You want me to wait?" Zee asked.

I got out of the car. "No. Make sure you leave."

I walked to where I'd entered last time.

There was only one way to get into the Shadowlands, and that was to talk to a crawler, and I didn't have an anchor.

"I need an entrance," I said to the closest crawler, before I lost my nerve.

The air shimmered in front of me, and I leaned in. Without Kane's hand in mine, the entrance was more like a vacuum that sucked me in the rest of the way.

Asher was standing in front of where I'd fallen. "What are you doing here?" he asked me. "It's not safe for you to be alone. You've got to go back."

He must've noticed my hand not gripping Kane's, because how else would he know? "I can't. I'm looking for someone. Another Shadow Walker. She got stuck here."

He helped me to my feet. It was the first time Asher had touched me, and he tried to steer me back to where I'd entered.

"I can't leave," I said, stepping away from him. "I need to find Penny."

Suddenly, the place glowed. Asher dragged me down, covering me as debris flew past us. It quieted quickly, the light going fading away.

Asher moved, and helped me back up. The trees were all flattened, charred, and broken. It was as if a bomb had gone off, destroying the landscape. That was when I noticed some of the crawlers heading toward us. Not enough to worry over, but enough to hit my radar.

"That was the explosion in your world leaking through into ours," he said.

"You must leave. The Shadow Walker you are looking for, she can't go back."

"I can't leave her. She's lost."

He urged me toward where I'd entered again, but I pulled out of his grasp.

Asher seemed panicked as he tried to grab me again. "You must. She's not lost. Her soul is stuck. So will yours be if you don't leave." Asher dropped his arms, giving up on trying to drag me. "There's nothing left for her soul to return to. She can't leave because there's nothing left to go back to."

Kane hadn't lied or been mistaken. Penny was dead. There was nothing I could do to save her. Her soul was stuck here.

A spell to merge a soul and a body.

That was what Kane was searching for, and it couldn't be for Penny. She'd died after he was looking for it. Then who?

"Ollie, you have to leave." While we'd been arguing, and I'd been constructing the pieces, more crawlers had come.

The creatures were getting so close that I could feel the chill off their skin.

"You're ours now, Shadow Walker," one of the larger ones said as it approached.

"They know you're alone. I won't be able to hold them back. You must leave."

I took the few steps to leave, turning to say, "Thank you."

I went to step through, but it wasn't as easy as I'd expected. The same force that had pulled me in was pushing me away now, not letting me exit.

Asher was quickly getting overwhelmed by the horde of crawlers trying to get to me, until I couldn't see him anymore. I pushed with everything I had, but it wasn't enough, as their hands started to claw at my clothes, my skin, my hair.

Then I felt the heat of a hand grabbing mine.

29

I was lying on charred ground, not twenty feet from a blazing forest fire. I could hear fire engines on their way in the background as Kane scooped up my trembling body and carried me quickly to his car.

He didn't speak until we were a couple of blocks away. "What were you thinking?" he asked, but the tone of voice translated it into, *You are a complete idiot.*

My teeth were chattering too much to respond. It was strange how while I was in there I'd been cold, but now I felt as if I were freezing to death.

I leaned my head back and rested, not caring how the anger poured off Kane. All I cared about was that he had the heat on full blast and he'd leaned over and directed all the vents toward me.

He didn't say anything as he shifted the car into a higher gear, but he didn't have to. It was nearly impossible to breathe with the amount of anger flooding the small space. He swerved into the alley behind the Underground in half the time it should've taken.

He got out of the car, but I couldn't follow. I was pretty certain standing was going to be an issue, considering how my feet were feeling. Were they frostbitten?

Kane opened the car door. "You can't stand, can you?"

No way did I feel like telling him the truth right now. I was already wading knee deep in *I told you so* stares as it was.

"How bad?" he asked, right as a wave of sharp, stabbing pain hit.

I was gritting my teeth through the pain, so could only nod. He appeared to get angrier.

He leaned down and lifted me in his arms, then kicked the car door shut.

As we neared the door to the Underground, all I could think of were the eyes on me as he carried the weak paper doll inside.

"Put me down. I don't want everyone seeing me getting carried in." I tried to shift out of his grasp.

He hoisted me higher instead. "If I don't carry you, you're going to be lying in front of the door like a lump for everyone to step over as they enter."

He shouldered the door open before I could argue the point.

The people in the Underground glanced over, but no one seemed to be overly interested as we walked across the floor. Butch was waiting by the bottom landing.

"She went in alone," Kane said as we passed him and he took the flight two stairs at a time.

Butch was right behind us. "How bad?"

"I don't know yet. Lock the door." Kane crossed the room and set me on the sofa.

He immediately knelt in front of me. He unlaced my boots one at a time as I sucked in air and fisted my hand on the pillow.

He pulled off a sock, and I gasped as I saw the blackened skin.

His hands on my feet grew still as he looked them over.

Whatever was happening to them looked as bad as it felt. The blackened skin on my feet was slowly creeping upward, vines branching out and growing up my legs. As I stared, smaller threads were working farther upward.

Kane wasn't saying anything, his head bent in concentration. Butch was standing behind Kane and looking at me as if I were already lying in a coffin.

"What is it?" I asked Butch, who shook his head.

"You went in without an anchor," Kane said. "It's going to creep up until it covers your entire body."

I knew what it felt like now, only on my feet. If it didn't kill me, I'd surely be begging for death. "Can you stop it? Am I going to die?"

"No. I didn't wait this long to lose the best Shadow Walker I've ever met to her own damn stupidity." Kane grabbed me under the legs and scooped me off the couch.

"What are you going to do?" Butch asked, standing back as Kane turned with me in his arms.

"The only thing I can." Kane took a couple of steps toward his desk.

Butch stepped out of his way, but not before I saw the shock on his face. "You can't do that."

"I can do whatever I want."

"But if they—"

Kane swung around. "Either help or shut up. Those are your options."

"This could be bad. Real bad," Butch said, but instead of leaving, he walked into the supply closet off the office. Kane followed with me.

I waited for a wave of pain to pass before I said, "What are you going to do?"

Butch looked at me and gave a little shake of his head.

"It's better than death. The less you know, the better."

Butch bolted the supply closet closed from the inside and moved a couple things around, and the back wall, with the shelving, slid open. A tunnel lay beyond it with a staircase going down, but I couldn't see anything beyond fifteen feet.

Kane and I entered first, and I shut my eyes, not wanting to know when the door shut, eliminating the only light source. That was the problem with knowing monsters existed. You aren't *afraid* that there's a monster hiding in your closet. You *know* there's one.

"What are you going to do?" I repeated as I heard the creak of a large, heavy door opening, and a cold draft hit me as we entered a larger area.

"Save you. That's all you need to know. Butch, light torches."

"Torches?"

"No electricity down here. It interferes." He placed me on what felt like a cold, hard surface, like a rock table.

A torch blazed to life, and then another one as I realized I was in a cave. A cave underneath the Underground?

Butch lit another torch along the wall. "Are you going to give her something to knock her out? It's going to hurt like hell."

"It'll hurt less than what's happening now," Kane said, as he pushed my shoulder down so I was lying on the slab.

Butch walked over to where he was standing beside me. "If she fights it, it might not work."

The vines had crisscrossed and spread out until there was only black now below my pants hem. Kane pushed my pants up to see how far it went, then nodded. "I'll be back. *Watch* her this time."

I was alternating between breathing rapidly and not breathing at all, depending on how the waves of pain hit.

"What is he going to do?"

"Like he said, save your ass. You don't want to know anymore."

"I'm going to die." It wasn't until these moments, so close to the edge, that I realized I didn't really want to jump off the cliff. Had I ever really wanted to die, or had things changed that much?

"Kane won't let you die," Butch said, although I hadn't been speaking to him.

The monsters, back now that Kane had left, closed in on me, hovering on every side, whispering strange words and sounds to each other, like they knew exactly what was happening and it excited them. One of the largest I'd even seen this side of the Shadowlands stepped close, the smaller ones parting almost in reverence.

"Asher," it whispered awkwardly. "Help."

Was it asking if I wanted help from Asher, or was it offering help? I couldn't ask either way. The last thing I needed now was to blow the place up on top of everything else.

The large beast started chanting, luring me into its strange melody, its spell.

It was as if it were singing me a memory. I knew this song. From where?

The day Asher had shown me the jeweled swans. It was his song.

He'd sent me something to fix me. I lay back, not looking at the crawler, but letting the words ease into my mind.

Then I started repeating them, as if I'd already had this spell in my head. Maybe I had. Had Asher given it to me that first time and I'd not even known it was another spell?

Butch's hand left me from where he'd laid it comfortingly on my shoulder. I saw him backing away as I repeated the words, over and over again. I didn't blame him for backing up. As I chanted, it felt like I was splitting the atom, and it only made sense to want to avert the blast.

The more the words came, the stronger they came. A warm cocoon of air grew around me, the cold receding. I felt a heat seeping into me as if I were lying on the desert sand at noon. It grew, filling me and spreading down my limbs. The pain in my feet grew weaker.

I kept going until there was nothing left in me, until the final words drifted out as a whisper. I didn't know how long I'd been reciting them, but it must've been longer than I realized. I lay so utterly drained that it was as if I were glued to the table.

"What was that?" Butch asked. I used the last of my energy to turn my head to the side where Butch now stood beside Kane, across the room.

Kane's attention didn't waver from me as he responded, "I'm hoping it's not what I think."

Kane walked over and examined my feet and legs. He was silent as he did it, but when his eyes shot back to my face, he was calling me all sorts of names.

I was too tried to fight but too mad for it not to show. Had he wanted me to die? I still didn't know what they'd planned on doing to me or if it would've worked.

He walked closer to where I'd pushed myself up on my elbows, and I sank back down flush to the table.

He leaned over me, until he had a hand planted beside my head and was hovering.

"You weren't supposed to continue to talk to him."

There was only one him he could mean. I didn't know how he knew, but he knew.

"Yes, *that* him. You don't know what you're getting mixed up in."

He walked away, stopping beside Butch. "Help her upstairs."

"Kane, it's better than the alternative."

"I wouldn't be so sure."

Kane walked from the room, and Butch followed him.

They were probably talking about me, but I was too tired to get off this table or care what they said.

Butch's big head entered the room a few minutes later, and he strolled over. "He's a little put out right now, but he figured you might need a hand."

"Put out? You mean boiling angry."

"Well, technically he said, 'Go help her, because if I do it I might kill her.'"

I looked up at the ceiling, my only safe zone when Kane was gone.

"I understand why you did it," Butch said. "He'll get over it."

Except that wasn't what Kane was put out about, but I was too tired to care. Now that the pain was gone, all I could think of was Penny.

"I had to try and get her. Is that what might happen to me? Not just death, but an eternity in that place?"

"Pretty darn ugly, right?"

Very ugly. A soul trapped forever in that place, severed. It had to be connected.

"That's what he wants the spell for, isn't it? Someone stuck in there."

"I don't know. Let's get you out of here." With an arm around my back and one under my knees, he hoisted me up, while I struggled to loop my arm around his neck.

I didn't bother with any more questions, although I was sure Butch had the answers.

He walked back toward the stairway that had led us here. He climbed the stairs as he said, "That was a doozy of a spell. Where'd you get that?"

"Yeah, it was. What was the thing that Kane was going to do to me?"

"I'm not sure. So you feel better?"

"Pretty good." We were halfway through the office and neither of us had really answered a single question. He put me in the chair as he went back to hide the tunnel.

"Wait," I said, halting him before he picked me up again. "Don't you have some other secret tunnel to get me upstairs? I can't go back through the main room being carried."

Butch raised his upper lip, like there was a fishhook in it. "How many secret tunnels do you think we have?"

"Really? You've only got one?" There was a cave underneath the building with a staircase in the closet. Expecting a few more hidden passages was far from unrealistic.

"How many do *you* have?" Butch snorted at me.

None, unfortunately. He took another step toward me. "Stop," I said.

He did, and we stayed like that for a few minutes while I went over my options. It didn't take long, as there weren't many.

I reached for his hand. "Help me to the door."

"Uh, Ollie?"

"Yes?"

He did as I asked, but not without getting his two cents in. "You couldn't move off the table. Ten minutes before that, your feet were rotting off."

"I can do it." After he got me standing, anyway.

I shuffled my way across the office, using Butch for support. "I won't have everyone see me getting carried again."

We got to the door, and he slowly let go, as if waiting for me to collapse.

"You ready?" he asked, still leaning forward, his hands hovering a few inches from me.

"Yes. Open the door and don't get too close."

Butch stepped back and opened the door.

I paused before I walked out, and not because I was having trouble moving. "Butch?"

"Yes?"

I smiled as widely as I could after everything that had just happened. "Still alive."

"Still alive," he said, smiling back.

My legs were shaking as I made my way down the stairs two minutes later.

Butch, as instructed, stayed several feet away. My eyes shot across the room, somehow drawn to where Kane was standing about twenty feet away, talking to Jerry.

Kane didn't move or say a word, but he watched me, as if daring me to make it.

I stopped looking at him and continued forward. I'd make it. It was a little tougher once I got down the stairs and didn't have the railing. My feet didn't feel like they were in agony, but they sure felt like they'd been roughed up a bit.

Step by step, I walked through the Underground with my head up. No one here was going to know if I was strolling because I had free time or if I was struggling, as long as I kept my composure. If I could get to the wall that divided the Underground from the elevators, I could pretend I was stopping on purpose and not because I had to.

I made it to the wall, but with a thud. Ten more feet. I could do it.

As I took my break, Kane headed over.

He reached out, grabbed me under my arm, and half dragged me across the hallway.

He let go as we stepped into the elevator, shifting his hand from my arm to my waist. I slumped against him, not caring how mad he might be.

"Why did you do that?"

"Don't ask me to admit to doing something nice for you right now." His voice was cold.

He might've just helped me, but that didn't mean he wasn't still boiling. *Did* he help me, though? I might've made it. Maybe he did it for himself?

"Do you think anyone noticed? I don't want them to think you're stronger than I am."

"That won't shock anyone. Trust me."

"I'm not weak." It was a bit of a ridiculous statement—my cheek was pressed against his chest as he held me up.

"I might think you're a little stupid at times, but no one thinks you're weak."

His voice sounded nice and rumbly when I listened to it like this. "And I'm not stupid."

"You prefer stubborn?"

"I can compromise on stubborn."

The doors opened and he half supported, half carried me out.

"I can walk," I said, moving toward my door.

He let go, took a step back, and crossed his arms. God, he was so arrogant that I could nearly taste it.

I took a step, wobbled, and took another step, keeping my eye on the prize, which was my door.

One knee gave out.

Kane was in front of me, hefting me over his shoulder in the next second.

"I would've made it," I said as I flopped over him like a limp noodle. I wasn't even al dente. "I know what I looked like, but I would've."

He turned and walked to his door.

"Fine. You would've made it." He walked through his apartment and dropped me onto the middle of his bed.

I pulled the pillow from the top of the bed, down toward the center, instead of relocating.

"Why am I in your room?" Not that I could've gotten up. It was way too soft and comfortable.

"Because I told Isabella to give yours away before I left to find you. I'm not sure if there's someone in there or not. She might've acted quickly."

"So you *have* noticed she hates me." My eyes were already closed.

"I'm not blind."

I reached a hand out, feeling for another pillow that magically appeared. "Why would you do that? I thought you liked to keep those rooms empty anyway."

"I figured it would piss you off."

My cheek was smushed against his pillow, and I was surrounded by the woodsy scent of him. "It does."

"Well, at least I've got that, then." I felt the comforter being pulled from the side and wrapped over me.

"I'll tell her to get them out if they're in there."

"Thank you." I smiled.

30

I didn't care if Kane was going to speak to me, or even acknowledge me, after last night. If he wanted his spell, he was going to let me sit in his office whether he wanted me to or not, because I was officially bombarded by crawlers. It was getting to the point I couldn't breathe without thinking I'd brush up against one. I'd barely made it into my rooms and changed without losing my mind.

I walked through the Underground, toward the stairs, and couldn't help but notice a few of the witches were back. Mostly I noticed because the two about to cross my path seemed intent on scrambling out of my way.

I took the stairs at a jog and saw Isabella leaving Kane's office. At some point since the truffle incident, we'd moved past the pretense of hellos and straight to glares.

Instead of moving out of my way, Isabella stepped back in front of me at the last moment and clucked her tongue. "You might still be on the sixth floor, but don't let that confuse you. You're up there because you're a useful pet he likes to keep an eye on, nothing more."

Getting my room back must've been the salt on her Cheerios this morning.

"Isabella, I think it's time to come to terms with the fact Kane doesn't want to sleep with you. You're not going to become his little wifey."

"And you think you will? It's in your best interest to remember he doesn't sleep with the help."

Why did that burn so bad? "Who says I want something more?" Why was I arguing with her? How had I let her goad me into this conversation?

I was not, absolutely not, continuing this.

"Get out of my way before I spell you with a nasty wart on your nose."

She narrowed her eyes but stepped out of my way.

I didn't knock before I entered Kane's office in case he decided to not answer or tell me to go away. He didn't bother looking up as I shut the door and made my way to the couch.

"The one you've been talking to in the Shadowlands—watch yourself. Ollie, everything has a price."

So, he was talking to me. Not about something I wanted to discuss, but it was a beginning.

"Warning heeded."

His eyes met mine across the room.

"I hear you."

He didn't budge for a minute, a silent accusation that he wasn't so sure.

"I get it." I did. I'd been thinking of it since this morning. If Asher could send me a spell over from the Shadowlands, better to cut connections with him now than to find out what else he was capable of doing.

"Where we going tonight?" I asked, as if our destination tonight was a pressing emergency. The really pressing matter was moving off the topic.

"My place," he said, flipping a piece of paper over. "I've got a few ideas that might help you get a little more space for the time being."

This was where it got a little tricky, since I'd never admitted to the fact that I was having a hard time with the crawlers. I still hated admitting it, but when he put the paper down and saw me, my stare said, *Now you tell me?*

He stared back, cleared his throat, and said, "I didn't have it before."

Figured he'd blurt it out when I clearly wasn't interested in that kind of communication. Damage done; I might as well get some more details. "Would it be space like you have?"

"You won't clear a room, but you might be able to clear an area."

A little space wasn't *space*. I wanted them gone. I wanted to be able to run around with my arms stretched out like a human pinball and not worry about banging into them. I didn't want compromises. I was sick of staring at ceilings.

"Why aren't we going to get your spell?"

"We might not find my spell for months. I can't afford to have you lose your shit. You're an egg with visible cracks about to splatter all over my floor."

"Even if that's what you think, you can't soft-pedal it with *I'm concerned for you*? or *You seem a little fragile*?"

"Do you want to try this, or would you like to roll the dice and see how many crawlers you can squeeze into bed with you tonight?"

"All I'm saying is you could be a little nicer."

"Because you've had a tough life?" he asked. "Talk to the few thousand Shadow Walkers before you and ask if they feel bad. That's right. They're dead."

I wanted to say yes, I'd had a crappy life, and that was why he should try a little and be nice. Then he had to go mention all the dead Shadow Walkers, and screw me, because now I'd look like a jerk if I said yes. "You're mean."

"You're alive." He sipped his coffee.

"I guess it wouldn't hurt to try. Why don't we do it now?" The smell of the French vanilla drove me to the Keurig machine.

"Because I won't have what I need until tonight."

I was going to ask him why, but I suddenly had bigger issues. "Where's the French vanilla?"

"Leon ran through them all. I was lucky I got one cup."

With an annoyed sigh, I put in the hazelnut. "You're going to have to do something about this." I brought my hazelnut coffee over to the window that overlooked the Underground, trying to see if I could spot him.

No Leon, but I could see the table of witches looking up this way, and I knew they were talking about me.

"What?" he asked.

Figured he'd hear that small *hmmm* noise I made. "It's kind of stupid." Better to preempt the mockery.

"When has that ever stopped you?"

Clearly, there was no thwarting his talents. Although instead of feeling like harassment, this felt a lot closer to teasing. "You're going to think I'm crazy."

"Already do. Still waiting to hear a valid argument." He wasn't smiling, but it was clear he was amused with himself.

I bit a thumbnail. "The witches, they're acting weird."

"Because they won't eat with you?"

I sipped my coffee as I watched them below. "No. That I got used to."

"Then what?"

"I think…" I hitched a foot up on the bottom rail of the nearby table.

"You think what?"

He was going to get a good laugh over this one. "I think they might be afraid of me."

He laughed.

"Why is that funny?" They'd looked scared. They'd done everything they could to get out of my way. It was a reasonable assumption.

"Some of them still can't come into the building because they're being rained on, and you wonder why they're steering clear of you? There's a certain level of amusement to be had there."

Oh, it was funny because it was obvious. I laughed a little. Maybe he was right *this* time.

His phone vibrated on his desk. He hit the screen and answered, "Yeah?"

He looked over at me. That was how I knew I was involved.

"Leave it in my living room." He hung up the phone and pocketed it as he stood. "Let's go."

"Where?" I asked, still sipping my coffee.

"See if we can get you some space."

* * *

He was reading the sheet of paper that had been lying on his coffee table when we got to his room. My eyes bounced back and forth between the paper and his face.

"Well? Is that it?"

When he didn't answer immediately, I walked around to his side and lowered his arm so I could read it too. "Is this a spell?"

"Yes." His full attention was still on the spell, as was mine. Even in my head, I couldn't seem to get my mind around the words.

"Could I have gotten this in the Shadowlands?"

"No. Magic from the Shadowlands can't repel other magic from the Shadowlands. It's impossible."

"Then how are you going to get rid of them for good?"

"By obliterating the connection, which is different."

"If not from the Shadowlands, where did you get this?"

"I called in a favor."

I knew what that meant. "Who do I owe now?"

"*I* called in a favor. You owe no one. Consider it part of our deal."

"Oh." I leaned back, not sure what to say now. Why would he do that for me? It was so…nice.

He scanned the sheet one last time and then handed it to me. "Here. It looks correct."

"Should I say it?" I asked, taking the sheet from him. The moment I touched it, I felt like I was holding on to a low-voltage charge, so I placed it on the coffee table in front of me. "It feels strange."

"Try and speak it."

I sat on the couch, leaning forward so I could read it without touching it.

I hadn't expected to understand anything on the sheet, but somehow figured the words would flow from me that way they normally did. They didn't. I couldn't get my mouth to form them. Not a one. I couldn't say the first syllable.

I shook my head. "You sure about this? I can't seem to get my tongue around them."

He sat down across from ne, pushing the sheet closer. "It's not going to come as easily as shadow magic. Keep trying."

"What kind of magic is it?"

"Different kind."

"Well, that helped," I said, rolling my eyes a bit and thinking back to what Butch had called "Kane explanations." At least it wasn't only me.

I stared back down at it, trying to concentrate.

"It might take a while," he said, after another ten minutes passed.

"That's the understatement of the year." It might take forever with the way the words didn't want to stick. "How do you keep them at bay?"

"I told you. It's the way I am. It's not something to be taught."

"Can you say this?" I asked, and forced myself to touch the sheet and slide it toward him.

"It doesn't matter. You have to."

He said he wasn't a Shadow Walker, and yet he was the only other person here who could see the crawlers, even as they scattered from him like roaches in the light.

"What are you? Why is it that the crawlers, who cling to me like I'm the cone for their cotton candy, scamper away whenever you appear?"

"That's not a question you should ask someone." He was staring at me with a hard edge I hadn't seen in a while. I didn't know if he was going to lose it on me or freeze me out until I never asked another question.

"I'm asking anyway. What the hell are you? You're not human."

"You wouldn't understand. What I am you won't find in a book." There was a warning there, one I'd often given myself when people had asked too many questions.

Just as they'd done to me, I kept going with him. "Then give me the non-literary version."

"Survive a few years and maybe I'll explain it to you."

I knew when I'd hit a dead end. "I'm going to hold you to that, just so you know."

"Hope you can." He slid the spell back to me.

I leaned back over, concentrating as hard as I was capable with an already fried brain. Lately, I felt as if I'd stepped onto a mudslide and was trying to stop myself halfway down. The only way off the ride now was to wrap my arms around myself and plunge the rest of the way.

And plunging all the way at this point was putting all my concentration into getting him his spell. That was the end of this.

"This is obviously going to take a while. We need to keep moving forward to find your spell."

"Can you?" he asked, making it clear he knew how close to the edge I was.

"One way or another."

He'd said I was about to crack earlier. I'd said he was mean; I hadn't said he was wrong.

"Be ready tonight."

31

We'd gone somewhere new for the last five days, and every crawler I'd asked for the spell disappeared afterward. Every morning, I'd show up in his office, and somehow the spell would be sitting on the table in front of me, waiting. Even when I'd crumpled it and thrown it in the trash, it magically appeared the next day.

I'd burned it with matches last night. I didn't know when I'd started hating that spell, but I did.

"You're not trying hard enough."

I glanced over to where he was sitting with his laptop, and the suspicious sound of electronic cards swishing.

"I. Am."

Swish. Swish. Swish.

"Nope." *Swish, click, swish.*

"You're playing blackjack online while you tell me I'm not trying hard enough?"

"I do it because I like the feeling of success." He looked away from the screen, toward the paper, shook his head a little, and went back to the screen.

Swish, swish, swish.

This man could drive a saint to murder. Sometimes when he was like this, I wanted to haul off and punch him in the mouth. That was saying a lot, since I'd never punched anyone.

I stood, having about had my fill of him today. Until I looked over at the door and thought about what lay beyond this room. Kane or the crawlers? When he was like this, it was a closer race than usual.

I sat down on the couch again and kicked my feet up on top of the spell as I thought about tonight, where we'd go, how I wouldn't find the spell and then chug the last of my NyQuil. At some point in life, I needed to stop thinking things couldn't get any worse, because as soon as I did, they did.

Not to mention, people were starting to talk about how I was always beside Kane. I'd be talking too if I saw the way I dogged his steps. Today had been the worst.

"Did you notice the way everyone seems to be staring at me lately?"

"They're wondering if the rumor is true." *Swish, click.*

I moved my feet off the spell, as the tingle was vibrating through my shoes. "What rumor?"

"The one about you retrieving a super-powerful spell and how I'm afraid you'll escape my clutches so I'm forcing you to be by my side."

My eyes narrowed. "Why would they think that?"

"Who knows where they get these things?"

So they didn't view me as the weakling who needed a constant companion because Kane had started a rumor. I was beginning to realize Kane operated on the opposite spectrum to most. He'd tell you the horrible stuff, but he didn't like to fess up to good deeds.

I leaned back, thinking again of tonight and the odds of it being a failure. I'd give it ninety-nine percent against in my current mood.

"Why is magic stronger in certain places other than the obvious reasons of catastrophe and such?"

The swishing noises stopped for a moment. "Sometimes it's the history of a place, or length of history."

I toyed with a nail head on the front of the couch arm. "Has this soul-merging spell ever been used? Are you sure this can be done, or are you guessing?"

"Yes. I'm sure," he said. The swishing started back up.

"When was the last time?" I moved on to another nail head that was looser and more interesting to run the ridge of my nail under.

"Centuries."

Oops. The nail head popped off into my hand. I glanced over to see if he'd noticed. He had. And he didn't like it, either.

I leaned forward so I could see its hole and shove it back in. Almost as good as new, but with an interesting slant that lent it character. "Do you know where it was used?"

He was still staring at the new, improved nail head placement. Unlike myself, he didn't seem to value character.

He let out the longest sigh I'd ever heard before answering. "From my research, it was used somewhere near Quebec."

"Quebec?" I toyed with another nail head, but then switched to the laces of my shoes when his eyes narrowed.

I lay back on the couch, letting the ideas percolate while staring at the ceiling. "That is interesting."

"Expand."

I hid the smile, feeling stupid that I liked when Kane wanted to hear what I had to say.

"Well, if we need magic that has, for all intents and purposes, basically become extinct here, and different places seem to affect what we can access, why don't we go somewhere ancient?"

"Because there isn't an older place. Every place on this earth is the same age. Only human history is different."

"You say that, and it might seem logical, but you're wrong." I *really* liked when I knew something he didn't.

I lounged on his sofa, making him work for the rest, and I knew I had him.

"Please, inspire me with your magical wisdom."

"It's not magical wisdom. It's logic, and I have as much of it as you do."

"Then go ahead, dazzle me with your logic."

"Okay, I will. You may say the earth is all the same age, but is it really? I happened to have read an article about how scientists have discovered that that bedrock in Quebec, Canada might be the oldest surface on earth. Kind of interesting that that's the last known location where the spell you're hunting for worked." What was more curious was why if it were the last location he knew, we hadn't gone there. Maybe I'd simply outthought him. I liked that theory.

He'd stopped playing, and leaned back in his chair, as if assessing my logic, which I knew was damn solid, no matter how he might like to drag at this pretense.

I put my arms behind my head as one foot swung where it hung off the couch. "So? You think I might have outwitted you on this?"

"Don't gloat. It doesn't become you." His expression said otherwise.

"I happen to think it looks spectacular on me, better than even the black dress I wore to the party." I had looked good in that number.

"Now you're really talking nonsense."

Did he just admit I'd looked good that night? No way. The glow of having this man, who didn't compliment me ever, admit how good I looked was short-lived.

All the playfulness vanished. "There are places in Quebec that are very bad for Shadow Walkers. Are you sure you want to do that?"

To finally be free of the crawlers? "Yes."

"I'll call for the plane now. We'll leave in an hour."

I had a very bad feeling he might've been trying to spare me Quebec.

32

It had taken four hours to get here, and there was nothing but rock, trees, and water. Oh, and more crawlers than I'd known existed. It also appeared to be the place where the worst of the worst were. The place was going to be bad news. On the mudslide of my life, I'd hit maximum speed.

Kane was standing there silently beside me, the Humvee we had picked up at the private landing strip running behind us. "Get in and out—quickly."

I tilted my head toward him with raised eyebrows. "You're singing in the chorus."

"It's singing to the choir."

I shrugged. "My version makes more sense."

For once, he didn't argue.

I called over the nearest crawler, not having to worry about size, since they were all huge, and went in.

I didn't waste any time in the Shadowlands. I asked the biggest of the biggest in there, not wanting to mess around. The thing looked as big as a whale, and I trembled when it got close.

I demanded the spell, confident this time would be different, but it vanished, like all the others I'd asked before.

I stepped back out, and even with Kane there, it was a monster fest. They still kept a few feet away from him, but they were nearly breathing down the back of my neck.

"It's the place. Once you went in, it got worse. It'll get better once we leave," he said, tugging me closer as we made it back to the Humvee.

He pulled me over toward the driver's side. I knew it was so I could keep within the buffer.

"Why is the truck off?" I asked as I slid in and he followed behind me.

"Hang in there," he said, as he hit the ignition button. And hit it again.

"What's happened? It was running when I went into the Shadowlands."

"The crawlers coming around it dropped the temps too low."

"Hit the brake again." He did as I asked, but I was pretty sure he was humoring me as I leaned forward and pressed the button another five times.

He pulled his phone from his pocket. "Yeah, I need a lift out of here." He continued to tell them where we'd turned off, and gave them a few landmarks. He pocketed the phone.

"How long?"

"About thirty minutes."

"Let's walk."

"Let's not. You could freeze out there. It's too cold and it's too far. We're better off hunkering down in the car while we wait for a ride. It's not that long."

I didn't ask why he wouldn't freeze, because I knew I wouldn't get an answer. It wasn't because I'd missed that little nugget of information. Plus, I was too busy holding my nerves in check.

The more the crawlers circled the truck, the more it affected my mental equilibrium somehow, until I was shivering though the car was still warm.

"Come here," he said, tugging me closer to him.

"What?" I asked, knowing that I sounded as on edge as I was feeling.

"Turn around. Don't look at them."

If it were only that easy.

His hands went to my waist, and he shifted me so I was facing him. He shifted his hand up my back and pressed me close until it felt like we were hugging.

"What are you doing?"

"This is survival basics. Haven't you ever read anything about this?" He was taking the edges of his jacket and wrapping them around me. "We can share heat now."

Except he didn't get cold, ever. I took the excuse he gave me anyway.

The more of his heat that seeped into me as his arms wrapped around me, the farther away the crawlers seemed. I found myself relaxing and fitting myself to him. We both shifted here and there until we fit together from hip to shoulder.

His hand gently moved up and down my back over my jacket. "Don't worry, Ollie. I won't let the crawlers get you."

That first day I'd walked into Kane's office, I'd never thought we'd end up here, whatever here was. Colleagues, but maybe friends, too.

"Why do you do that thing where you pretend you're a dick?"

"Who's pretending?" His chest rumbled at his joke.

Our rescue was ten minutes early, and by the time they showed, I was hoping they'd be late. At some point, we'd ended up semi-reclined while Kane rubbed the knots from my back. I pulled my leg out of where I'd lodged it in between his legs, and then looked up to see he was fully awake.

His eyes were on my lips, and I wasn't sure what would've happened if the rescue team hadn't walked over.

* * *

We hadn't talked much on the way home, and it felt as if we were both taking a step back after getting a little too close for comfort. For once, Kane was as out of sorts as I was.

We got upstairs and I took a step toward my door, thinking of nothing but finishing off the last of my NyQuil.

"Ollie."

"Yeah?" I asked, turning toward him.

"I'm going to run out. You okay?" Knowing he was next door did something for my sanity. I didn't ever admit it, but he must've guessed.

"Sure. I'm fine." Or I would be after I took the NyQuil.

33

I had my back to the door and there was a swarm of them in front of me. Where had they all come from? I'd woken up two hours ago, when they whispered to me, breaking through my sleep.

Kane wasn't back. I'd knocked on his door and searched his room an hour ago.

I jumped when I heard the elevator door open. He was finally here. I held my breath. Gave it a minute. Didn't want him to think I was sitting here waiting by my door for him to get back—even if that's exactly what I was doing.

Then I heard Butch. "I handled that earlier."

I turned back around and slid down the door. He wasn't alone. It was only Butch, but if I ran out there, interrupting whatever business they had in my current state, it would be obvious I was on the fringes. I didn't want everyone to know I was struggling. I was sick of struggling.

With my head resting against the door, I heard them cross the hall.

"What about that other matter?" Kane asked.

"Handled. But we might have another issue.

"What's wrong?" Kane asked.

"She's off."

She? Odds were they were talking about me.

"You think she's cracking?"

Had to be me. Was I cracking? How insulting was that? Or would be if I weren't huddled up against a door, exactly like someone who might be cracking.

But how had Butch known? There must be some sort of cameras up here. Maybe in the hall? Had he seen me banging on Kane's door earlier? I would've banged my head against the wall if that wouldn't have given me up.

"I think she's getting close."

"Where is she right now?" Kane asked.

"In her rooms. I had the gargoyles slip something into her food to knock her out."

"So the problem's managed."

It would have been, except the gargoyles wouldn't slip me anything anymore. I wished they had. Although they hadn't told me someone was trying to doctor my food again, either. But I guessed I could only expect as much when it was Butch they were going against.

"Kane, are you sure you want to keep going forward with this?" Butch asked. It had the ring of a conversation that had been held before. "I think you're making a mistake. I think you—"

"Butch, I'm done discussing this with you. Keep an eye on her so I can get this spell. That's what I care about."

I heard buzzing before Kane asked, "Yes?" as if he were answering his phone. "Coming."

I waited to hear the rest of what they'd say, but instead I heard feet moving and the sound of the elevator doors shutting.

I'd lost my chance.

* * *

"Ollie?" Butch whispered as he walked through my living room. I'd known it wasn't Kane when I heard someone come in because the crawlers were still around.

If I stayed quiet, maybe Butch would leave, even if he came in my bedroom and saw the bed empty. He might think I'd gone for a walk or something.

I heard the door to the bathroom open.

He walked over to the shower stall, where I was sitting cross-legged with the glass door closed. It had been the smallest enclosure I could find.

Butch didn't need to say a word as he stared down at me. I tried to smile. I faltered.

When he finally did speak, he said, "Fuck. You cracked."

"No, I'm good. Just needed a minute."

A second "Fuck" made it clear how convincing I was.

He was shaking his head as he dug his phone out of his pocket.

"What are you doing? Who you calling?"

"You know who."

"Don't call—"

"You're cracking. I gotta call."

"I'm fine." I stood up. *See? Look at me, I'm standing in the stall.*

He dropped the phone from his ear and stepped back, forcing a crawler he couldn't see to move out of his way with a growling noise.

He opened the glass door. "Step out of the shower and I won't call."

I lifted my foot then froze inside the shower as crawlers moved forward.

"Why's it so cold in this place?" Butch asked, distracted from the crazy picture I presented for a minute.

"Because they're crammed in here."

Butch looked around the bathroom and said, "Fuck," for the third time, but this one seemed more focused on the room. He lifted the phone back up.

I leaned forward and grabbed his wrist. "Butch, you don't need to call him. I'm going to be fine."

His eyes narrowed. He started calling someone but held his hand to block me when I went to grab his phone.

"I'm calling Leon. That's my final offer, unless you come out of that stall."

I sat back down. Leon wasn't so bad.

"Come up to Ollie's? We've got a little situation."

He pocketed his phone, and I leaned my head back.

Fifteen minutes later, Butch, Leon, Jerry, and Flip were all gathered by the entrance to the bathroom, whispering about what they should do with me.

"Let's drag her out," Leon kept saying.

Flip would intervene and call him brutish. Butch would jump in and defend Leon, then Jerry would defend Flip. We were currently on our third go around.

Then someone must've ordered drinks, because Zee popped in. She took one look at me and decided she needed to be involved, concerned that if someone didn't fix me, she wasn't going to get the rest of her favors paid off.

Butch was leaning against the bathroom sink, next to where Flip was sitting on it, sipping a martini. Jerry, Leon, and Zee were betting on something on Jerry's phone.

I rested my forehead on my knees as I heard the footsteps heading our way.

The crawlers scattered, and I groaned, knowing Kane's appearance was imminent.

Even as I dreaded seeing him, the tension eased from my shoulders. It was safe now. At least while he was here.

I didn't look up when I heard him walk in the room. I was sitting in the shower stall. There was no way to save face on this one. It was all I could do to not turn beet red from the humiliation of it all.

"Everyone, clear out."

There was a mass exodus, and it took a minute before I could see the bottom half of Kane approaching.

I didn't want to see his face, the judgment there, or hear what he'd say.

I already knew what he was thinking. I'd turned out to be exactly like the rest of them—fragile and disposable. A paper doll. I'd merely taken a bit longer to get there.

The shower door opened, and I could see Kane's bare feet.

He bent down, crouching in front of me, sweatpants hugging low on his hips and his torso bare, showing off a perfect blend of muscle and sinew.

"Ollie." His voice was soft. "What's going on?"

"I'm fine."

I wanted to look at him, but this was the most embarrassed I'd ever been in my life. No matter how many times I told myself to look up, I just couldn't do it. I needed to get up and pull it together.

"Ollie, you're sitting in the shower with your clothes on." Somehow Kane made that sound funny instead of pathetic.

"I was looking for a quiet place to rest for a minute. You can go. This looks worse than it is. I'm good."

"Ollie, I can't leave you in the shower." He said it slowly, but I knew that tone. I could leave the shower stall willingly or I could leave the shower stall Kane's way. But I was leaving the shower.

"I can't talk to you while you are like this."

After what seemed like forever, I dragged my eyes up to his face. There wasn't any mockery there.

"Do you want me to get rid of the crawlers?" He was offering, but he didn't seem convinced himself that he wanted to do it.

"But…" I couldn't have moved no matter what was said after that. I'd never thought it was a possibility with him. "I haven't gotten you the spell."

Arms resting on his knees as he sat there waiting, he said, "I'm aware."

I thought I'd gotten past the point in life where someone could shock me. It was hard to get my head around the idea, that after all he'd gone through, he'd let me off the hook. "But that was the—"

"I know what the deal was."

"Why?" Now I couldn't stop staring at him.

His expression was guarded. "It doesn't matter why."

I didn't know what or who he needed this spell for, but I had a vested interest in it now too, or at least I thought I did. "The spell you want. Could that put Penny to rest? Could it be used for her?"

"It could."

I dragged my knees upward and let my forehead rest on them. I knew what I wanted to do, and that meant being haunted by Penny, crying for help, for the rest of my life.

Then there was Kane. He'd never told me what he was going to do with the spell, but there was probably another lost soul out there, suffering. "I need to keep going." The words weren't said with confidence, but I was committed to them.

He appeared relieved as he stood, holding out his hand. "Come on."

"Where?"

He grabbed my hand and pulled me up when I took too long. "My place. I'll try and stay with you as much as I can until it's done."

He towed me forward out of the bathroom and halfway through the bedroom. "Can't you stay here?"

He stopped pulling me forward, looked around the living room, and said, "No," before continuing onward.

He let me go once we got into the hall and I shut my door.

He pointed toward the bedroom. "It's all yours."

He walked into the living room, looking like he was going to get comfortable on the couch.

The open double doors framed the king bed inside.

I stepped inside the bedroom and then paused before I made it more than a foot from the doors. "Do you mind if I leave these open?" I asked.

"Nope."

He walked into the kitchen area, and I edged back out of the bedroom, watching what he was doing.

"Did you want a drink?" he asked as I looked around.

"Um, no."

He headed back into the living room. "I was going to watch some TV," he said, walking over toward the cabinet beneath the hanging flat-panel.

"What are you going to watch?" I asked, settling onto the loveseat.

"I'm not sure. Did you want to watch something?" He opened one drawer and then the next one. He lifted several remotes, hit buttons, and put them back, before repeating the process.

"I'll watch whatever."

"You can choose."

"How about *The Strangest Times*?" It sounded like it could be a TV show. I wondered if he'd catch the irony.

"Sounds good," he said when the big screen hanging on the wall flickered on.

"Here, find your show…" He waved his hand toward the TV before he handed me the little box and then settled onto the couch.

"You know, I don't think that show is on right now." Remote in hand, I flipped through the channels, trying to find a movie or show that actually existed.

"About that drink—you don't have any hot cocoa, do you?" I rolled onto my side, my face a couple feet from where his head was.

"I'll call a gargoyle."

"Thanks." I settled some of the pillows into the perfect spot and realized something incredibly strange was happening.

In the middle of all of this turmoil, lying feet from a man who I knew wasn't human, I felt more normal than I ever had in my life.

34

The moment the gap between Kane and I was big enough, they swarmed me. I'd been trying to say the spell since this morning, and it was now two in the afternoon. I stared at the words before me and tried to force the sounds from my lips.

And tried, and tried.

"What if you said them first?" I asked, holding out the sheet to Kane where he sat at on the couch.

"This spell only works once. If I say it, even though I don't need it, it won't work again."

I pointed to the first word of the spell. "What if you say only that one? Maybe if you said it, I'd be able to repeat it and the rest would flow?"

"Doesn't work that way."

Kylebah. That was the first word. It didn't seem that bad. I could hear it in my head, could feel the K on the tip of my tongue, but I couldn't even get the first syllable out.

If the spell wasn't going to work, I'd never get enough space from the crawlers without getting rid of them completely, and everything that went with that.

That had always been my plan, getting rid of them for good. Except now I knew what I'd be giving up. I liked magic, and I had a strong feeling I'd like it even more as I went.

I hadn't been able to live life as a normal person before. Now I could go back there and do just that if I wanted, but lately, that life didn't seem as appealing as it used to.

"Can you leave the apartment for about ten minutes? Maybe if I have no choice but to be surrounded by crawlers, it'll help force the words out."

Kane appeared as skeptical as I felt. "Or maybe you'll lose your shit?"

"I don't go bonkers that quickly, thank you. It takes a few hours at least."

Kane shook his head but did as I asked.

The crawlers were back immediately, and then they seemed to part. Seriously? He didn't think I could make it more than two minutes?

I looked up, expecting to see Kane, and didn't.

A very large crawler, the same one I'd seen in the cave, which had twisted horns that grew from his head, stepped forward. The smaller crawlers all backed away, giving him space.

"Asher," it said, in a raw voice.

It appeared to be waiting for an acknowledgment. I nodded, afraid to speak to it.

"Spell. Cemetery." It stepped away and then faded as if it had never been. The other crawlers swarmed back in, filling the void.

Asher had a spell for me. Did he have *the* spell? I was still debating that when Kane walked back in.

"Well?" he asked, plenty of skepticism in his voice, expecting me to confirm it didn't work.

"Yeah, no good."

He walked past me into his bedroom as I still flip-flopped. Would it really hurt to just see what Asher had to offer? I didn't have to accept anything he offered. Although what was the difference? Kane implied there might be a difference, but he was a crawler, like the others. What difference was there in which crawler I got the spell from?

I heard him moving around the bedroom before he said, "We need to go to the office."

That meant he needed to go to the office and I was the person who would go crazy if left alone.

Fuck it. I had to try. "Kane?"

"Yeah," he yelled back.

I got up and walked to the door, and he turned to see what I needed.

I leaned against the door. "Remember that cemetery we went to on one of my first trips?"

When he nodded, I said, "I want to go back there, tonight."

"Why?"

I was holding out on him, and he knew it the same way he knew everything else. He read people the way most of us read the news.

"I just do. Call it a hunch." He knew there was more, and it was all going to come down to how much he wanted the spell. Was he willing to look the other way and go along if it meant he got what he wanted? How badly did he want this?

He nodded. "Okay. We'll go tonight."

Looked like he wanted it as badly as I did.

35

Kane walked over and stood beside me. "Here we are."

He didn't know why we were here. What was driving me back here, one of our original spots, for something we'd been searching high and low for.

He took my hand. "I don't know why we're here, but if you can get it, it's going to be tougher."

I turned to him, wanting to tell him what or who I was looking for. I wanted to run all my ideas past him for some crazy reason. I wanted to swing open the doors to all I was holding back and invite him in, but I didn't think he was looking for that kind of invite. He wasn't that guy.

But could he be? Did he just need a little more time? "Are you ever going to tell me what you need the spell for...or who?"

He kept looking forward. "Maybe in the next life."

I nodded, more to myself than him. I didn't have that kind of time to give.

He made his choice, and whatever I thought I saw wasn't going to be.

I made my choice as well. I didn't tell him what had drawn me here. Hopefully I'd be able to move past this part of my life after tonight.

His hand firmly in mine, I sought a crawler that would take me to the Shadowlands, and didn't waste any more time wondering about what might've been.

It was colder than it had been the last time I'd entered, and I held on to Kane's hand firmly. I felt the difference Kane had alluded to. It wasn't just colder, it was bleaker.

I took a few steps and then felt him. Asher was here somewhere, and heading toward me. I waited, preferring he come to me, closer to the exit.

He turned a corner, walking out from behind a mausoleum.

He stopped a few feet from me, a soft smile on his face. "I knew you'd come."

"I came because of the message." I wrapped my arms around myself as the crawlers nearby drove the temperature down. "I thought you couldn't help."

He took another step forward. "I said that very few had that spell, not that I couldn't get it."

"You knew what I was looking for. Why now?"

"Because I want to help you. I care for you, Olivia. I don't want you to leave here…leave me. I wanted you to keep coming."

That sentence was wrong in so many ways. How did he know I was leaving? And there was no way I was going to come back here for him, not even for spells. Not now. "How do you know I'm leaving?"

"I told you—I hear things." His hands clenched and unclenched.

I kept feeling like he was barely staying put. I needed to shut this down now. Spell or no spell, I needed to get away from him. "I want to thank you for all you've done for me, but I won't be seeing you again."

His face convulsed as if I'd caused him bodily pain. "Why?"

"Because if there's a way to stop being a Shadow Walker, I'm going to do it."

He reached for me and was grabbing my arms before I could stop him.

"I can help you. I'll be there for you. I can ease the pain and struggle you go through every day. I can give you something that will drive them away from you."

If he could do something that would keep the crawlers at bay, maybe I wouldn't live just a normal life after this, but one with unlimited possibilities. Asher might've been a crawler, but he wasn't like the others. Face to face, looking into his eyes, my hunch was he didn't want to hurt me. He was genuine in wanting to help.

If it hadn't been for something my father had told me long ago, I might've kept ignoring the inclination to accept. He'd said hunches aren't the same as guesses. Sometimes your mind is picking up on all sorts of details you aren't aware of. A hunch is your subconscious trying to point you in the right direction when your waking mind can't see past the clutter around you to the truth of the matter.

Asher must've sensed my willingness, because he held out his hand to me, and I took it. I felt the tingle of something going through him and into me, and I had to force myself not to panic. Then he was letting go, smiling at me.

"That's it?" I asked.

"That's it."

I didn't feel any different, and the crawlers were still circling us.

"It won't work in here."

I nodded, knowing that would've been too much to ask for. "What of the other spell?"

"If I give it to you…" He paused and turned his head to look at all the crawlers that had moved our way. "They are going to do everything they can to stop you. It'll be worse than ever before. Know that you'll have to fight your way out."

"I know it won't be easy." I saw them all coming, as if they sensed the magic that was about to be passed and it agitated something deep within them.

"It will be near impossible."

Asher didn't want me to do this, and yet Kane did. But Asher was the one I was supposed to fear. Nothing in this world was making sense to me, but I knew I needed to get out of here.

"If I can't do it, I'll leave it behind."

"Once you have the spell, you won't be able to, not with this one."

Was I scared? I was petrified. And I was going to do it anyway. I just needed to remember that, no matter how scared I was, it couldn't come close to how terrified Penny must be day in and day out roaming this cold and dark land. "Please, give it to me anyway."

Asher did as I asked. He didn't want to, but he respected me enough to do it anyway.

"I'll try to help you as much as I can," he said before the words drifted from his lips, filling the air, filling my mind, and calling to every crawler in the area. It was short, only three lines, but it was potent. It settled into that special place in my mind.

I felt them closing in around me as soon as he stopped, and in numbers I'd never seen before. Then I was jarred into action by Asher.

"Run!" he screamed, pushing me toward my exit, which had somehow grown farther away without my notice.

I spun and took off toward the entrance. It only took one step before they were on me. It was as if every fear I'd had was coming to life in this moment. This, exactly this, was what I'd been waiting for all those years. It was if somehow I'd known I'd end up here.

I saw flashes of claws coming before I felt the burn as they tore past my clothes and dug into my skin. The way back couldn't have been more than five feet away, and yet it felt like it was five miles as they swarmed around me. I lashed out with both hands, making sure to keep my grip on Kane, and using that hand as a bludgeon even as I felt the weakness in his grasp.

I didn't know how many were on me as they drove me to my knees. The pain was coming from everywhere as claws dug furrows in my back and legs, more blows raining down upon my head.

But they weren't holding me down. It was if they couldn't maintain a hold on me if they wanted to, their blows hitting and then sliding off.

I tried to get back to my feet again as another blow drove me down. But I looked forward, seeing glimpses of my destination in between the legs of crawlers as they moved.

I wouldn't die here. It turned out that what my weakest moment revealed was that I didn't have any desire to die at all. Would give anything to live.

I kept my eyes forward as the blows kept coming.

If I couldn't walk, I'd crawl.

I'd only cleared my head and shoulders when Kane dragged me the rest of the way out, his grip finally strengthening.

I fell on my back as he leaned over me. "Ollie?"

The shock in his eyes told me I looked like I felt, and his hands ran my length, feeling the various injuries, of which there were many.

I held out my hand, a pristine white pearl in the center of my palm dropped on the ground as my hand shook from loss of blood. I was going into shock.

His eyes shifted to the pearl and then back to my face.

His fingers were touching my cheek. "Hang on. You hear me?"

I nodded. My body might not have much strength, but my soul had fight in it for days.

36

I must have blacked out, because when I heard the voices and tried opening my eyes, I was in that secret place beneath the Underground.

I was lying on the table with a blanket draped over me.

"It's working," Kane whispered as he looked at one of my legs. Butch, Leon, and Jerry were standing nearby.

Kane walked over to my head, fingers gently brushing the hair back from my face.

"What are you doing?"

"You're going to be okay," Kane said. "Sleep."

I didn't want to sleep, but it came anyway.

* * *

Everything hurt down to the roots of my eyelashes as they fluttered open. This time I was lying in Kane's darkly lit bedroom, surrounded by his smell. The man himself walked into the room, as if he had sensed me awakening.

He walked over and sat down on the corner of the bed. He didn't say anything for a minute.

"You almost died in there." His eyes wandered away from my face, and he stood as if he were restless.

He walked over to the window and looked out. "You shouldn't have any scars."

I nodded. That was the least of my concerns. Being able to get out of this bed, that was a concern.

I forced myself upward then stopped him with a hand when he would've come and helped me. He watched from across the room as I managed to get into a sitting position.

"Ollie, are we okay?" Kane asked, still in his spot across the room.

I knew where the question was coming from, could see the guilt as he looked at my injuries.

"We're fine," I said. We weren't good. I didn't know what else I could say. I wasn't sure myself beyond that. All I did know was I needed space right now.

I swung my legs free and then grabbed the robe laid out on a chair nearby, and the whole time Kane seemed to be fighting the urge to help me.

With a lot of effort, I slipped the robe on over the t-shirt I didn't recognize, and stood.

"Where are you going?" he asked.

I walked slowly toward the door. "To my rooms."

"Alone?" he asked.

I paused, with my hand on the door. "Yes."

His eyes narrowed. "You sure?"

"Yeah, I am. I'll find you when I'm ready."

I walked away from him, feeling his stare on me the whole way out.

As I made my way to my rooms, the crawlers were there, as if they'd been waiting.

But something was different. They weren't hovering anymore, but keeping their distance, almost like a bully that had gotten a black eye in a fight.

I purposefully walked closer to one, and it shifted out of my way. Asher had been true to his word.

37

I woke the next day in a bed occupied solely by me. I looked around and saw some crawlers peeking in at me from the living room. I got up and shut the door. I looked in the mirror, not afraid of what I'd see behind me for the first time in my life.

I dressed with care, putting on a pair of black pants and a blouse. Every strand on my head was perfectly smooth, and I put on makeup supplied by Zee.

I walked into Kane's office forty minutes later.

Kane, Butch, and Leon turned to look at me, Leon letting out a low whistle.

"Still alive," I said.

"Still alive," Leon and Butch repeated. This time, even Kane smiled.

With a nod in my direction, Butch left the room, Leon patting me on the shoulder before following him out.

I took the seat in front of Kane's desk instead of the couch.

"I used the spell on Penny's grave this morning."

I'd walked in here with a mental list. Kane had just checked the first box.

"Thank you." There'd been a time I'd hesitated to thank him. Whether he wanted to accept thanks from me wasn't my problem.

"And here we are," he said.

"I fulfilled my obligations. You said, 'Get me the spell and I'll shut the door for you. Then we can go our own ways.'" At the time he'd said it, I hadn't realized how much I'd be giving up. Or the true risk he'd been putting me through to obtain his goal.

None of that mattered. He'd made a promise. Now it was time to see if he'd keep it. If he couldn't do that, there was no future, not here.

"I know what I said."

He leaned down, lifted a suitcase from underneath his desk, and laid it before me. "It's all there. Feel free to count it."

"That's okay." It had never been about the money.

"As soon as you're ready, we can go below and finish it."

I didn't need Kane anymore—not for this spell, anyway. Whatever Asher had done, while not perfect, was tolerable.

If Kane finished them off, I would be a normal person for the first time in my life.

Maybe go back to school, get a career, whatever I wanted. I could have a normal life from here on out. It was exactly what I'd always wanted. So why wasn't I running to grab my things and get the hell out of here?

Was he really going to let me leave? There was too much at stake. I had a limitless amount of magic virtually at my fingertips. He wouldn't allow me to throw that all away, would he?

Could I?

"So that's it? We could go right now?"

He nodded slowly as he reclined in his chair, every ounce of him saying it was so. "Right now, if that's what you want."

I rose and walked toward the supply closet that led to the hidden stairs. "What about my other debts? You said they'd follow me."

He stood. "I'll handle them."

I stared at him, daring him to show his true colors while he stared back, waiting for me to open the door.

I was standing there with my hand on the knob.

I could have a normal life, maybe get married and have kids. Grab everything I'd always wished for that had always been so far out of reach.

Except I didn't think that was the life I wanted anymore.

My hand dropped from the knob. "What if I want to stay? Maybe leaving isn't the best choice."

"I'm listening," he said, as he sat on the corner of his desk.

I took a couple of steps back toward his desk. "I need an anchor. I'm sure there are other spells you need."

"You want to keep going?"

"It seems like a waste not to."

"You think you can handle it?"

"That's not really any of your business, is it? And that's what this relationship would be. I want to make that very clear. Business." I'd thought for a small blip that maybe it could be more. And whether I'd wanted to admit it before or not, part of me had wondered what it might be like to have a different kind of relationship altogether. But the type of relationship he was capable of wouldn't be enough. I could admit that now. I had to be completely honest with my emotions, if only to myself, so that I was always extra vigilant nothing like that would ever happen.

"Business only. Completely clear." His tone said something else entirely. "I could use some help if you want to hang around."

"I think I'll be okay. Actually, I know I will.

A slight smile curved his lips as he walked closer to me. "You could hang around anyway."

I knew what he was offering. I deserved more.

"Maybe in another lifetime." I smiled as I moved to exit his office.

"Olivia? Would that be a human lifetime?"

I didn't laugh until I had shut the door behind me.

Somebody was going to have to stick around and do something about this man's ego.

* * *

I walked into my rooms on the sixth floor. I was still here, next to Kane, but I felt like a lifetime had passed, and I was a completely different person than the woman who'd barely had the will to get off the couch. The crawlers I'd longed to get rid of, the ones that had nearly driven me to insanity, still lingered on the outskirts of the room, but I was master of this domain.

I strolled into the bedroom, not fearing what I'd see and bumping limbs on furniture because I refused to open my eyes.

I unbuttoned my blouse, wanting to do nothing more than to throw on a t-shirt and watch TV from a normal viewing distance as I thought about what spell I might want to get tomorrow.

"Olivia."

My fingers faltered on the third button. Had I imagined that?

"Olivia." The voice held more excitement this time.

No. It couldn't be.

"Olivia." I felt a hand touch my shoulder.

I turned around, hoping I was mistaken.

I wasn't.
Asher was out of the Shadowlands.

Ollie's story continues June 2017 with A Walk in the Dark.

Find out more about Donna on www.DonnaAugustine.com

Also by Donna Augustine

The Wilds
The Wilds
The Hunt
The Dead
The Magic

Karma
Karma
Jinxed
Fated
Dead Ink (A Karma World Romance)

The Keepers
The Keepers
Keepers and Killers
Shattered
Redemption